MURDER IN MAUI

A Leila Kahana Mystery

R. BARRI FLOWERS

D1518270

Murder in Maui: A Leila Kahana Mystery is a work of fiction. Names, characters, places, and incidents are either the product of the author's imagination or are used fictitiously. Any resemblance to actual events, locales, business establishments, or persons, living or dead, is entirely coincidental.

ISBN: 1475202849
ISBN-13: 978-1475202847

This one is for my wife and best friend, H. Loraine, and the great memories we share from many trips to Maui, which is arguably the most beautiful place on earth.

And to my mother, who put me on the right track many years ago toward living my dream to become a writer.

Lastly, to all who share my love for Maui and its many wonders. I hope this mystery novel captures the true spirit of the island, while giving readers a heart-pounding tropical police procedural to enjoy one page at a time.

* * *

ALSO BY R. BARRI FLOWERS

NOVELS
Murder in Honolulu (A Skye Delaney Mystery)
State's Evidence (A Beverly Mendoza Legal Thriller)
Persuasive Evidence (A Jordan La Fontaine Legal Thriller)
Justice Served (A Barkley and Parker Mystery)
Dark Streets of Whitechapel (A Jack the Ripper Mystery)
Dead in the Rose City (A Dean Drake Mystery)
Killer in The Woods (A Psychological Thriller)
Ghost Girl in Shadow Bay (A Young Adult Haunted House
Mystery)
Danger in Time (A Young Adult Time Travel Mystery)

TRUE CRIME
The Sex Slave Murders: The True Story of Serial Killers
Gerald & Charlene Gallego
Serial Killer Couples: Bonded by Sexual Depravity,
Abduction, & Murder
Mass Murder in the Sky: The Bombing of Flight 629
(historical short)

SHORT STORY COLLECTION
Edge of Suspense: Thrilling Tales of Mystery & Murder
Love Aboard the Titanic/Billy The Kid's Wife (Timeless
Romance Shorts)

What Bestselling Crime and Thriller Writers Say About MURDER IN MAUI: A Leila Kahana Mystery

"A police procedure of the highest order, mixing equal parts Sue Grafton and Jeffrey Deaver with a sprinkling of Patricia Cornwall at her best. MURDER IN MAUI is Hawaii 5-0 sharpened to a dark edge beneath the brilliant sunshine." — *Jon Land, internationally acclaimed bestselling author of STRONG JUSTICE and STRONG ENOUGH TO DIE*

"A masterful thriller set in the dark underbelly of Maui, with lots of fine action, down and dirty characters, and the vivid details of police procedure one would expect from an author who is also a top criminologist. A terrific read!" — *Douglas Preston, New York Times bestselling author and co-creator of the PENDERGAST series of novels*

"A gripping and tightly woven tale you won't want to put down. Flowers neatly contrasts the natural beauty of a tropical paradise with the ugliness of murder and its aftermath. Treat yourself to a vacation in Hawaii. You'll want to return again and again." — *John Lutz, Edgar winner and bestselling author of MISTER X and NIGHT VICTIMS*

"From one of the best true crime writers around, R. Barri Flowers now has combined his impressive criminology credentials and literary talents to create Maui homicide detective Leila Kahana, a fascinating and complex heroine. Fans of CSI and Hawaii 5-0 will love this one and scream for more!" — *Deborah Shlian, award-winning co-author of DOUBLE ILLUSION and DEVIL WIND*

"A combination of grit, action, and incredibly realistic police procedure. That's the recipe that keeps me turning pages until the sun comes up. Author R. Barri Flowers dug deep into his extensive background as a criminologist to plot MURDER IN MAUI, a tale so genuine that even I was tempted to call for backup a couple of times." — *Lee Lofland, former detective, author of POLICE PROCEDURE AND INVESTIGATION, and founder of the Writers' Police Academy*

"Flowers delivers the goods. An exotic setting, winning characters, and realistic procedural details make MURDER IN MAUI a sure hit with crime-fiction readers." — *Bill Crider, Edgar winner and New York Times bestselling author of MURDER IN THE AIR and MURDER IN FOUR PARTS*

"MURDER IN MAUI is a page-turning mystery featuring the debut of a fascinating character, Detective Leila Kahana. Leila is smart, funny, talented and on top of her game as a detective and police sketch artist. The ending definitely has me saying, More please, Mr. Flowers." — *Jan Grape, Anthony and McCavity winner and author of WHAT DOESN'T KILL YOU and co-editor of MURDER PAST, MURDER PRESENT*

"MURDER IN MAUI is terrific. Gripping writing, wonderfully rounded characters you really care about, and vivid locations—this novel is a real and rare treat." — *Peter James, international bestselling author of DEAD SIMPLE and DEAD LIKE YOU*

"MURDER IN MAUI launches a series detective in a beautiful setting with a thoroughly puzzling mystery to solve. If you love Hawaii or a good head-scratching mystery, you'll enjoy this book. Very entertaining." — *William Bernhardt, bestselling author of CAPITOL BETRAYAL and CAPITOL OFFENSE*

"Starts with a bang—literally—and drops you right into the deep end of murder. A by-the-book mystery that keeps the suspense taut and edgy." — *Joe Moore, international bestselling co-author of THE 731 LEGACY*

Reviews Of Other Crime Fiction By R. Barri Flowers

STATE'S EVIDENCE

"Flowers once again has written a page-turner legal thriller that begins with a bang and rapidly moves along to its final page. He has filled the novel with believable characters and situations." — *Midwest Book Review*

"This legal thriller will have you on the edge of your seats. The courtroom scenes are unforgettable and very believable.... The author gets into the mind of the criminals and you'll feel privileged to information that the other characters don't know. State's Evidence is a must have for any fan of suspense books." — *Shades of Romance Magazine*

"R. Barri Flowers's book STATE'S EVIDENCE is a well-written thriller with an opening scene that would cause anyone to keep turning the pages. STATE'S EVIDENCE will make the top sellers list because it's fast-paced, intriguing, satisfying, and I highly recommend it to you." — *Romance Reader At Heart*

"STATE'S EVIDENCE, the new legal thriller by R. Barri Flowers, is a mixture of murder, mystery, madness and mayhem. The story was well written and believable, and at times erotic. Flowers inflicted the characters with human flaws, among them the desire for love and revenge." — *RAWSISTAZ Reviewers*

"Just when you think you have figured the plot out, R. Barri Flowers throws another curve. One of my suppositions did prove out but was clouded by the red herrings being thrown around.... It was well worth the time taken to read it." — *Roundtable Reviews*

"STATE'S EVIDENCE has a varied, multicultural cast of interesting characters, both good and evil.... Plot is clever and intriguing with unusual twists, with the suspense escalating rapidly." — *Romance Reviews Today*

"An intriguing story of murder, madness and mayhem, with a slight blend of mystery. Flowers depicts believable characters in this suspenseful legal thriller." — *Romantic Times*

"R. Barri Flowers has written an electrifying and enthralling legal thriller that will appeal to readers of Nancy Taylor Rosenberg and Barbara Parker. The courtroom scenes are very realistic and the heroine is someone readers will empathize with and admire as a role model for minorities and women. STATE'S EVIDENCE would make a great action packed movie." — *Harriet Klausner*

JUSTICE SERVED

"A clever mystery with many suspects.... Vividly written, this book holds the reader's attention and speeds along." — *Romantic Times*

"An A+ suspense/mystery with a touch of heartfelt romance.... Is not just simply compelling, it also activates reader's consciousness.... Powerful legal suspense is riveting." — Fresh Fiction

"This author weaves a magical web, as well as, a tangled one [and] wraps up the mystery thriller beautifully.... Will be recommending this title to many!" — *Huntress' Book Reviews*

"Justice Served is a model of crime fiction.... Flowers may be a new voice in modern mystery writing, but he is already one of its best voices." — *Statesman Journal*

"The magic behind R. Barri Flowers' terrific suspense thriller is that the serial killer is in plain sight as the clues are laid out for the audience to determine.... Fans of police procedural serial killer thrillers will want to read this fine tale while anxiously waiting to follow the next investigation." — *Harriet Klausner*

"R. Barri Flowers has created a superb mystery.... There's just enough romance and romantic triangles to keep the interest going. It's a great book that any mystery lover will adore." — *RAWSISTAZ Reviewers*

"This novel has lots of twists and turns and is a very fast read with believable characters and a very tense setting." — *Midwest Book Review*

PERSUASIVE EVIDENCE

"Compelling detective mystery." — *The Best Reviews*

"A superb legal thriller." — *Midwest Book Review*

"Raw, primal, thrilling, incredible—one of the best books that I have read. I was completely riveted from the first page." — *Romance Reader at Heart*

"It has all the aspects of a perfect mystery, and thankfully, it isn't so predictable you figure out what's going on." — *RAWSISTAZ Reviewers*

"An excellent look at the jurisprudence system.... will appeal to fans of John Grisham and Linda Fairstein." — *Harriet Klausner*

"Interesting 'whodunit' that kept me guessing until the end...found the story to be quite engaging with all around solid pacing, plot and delivery." — *APOOO BookClub*

"An absorbing legal thriller.... Flowers' forte lies in the vivid well-developed characters he creates. The interactions of his characters and the conflicts that arise serve to make the story a compelling page-turner." — *Romance In Color*

"All the elements of a great mystery book, suspicions, red herrings, evidence and witnesses. If you are into mysteries, this would be the book for you." — *Romance Review*

"A story that keeps you on the edge of your seat.... A page turning story I couldn't put down." — *Romance Junkies*

PROLOGUE

The handgun was loaded methodically. Time for payback. Now they would know what it felt like to be humiliated. And only then could some peace of mind come.

And just maybe a life again.

First things first. There was a job to do and the doer was determined to exact some vengeance against those deserving.

Stuffing the gun in a pocket, the soon-to-be-killer downed the rest of a glass of liquor before heading for the door.

It was a relatively quiet evening by Maui standards, what with the constant throng of tourists practically taking over the island. This was a good omen. No need to draw undue attention or have to take out someone who didn't deserve to die.

The doer got into a vehicle and began the drive down Mokulele Highway toward the South Shore.

Arriving in Wailea, the car was parked not far from the Crest Creek Condominiums.

Then came the wait, certain they would show up. After all, their routines had been studied and memorized.

Ten minutes later both arrived in separate BMWs. The tall, handsome man left his car first and casually looked around as if lost before heading toward a condo.

The woman waited an appropriate amount of time before stepping out of her car. She was attractive and leggy with long blonde hair.

She joined the man in the condo.

It didn't take much to imagine what they might be doing inside, having already witnessed it firsthand.

She was the loud type; while her lover was more focused on rough actions speaking for him.

Glancing at a watch, the doer decided it was time to get this over with.

Moving quickly toward the condo, the doer resisted the temptation to look around in the dim light, knowing this small impulse alone might cause someone to hone in on a passing stranger.

Pausing at the unit and listening carefully for any sounds within, there was nothing perceptible due to the thick walls, which would work well for the purpose in mind.

The gloved hand turned the doorknob, slowly opening the door.

Inside two goblets of wine sat on a table in the living room. Clothes were strewn about the hardwood floor as if they couldn't get them off soon enough. Muffled sounds could be heard upstairs.

The doer climbed the steps, moving steadily. The master bedroom was just down the hall. Laughter and moaning grew louder, along with the frenetic movement of bodies.

The two were on the bed naked having sex. She was on top, galloping like a stallion, while he had one hand clamped firmly on her breast and the other gripping a buttock.

Removing the gun, a few brisk steps toward the pair followed. Before they were even aware of another presence in the room, it was too late. Bullets were systematically pumped into the pair until the killer was satisfied there was no life left in the room other than one.

CHAPTER ONE

Leila Kahana had been with the Maui County Police Department for seven years, working in the Criminal Investigative Division as a detective and composite sketch artist. She'd joined the homicide squad three years ago and had seen her share of murder victims in various types of positions, ranging from fetal to awkward to dangling. But none made her olive skin flush like the present victims. A Hawaiian man and white woman, both in their thirties, were naked and locked in coitus; the woman slumped astride the man.

Identified through their driver licenses as Doctors Larry Nagasaka and Elizabeth Racine, both had been shot at point blank range in the head and the woman had bullet wounds in her back. The two were literally lying in a pool of their own blood.

The call had come in this Tuesday at 8:30 p.m. with a report of gunfire at the Crest Creek Condominiums, one of the new and expensive developments in the exclusive Wailea Resort. Neither victim lived at the residence that, according to records, was owned by the Medical Association of Maui.

3

"Looks like they went out with a bang, no pun intended," her partner, Detective Sergeant Blake Seymour, said as a police photographer took pictures of the decedents.

Leila winced, hoping Seymour didn't notice how uncomfortable she felt seeing the victims locked in the sex act. Not that she had anything against sex, other than being without for the past six months. It just seemed like some things should remain private and not exposed for everyone to see. Or at least not a bunch of gawking law enforcement personnel.

But then Leila didn't imagine the pair knew they would be murdered at the worst possible time. Or best, depending on how you looked at it.

"I guess we can pretty much rule out murder-suicide," she said, as there was no murder weapon found anywhere near the bodies. Not to mention they were shot multiple times and in difficult positions, making it all but impossible that either victim could have been the shooter.

"I agree. Not unless one or the other was a glutton for punishment and Houdini at the same time."

Leila wrinkled her nose. "There was no sign of forced entry either. And it doesn't look like anything was taken. Once you get past their messy remains and clothes scattered around, the place is immaculate. Not exactly evidence of a burglary."

Seymour flexed his latex gloved hand and lifted a shell casing, dropping it in a plastic bag. "Someone invaded the place all right, and found exactly who they were looking for. The question is, under what circumstances and who got the jump on the lovers?"

Leila made it a point to never try and get inside a killer's head too soon. The evidence had a way of leading them down the right path, even if less than straight and narrow. She looked again at the victims.

"No reason to believe they were expecting company. Obviously it didn't deter the killer. Whichever way you slice it, this was definitely personal."

"Sure looks that way. Whoever did this definitely wanted to make a statement. They didn't have a fighting chance."

"So we'll fight the fight on their behalf."

Leila stepped aside as the photographer took pictures of the corpses from a different angle. She believed the killer not only wanted to execute the pair, but humiliate them, too.

She instructed other CSI members to document the crime scene including identifying, collecting and processing any possible physical evidence.

Following Seymour downstairs, Leila couldn't help but wonder if anyone ever used the place other than for sex. If only her house were as tidy. Or maybe that would make it seem too artificial rather than a place to live.

She noted the door key on a cabinet off the foyer. "I'm guessing one of the victims used this to get in. Probably left the door unlocked and that's how the killer got in."

Seymour looked. "Yeah, you're probably right. Still, you never know. If the killer had a key, he or she might have tossed it aside, no longer needing it once the deed was done." He said to a nearby CSI, "Dust this key for prints."

"Sure thing."

Seymour did a quick scan of the area. "Would've helped if they'd had a first rate security system."

Leila blinked. "Maybe the association didn't feel one was needed."

"A costly error in judgment, though something tells me the victims were here on their own time taking care of business, so to speak."

"Yeah, right." She rolled her eyes.

Seymour managed a weak smile.

Leila approached Officer Tasia Gould. "Who called this in?"

"A neighbor." She lifted a notepad. "Barbara Holliman."

"We'll need to speak with Ms. Holliman."

"And anyone else in the immediate area who was home when the call came in," Seymour added. "Someone must have seen the shooter."

Tasia nodded. "That's usually the case, even if they didn't realize it at the time."

Leila looked up at Seymour, who was nearly a foot taller than her five-four with most of it muscle. "You think this is an isolated incident?"

He shrugged. "Guess that will depend on why someone wanted the doctors dead while caught in the act."

Leila refused to speculate on motive beyond the obvious that the killer knew the doctors. Not till they had more to go on regarding the victims.

And perpetrator.

* * *

Leila sat in the passenger seat as Seymour drove. Both were trapped in their own thoughts about the latest case to bring them out into the night. For her part, Leila never considered one investigation to be any less or more important than the next. When dealing with human beings and loss of life through violence, all cases deserved their best efforts.

She glanced at Seymour's profile. He was nice enough looking, if not the most handsome man she had seen. His salt and pepper hair was cut short and he'd recently grown a mustache, which Leila hadn't decided if she liked. They had been partners for two years and she still didn't know him very well. At times he could be moody, witty, or a million miles away.

Seymour was currently separated from his wife. Leila suspected he wanted to get back together with her, but tried to pretend otherwise. She wasn't sure what to tell him, having no experience in that department.

At thirty-two, Leila had never been married. Born in Hawaii to conservative Polynesian parents who believed it was her duty to marry an established Polynesian man, Leila wasn't opposed to marriage as much as being with someone she didn't love. That included her last boyfriend, who had turned out to be a real jerk.

Leila preferred to be on her own for now till someone came along who really made her want him.

She looked again at her partner. "Why are you so quiet over there, Seymour?"

"Just thinking about disappointing my daughter." He paused. "I was supposed to pick her up for the night. Then duty called."

"Is it too late now?"

"She's probably asleep."

"She knows you're a cop. I think she'll understand." Easy for her to say.

"Yeah, I suppose." Seymour sniffed. "I still hate letting her down."

"So find a way to make it up to her."

"I'll think of something."

Leila's mind returned to the grisly crime scene. They were on their way to notify next of kin before the press could. This was one of the hardest parts of the job, along with tracing the winding path that had culminated with a double murder.

* * *

The address they had for Larry Nagasaka was in nearby Kihei. It was a beachfront estate surrounded by swaying palm trees in a gated community. Seymour could only imagine what a place like this went for. Certainly way out of his league.

Apparently the doctor wasn't entirely at home here though, considering he'd chosen another location to have sex.

The door was opened by an attractive petite Asian woman with long raven hair, almost as though she'd been expecting them.

"Yes?"

He identified them. "And you are...?"

"Connie Nagasaka."

"Is Dr. Larry Nagasaka your—?"

"Husband. Yes." She frowned. "What is this about?"

7

"Could we please come in?" Leila asked.

Connie met her eyes and nodded. She led them into a large foyer. "What's happened to Larry?"

Seymour cleared his throat. "I'm sorry to inform you that your husband's dead."

A hand flew to her mouth. "How?"

It was always the initial reaction Seymour tried to gauge in determining if such news came as a total shock.

"He was shot to death."

"Where?"

"At a condo in Wailea."

Connie's nostrils flared. "Was he with *her*?"

"Who?"

"His lover."

Seymour glanced at Leila, deferring to her.

"You knew your husband was having an affair?"

"He made no secret of it. Neither did she."

Leila glanced at her notes. "Two people were shot to death tonight. Your husband and a woman named Elizabeth Racine."

Connie started to cry. "I told Larry she wasn't worth it. He never listened to me."

"Mind telling us how you spent your evening?"

She favored her sharply. "At home. By myself. I've gotten used to it."

Seymour chewed on his lip. "Do you know anyone who would've wanted your husband dead?" He was still trying to decide if she belonged on that list.

"Maybe Liz's husband, Kenneth," Connie answered matter-of-factly. "Few men can tolerate a cheating wife."

* * *

Leila eyed Seymour after they reached the department issued dark sedan. "She wasn't exactly a grieving widow."

"Not everyone takes the news the same."

"Especially when you have an adulterous husband who happens to be bringing in what has to be big bucks."

Seymour opened the door. "Think she did it?"

Leila imagined Connie pumping bullets into the lovers. "Anything's possible. Or maybe someone did the job for her."

"Like Kenneth Racine?"

"Hey, stranger things have happened. Maybe he'll save us all some trouble by fessing up."

She wasn't holding her breath. From Leila's experience, most homicidal spouses were anything but accommodating. They usually preferred to blame everyone else for their problems, including the victim.

Or, in this case, victims.

Seymour pulled into the parking lot at Maui General Hospital where Doctor Kenneth Racine was on duty as medical director of the Behavioral Health Unit.

Leila hated hospitals, an emotion born from fear of having her tonsils removed as a child and added to by the death of her father ten years ago after spending the last two months of his life in a hospital bed.

They were directed to the third floor, where a nurse pointed toward a forty-something, tall man with thick gray hair. He seemed agitated after snapping his cell phone shut.

"Dr. Kenneth Racine?" Leila asked.

"Yes?"

She lifted her ID. "We're detectives with the Maui County Police Department. Could we have a word with you in private?"

His brow furrowed. "Look, if this is about those parking tickets, I swear I'll pay them. Things have just been a little crazy around here, you know?"

"We're not traffic cops," Seymour said curtly. "This is a homicide matter—"

Kenneth's head snapped back. "My office is just over there..."

They followed him to the office, where he left the door open.

"You said homicide?" He looked at Seymour.

9

"Afraid we have bad news. Your wife, Elizabeth, was murdered."

Kenneth's eyes bulged. "That's not possible! Liz is at a seminar in Honolulu."

Leila blinked, wishing that had been the case for his sake and hers. "We believe a woman found shot to death at a condo in Wailea tonight is in fact Elizabeth Racine."

He lifted his cell phone and pushed a button. "Yes, I need to speak to Elizabeth Racine. She's a guest there." A few moments passed. "What do you mean there's no one registered there by that name?"

Leila regarded Seymour. She wondered if Racine's reaction was mainly for their benefit.

He hung up, eyes downcast. "They said she never checked in, even though she had made a reservation."

Leila supposed it had been smart to cover her tracks. That was, until someone made certain they ran out for good.

"Larry Nagasaka was also murdered at the condo," she said.

"Larry—" Kenneth gulped. "Are you telling me my wife and Larry were having an affair?"

"Sure looks that way."

"That bloody bastard."

Leila didn't disagree, but that was beside the point. "You had no idea your wife was seeing another man?"

Kenneth sneered. "Isn't the spouse always last to know?"

"Not always," said Seymour. "We need you to account for your whereabouts tonight."

"You're kidding, right? You think I actually had something to do with this?"

"Wouldn't be the first time a vindictive spouse offed his wife and lover."

Kenneth took a step backward. "Look, I loved my wife and would never have wanted her dead, no matter what. I've been working my ass off here since three o'clock trying to keep this unit together."

* * *

"His story seems to hold up." Seymour stood beside Leila in the elevator.

"Even in a busy hospital, people can sometimes see what they want to," she said.

"True. Wouldn't be too much of a stretch to believe Racine could've taken a break from his duties to get rid of a cheating wife and her lover."

Leila ran a hand through her hair. "Aren't doctors supposed to be in the business of saving lives?"

Seymour gave her a deadpan look. "That may well depend on whose life it is."

He drove on the Honoapiilani Highway to West Maui where Leila lived.

"Do you want to get a drink?"

Leila didn't look his way. "Tempting, but I think I'll call it a night, if that's okay. It's been a long day."

"You're right, it has been, and that's fine."

"Another time?" She faced him.

"Yeah." He turned to look at her and back to the road. A few minutes later Seymour dropped Leila off at home. "See you tomorrow."

"Count on it." She gave a little smile and waved.

Seymour drove off, thinking she was probably the most levelheaded cop he knew, including himself. And also the best looking, which may have been the problem. He loved her new hairstyle, a short bob with sloping edges. Of course he kept his compliments in check, not wanting to make either of them uncomfortable in what was a good working relationship. Partnering up with Leila might not have been his first choice, but she'd earned his respect and taught him a few things along the way.

Seymour took the Kahekili Highway to the place he was renting in central Maui. Unlike the resort areas on the west and south sides of Maui, there wasn't much here to excite tourists. The fact that real people like him lived and worked in central Maui made it more to his liking, aside from living alone for the time being.

He would've preferred going to the house he once shared with his wife, Mele. That was before he screwed up, got caught, and was kicked out four months ago. She had yet to file for divorce, but since there was virtually no real communication between them, he feared it was only a matter of time.

When they did talk, it was mostly about their eight-year-old daughter, Akela. They had adopted her when she was less than a month old after learning that Mele was unable to have children. Akela was the one thing in his life Seymour was most proud of. He hated having to disappoint her. But he was a cop and had been for twenty of his forty-six years. Someday Akela would understand that people like him were needed to go after the bad guys in the world. Or at least within Hawaii. Until then, he would continue to try and balance the things most important to him.

Seymour thought about the crime that left two doctors dead. There was nothing more to be done tonight other than hope they caught a break and made an arrest.

As to what drove the killer to taking the two lives was pure conjecture at this point. But it didn't mean he wasn't up to some guesswork. Obviously the victims thought they had the perfect place for their affair.

Well, they were dead wrong.

They had ticked someone off. Or maybe one had been targeted and the other was just collateral damage.

Either way, a killer was on the loose and that was always cause for concern for you never knew what one might do next after experiencing their first kill and finding it agreed with them.

.

CHAPTER TWO

The alarm clock went off at six a.m., giving Leila a start after being caught in a deep sleep. She managed to drag herself out of bed and into the bathroom to wash her face. Then she went downstairs to make coffee.

Leila lived in a two bedroom, plantation style cottage in Lahaina. It was built in 1934 and once owned by her grandfather, Ekewaka Kahana, a former County of Maui police chief. Leila had lived there for the past five years, taking over ownership from her mother who lived on the Big Island and had been renting the place before deciding to sell. Little by little she had managed to renovate the house, which still had its original wood floors and wood frame windows.

By six-fifteen, Leila was out taking her daily jog. It took only a few minutes to end up on Front Street, Lahaina's main thoroughfare, where she could see the ocean and pass by quaint shops and historical attractions before the crowds began to gather.

After showering, she headed off to work in her Subaru Impreza, admiring the West Maui Mountains and breathtaking glimpse of the coastline along the way.

The Maui County Police Department was located in Wailuku, the county seat. Leila made her way to the second story conference room where the homicide squad met each morning to go over their cases, new leads, and lost opportunities. The cold-blooded murder of two doctors would surely be at the top of the agenda.

Present was Lieutenant Paul Ortega, who was contemplating retirement now that his youngest daughter had gotten married, Detectives Trent Ferguson and Rachel Lancaster, and Detective Sergeant Blake Seymour.

"I thought for a minute you'd decided to give up all this for something less taxing," quipped Seymour.

Leila sneered, noting she was fifteen minutes early. She regretted not going with him for a drink last night. If only he were single in the true sense of the word, instead of hoping the wife might take him back.

"Wouldn't want to make your life easier," she retorted.

He laughed. "Trust me when I say that wouldn't happen."

She took that as a compliment, taking a seat next to him.

Lt. Ortega gained their attention. "I'll bring you up to snuff on the latest. First, whoever killed Doctors Elizabeth Racine and Larry Nagasaka is still at large, in spite of our best efforts to the contrary. The fact that both victims were married, but not to each other, makes it very likely we could be looking at a love triangle murder mystery. The spouses would have us believe otherwise. But we all know alibis can never be accepted at face value. Nor should they.

"Another possible angle is the murders could be work related. Racine, an internist, and Nagasaka, a hematologist, both belonged to the Medical Association of Maui—a group of medical practitioners on the island who banded together about ten years ago. Maybe someone handpicked these victims in particular. Or others could be targeted, too. Let's not wait to find out."

"Ballistics will tell us the type of gun and bullets used," Leila said, hoping this would lead to the perpetrator, though she knew they had to count on additional evidence to make the connection stick.

Ferguson clasped large hands. "Chances are the gun was either stolen or bought on the street."

Rachel snorted. "Or it's just as likely the perp bought the weapon legally."

"We know the killer pumped at least five to six bullets into the victims," Seymour told them. "The autopsy results will confirm and should give us something to go on regarding the shooter and murder weapon."

Leila nodded. "The killer had easy access to the condo, suggesting they probably staked out the place and waited to catch the victims off guard before shooting them."

"But why not just go after the one targeted?" Rachel looked nonplussed. "Why take an innocent life? Unless both doctors were the intended victims from the start."

Ferguson lifted his chin. "Maybe the killer didn't give a damn if someone else died who happened to be at the wrong place, wrong time. Most killers don't have a conscience."

"But they were killed having sex." Seymour sat up. "I doubt it was an accident. Our killer likely had every intention of executing both victims. The method and timing were choreographed. What it comes down to is this. Was this the ultimate price of infidelity? Or were they killed because they were doctors and belonged to the same professional organization?"

Leila agreed that his points had merit. "Whether the killer went after one person or both, the result is the same: we're left with two victims and more than one possibility as to why they were murdered. We've got our work cut out for us."

"Then I suggest we get going," Ortega said. "You and Seymour continue to take the lead on this one. Ferguson and Lancaster will work with you apart from other cases they're investigating. Get this killer off the streets!"

Leila gazed at Seymour, certain he too was already feeling the pressure of closing this case as quickly as possible.

* * *

Leila paid a return visit to the scene of the crime—Crest Creek Condominiums—to interview Barbara Holliman, the woman who reported the crime.

She was in her early forties and lived alone three units away from the condo where two lives were lost.

"Tell me exactly what you heard, Ms. Holliman."

Barbara fidgeted. "About four or five pops. I knew right away it was gunfire. My dad was a hunter, so I know what gunshots sound like."

"And that was at approximately eight-thirty?" Leila lifted a cup of tea that had practically been thrust upon her.

"Yes."

"What did you do then?"

"Well, first I nearly had a panic attack, wondering who was shooting who and if I should duck or what." She sighed. "When I calmed down, I called 911."

"Did you ever look outside to see if anyone was there?" Leila had noted the shooter would have had to pass by her condo to get to the other one from the street."

"Yes, when I got the courage I peeked through the blinds."

"Go on."

"I saw someone running," Barbara said. "It was kind of dark so I couldn't really tell if it was a man or woman. I have no idea if the person I saw was the killer or completely innocent."

"Did you see anyone else?"

"No, not till a few minutes later when the police showed up and people started gathering outside. There was a lot of commotion out there."

Leila set the teacup on a saucer. "Did you see anyone in the crowd you didn't recognize?" She suspected the killer had fled the scene, but there was a chance he or she had hung around to watch the aftermath, gaining a vicarious thrill while hiding in plain view.

Barbara rubbed her nose. "Yeah, maybe. I think everybody was just caught up in the moment and assumed it wasn't a random act; believing the shooter had already left."

Leila wondered if the killer had staked out the condominium complex beforehand, plotting out an escape route, and avoiding detection. That was assuming the person wasn't a regular visitor.

"Did you notice anyone hanging around that day or previous days leading up to the shootings?"

"No, not really." Barbara flushed. "I'm probably not as observant as I should be."

"How about cars?" Leila persisted. "Maybe there was one that caught your eye, seemingly out of place. Or the driver appeared lost. Or a car parked somewhere longer than it should have been."

Barbara twisted her mouth to one side. "Cars come and go around here. Mostly BMWs and other high-end cars. I can't really say that any stood out as not belonging. Sorry."

So was Leila. Either the unsub came there on foot or drove an expensive car, meaning they had more in common with the victims than being the last to see them alive.

Leila made mental notes. Even the most insignificant detail could be important down the line where it concerned murder. Only time would tell. Along with how careful or sloppy the killer was in covering their tracks.

* * *

Later that evening, Seymour went to pick up his daughter for pizza. It was the least he could do after being forced to abort the sleepover the previous night.

His estranged wife, Mele, lived in Kahului, Maui's largest town. Seymour had purchased the fifteen hundred square foot contemporary home right after they got married. Seemed like a good investment at the time.

Maybe it still could be.

Seymour noted Mele's red Honda in the driveway. He rang the bell. Mele opened the door. She was Filipino with long black hair she usually wore in a braid.

"Sorry I'm a little late."

She frowned. "So what else is new?"

"I don't want to fight with you." Or perhaps that was better than not talking at all.

"If you say so."

"Where's Akela?"

"I'll get her. You wait here."

Seymour stood in the living room, feeling like a stranger in his own house. He wished he could take back some things, but he'd just have to deal with it.

"Makuakane!" Akela said to him spiritedly.

He watched as she came bounding down the stairs. Tall for her age, Akela had long dark hair that was pulled back in a loose ponytail.

She ran into his arms and hugged him.

"Hey, honey!" He gave her a kiss on the cheek.

"I thought you weren't going to come again." She looked at him sadly through big brown eyes.

"Well, you thought wrong!" Seymour sometimes cursed his job. "Are you ready to get stuffed on some pizza?"

"Yeah, I think so."

Mele reappeared. "Don't keep her out long. She has piano lessons in the morning."

He looked at his wife. He was still attracted to her even when she was snippy with him. "You're welcome to come, if you like."

She seemed to consider it. "I'll pass."

Seymour forced a smile, if only for his daughter's sake.

* * *

Leila sipped a glass of red wine while taking a bath. She felt lonely and had for some time now. Even when she was with her last boyfriend, he'd been unable to fill the empty void in her life. She wondered if something was wrong with her in the inability to find someone with whom she could truly relate.

Had she set the bar too high?

Or was she simply looking in all the wrong places?

Her mind drifted to the murder investigation. How close were they to nabbing the killer? Were they planning a repeat performance?

Leila imagined the victims making love before being shot to death. She wouldn't pass judgment on their infidelity. It didn't rise to the level of being murdered.

She wondered what it would be like to make love to Seymour. Or wasn't he interested in her that way with a wife still in the picture?

Maybe it was best if she kept her focus on things more practical. Like solving murders.

CHAPTER THREE

Gabe Devane went for a usual morning jog with his dog Sal in Makena State Park. He liked being able to get Sal out of the backyard where he was cooped up most days while Gabe worked.

He felt the dog yank on the leash, longing to roam freely. "Sorry, boy, no can do. The last thing I need is for you to get into trouble."

Sal settled down and seemed to acquiescence to a leisurely, controlled run.

Gabe sucked in a calculated breath and thought about the nasty breakup with his girlfriend last week. He hadn't seen it coming. Should he fight to get her back? Or use his newfound freedom to scope out the marketplace with so many hot chicks in Maui?

Sal's bark snapped Gabe from his reverie.

"What is it, boy?" The dog was trying to break free.

Looking around, Gabe spotted an elderly woman being mugged. He ran in that direction. "Hey, leave her alone!"

The mugger saw him coming, grabbed the woman's purse, and knocked her down before bolting in another direction.

Gabe released the dog. "Get him, Sal!"

The dog was not vicious by nature. But Sal knew the bad from the good and wasn't afraid to go after someone who deserved it.

Gabe reached the old woman. She was lying on the damp grass, half dazed and bleeding from the mouth. She looked about eighty-five or so. It made him even angrier that the asshole mugger would go after someone so old and fragile.

"Are you all right?" Gabe could see she was anything but okay.

She moaned something indecipherable and seemed to pick at her thinning white hair as though searching for dandruff.

"My pur—" she stammered.

"Sal, my dog, went after him. Just stay down there and I'll get help."

Gabe flagged down a passing couple to call 911 and look after the old woman, while he went in search of his dog. And the mugger.

* * *

Leila had just poured herself a cup of coffee at work when she was approached by Detective Tony Fujimoto from the Property Crimes and Robbery Unit. He looked as though he'd been up all night. She wondered with whom.

"You busy?" he asked.

"I'm sure I will be soon. What's up?"

"We had a mugging reported this morning. A jogger got a description of the mugger and we think it's the same guy who has attacked elderly people several times in the last month. I need you to do a sketch. Maybe we can nip this problem in the bud."

"No problem. Is the jogger here now?"

"Yeah. He's waiting in room A."

Leila gave a weak smile. "I'll see what I can do."

"Appreciate it. Let me know when you're done."

So much for a coffee break to begin the day. She went to her desk to get a pad and pencils.

Seymour was sitting at his desk across from hers. "Are you ready to put this mug on paper?"

"You wish." Actually she thought it might be fun to sketch him sometime.

"Had to try. Someday you may surprise me."

"Maybe. Right now I have to do a composite sketch of a mugger."

"While you're putting your artistic talents to work, I'll pay a visit to the Medical Association of Maui. There's a good chance someone in the organization has become a liability."

Leila didn't discount that, starting with Elizabeth Racine's husband, Kenneth. "Let's see which way the wind blows. Catch you later."

She found the witness sitting patiently in the room. "Hi, I'm Detective Kahana."

He stood. "Gabe Devane."

Leila shook his hand. She speculated he was in his late thirties. "You witnessed a mugging?"

"Yeah, pretty much saw the whole thing while in the park with my dog. I hope that poor woman will be all right."

"We'll check on her."

"So how do we do this?" he asked. "Never described a mugger before."

"It's simple, really." Leila opened up her pad. "I'll ask you some questions and you just answer them to the best of your ability."

"I can do that."

"Did you get a pretty good look at the person?"

"I think so, though he was about fifteen feet away before I saw his face. Then my dog went after him, but somehow lost the no good bastard."

Leila twirled her pencil. "Let's start with the basics. About how old would you say the mugger was?"

"Between twenty-five and thirty."

"Race or ethnicity?"

"I think he was a native."

"Meaning...?"

"Hawaiian, I guess."

It didn't insult Leila when people referred to the "natives" as Hawaiians as this was more preferable than locals. As it was, true Native Hawaiians such as herself comprised only around ten percent of those living in Maui County. The majority of residents were classified as white or Asian.

Leila held the pencil. "How about a general description of the man's face?" She knew most people had difficulty regarding detailed specifics on a suspect, often rarely studying their features as if for a college exam.

"Let's see... His face was narrow, a little tanned, and I think he had a goatee."

She sketched this. "Did you get a look at his eyes?"

"Definitely black or brown."

"Were they close set?"

"I believe so."

"Long nose or short?"

"Short."

"Wide or narrow."

"More wide than narrow."

"What about hairstyle or color?"

He sat up. "Hair was black and worn in a short ponytail."

"That's good." Leila believed the way a suspect wore their hair was critical in a composite sketch. Surprisingly, relatively few criminals bothered to change their hairstyle to lower their risk of detection. "Did you happen to notice if he wore any jewelry, like an earring? Or had any distinguishing marks on his face?"

Gabe shook his head. "Wish I could help you there, but it all happened so fast."

"Not a problem. I think we have enough to go on." She worked in rapid fashion to complete her interpretation of the suspect's description before holding up her sketch. "Is this reasonably close to the mugger's face?"

Gabe studied it for a moment. "Yeah, I'd say that's damn close."

Leila sucked in a breath of relief. "Great. I'll get this to the detective on the case. Thanks for your help."

"Just doing my civic duty." He smiled.

Leila wondered if he was flirting with her. She noted there was no ring on his finger so he might be single. Too bad he wasn't her type, though Leila wasn't always sure who was.

She stood and shook his hand. "We'll be sure to let you know when we get the mugger."

"I hope it's soon, if only for that old woman's peace of mind."

* * *

Sometimes Detective Rachel Lancaster hated this job. Now was a perfect example as she stood outside the door, accompanied by two uniformed officers. She understood in a basic way why sixteen-year-old Carrie Poole had kept her pregnancy a secret, not even telling the father. Her parents were overly strict and ultra conservative, making the girl feel shame and fear as to how they would react. After all, Rachel's own sister had once gone down that same road, ultimately having the child and giving it up for adoption, something she'd regretted ever since.

In Carrie's case, she had gone to extreme measures to rid herself of a burden she wished would go away. She'd put her newborn son in a plastic bag and tossed him a dumpster like garbage. An autopsy revealed the partially decomposed baby was full-term.

It had taken more than a month of investigating till DNA evidence tied Carrie to the infant. She now faced multiple charges, including murder and concealing the birth of a child. Rachel had come to the modest home in Kula, where Carrie lived with her parents, to take her into custody.

She rang the doorbell, wishing the girl had found someone to talk to before making a bad choice that would haunt her for the rest of her life.

Carrie opened the door and stood there mute.

Rachel bit her lip. "Carrie Poole, you're under arrest for the murder of your newborn baby."

The girl made no attempt to resist, and actually looked relieved that this day had come.

In accordance with department policy, Rachel put the handcuffs on her, even as Carrie's parents appeared and mildly protested.

"There must be some mistake," her father insisted.

Rachel gazed at the teenager. "I wish that were the case, but it isn't."

"Carrie...?" Her mother waited for a firm denial.

It didn't come.

"I did it, Mama," Carrie cried. "I killed my baby."

Rachel led her away.

Afterwards Rachel did some paperwork at her desk. She stopped to look at the photo of her late husband, Greg. He died two years ago in Iraq when his tank was hit by an improvised explosive device. He'd had less than two months left to serve in the Army before his tour of duty was up.

Rachel had become a widow at thirty-four. She and Greg had put having children on hold while she got her career going in law enforcement. Now she wished they'd had a child to keep what she and Greg had alive. Instead she'd had to arrest a teenager who took away her child's chance at life. How fair was that?

* * *

Leila found Detective Fujimoto at his desk. "I've got a present for you." He looked up as she held out the composite sketch.

He took it, studying. "So this is the asshole who's been attacking the elderly?"

"The witness believes it hits the mark. I'll settle for a reasonably close sketch someone just might recognize."

"Yeah, that's what I'm counting on. We'll get this out there and hope for the best."

"It's all we can do," she said. "If that fails, he'll probably target someone else."

"That's what bothers me. How long before his aggression turns deadly and moves into your realm?"

Leila frowned. "Don't even think it. We have enough on our plates right now, thank you."

Fujimoto moved a hand though his raven hair. "I'll bet. Isn't killing doctors like the next worst thing to killing clergy?"

"There's no ranking for murder in my book," she said. "No one should have to die before their time."

"I agree. Unfortunately that doesn't stop killers from deciding when it is someone's time to go."

Leila knew that all too well. Didn't mean she had to like it. "Speaking of which, I'd better get back to the grind. Wouldn't want Seymour to claim he did all the work by himself."

Fujimoto grinned. "Isn't Ferguson working the case, too?"

She nodded. "Why do you ask?"

"Oh no reason in particular," he said quickly. "Guess I just wanted to make sure someone had your back in case Seymour was out of shouting distance."

Leila swallowed. "We all have each other's back. Just as I'm sure you do in robbery."

"Yeah."

She smiled. "Good. Had me worried for a moment there, Fujimoto."

CHAPTER FOUR

The Medical Association of Maui's main offices were located in West Maui's Kapalua Resort. Seymour parked in the lot and jammed a stick of gum in his mouth. He had no reason to believe the organization was directly connected to the double homicide at its condominium. But his gut instincts told him the location of the murders was more than pure coincidence.

Seymour went inside the one story building and was immediately struck by the marble floors, stone pillars, and other indications of overspending. How much of it was blood money? He wondered if greed could be at the core of losing two of their own.

He had an appointment with CEO Douglas Brennan, believing it was a good idea to start at the top.

"Thanks for seeing me." Seymour shook hands with the sixty-something man who was impeccably dressed in a gray suit.

"I'm happy to do whatever I can to help," Douglas said as he sat behind his desk. "We're all broken up over the deaths of Liz and Larry."

"I understand your organization owns the condo they were using?"

"Yes, that's right. We originally bought it as an investment property; then decided we'd use it as a place for prospective members to stay when in town."

"Does everyone in the association have access to it?" Seymour looked at him.

"Technically, yes. We keep a spare key in the office. Larry, who arranged for guests to stay at the condo, had the main one."

Seymour assumed the key left on the cabinet in the condo must have belonged to Nagasaka. But someone else who knew about the spare key could have used or duplicated it to enter.

"Where is the spare key now?" Seymour asked.

Douglas opened a desk drawer and removed a small envelope, emptying a key onto the desk. "Right here, like it always is."

"I see." This told Seymour that anyone would be able to borrow the key and return it when the CEO was out of his office. "Do you know anyone in particular who might've held a grudge against one of the doctors or had any other reason to want one or both dead?"

Douglas squeezed the tip of his nose. "This may sound cliché, but we're like a happy family. Everyone likes and supports everyone else. So to answer your question, no, I don't believe Larry and Liz's deaths were connected to this organization."

"Not all families get alone lovingly," Seymour couldn't resist saying. "In fact, some have proven to be downright deadly."

"I'll grant you that much. But I'm confident, Detective, that you're looking in the wrong direction."

From Seymour's experience that was cause for digging deeper. He doubted a CEO with his head in the clouds was as privy to all that was happening among the ranks as those beneath him.

"Was it common knowledge among the members that Dr. Racine and Dr. Nagasaka were lovers?"

Douglas flinched. "I'm sure Liz and Larry were discreet."

"Obviously not too discreet since they chose to use company property where anyone could have walked in on them."

"Our primary focus is treating our patients. We try not to regulate members' personal lives, so long as no laws are broken."

Seymour's brow furrowed. "Unfortunately, the law against murder was broken—twice. I'd like the names of every member of your organization."

Douglas raised a brow. "Is that really necessary?"

"Probably not. But with two of your group murdered, it's best to err on the side of caution. Don't you think?"

"Of course. Whatever you need, I'll have my secretary get for you."

"Thank you." Seymour wondered if protecting the company's image was more important to him than seeing that justice was served no matter the cost.

Douglas tapped his desk. "Oh there is one other thing I should probably mention, though it may or may not be relevant..."

"I'm listening."

"We have a cleaning service come in once a week—meaning they also have a key to the condo. If I'm not mistaken, yesterday was their day to clean the place. Maybe something went horribly wrong—"

Seymour's lashes flickered. He thought about how clean the condo had been. Would a killer have taken time to tidy up the place after executing two people?

"What's the name of the cleaning service?"

"Ocean View Housekeeping."

Seymour left with more than when he arrived. He would bring Leila up to snuff and see who was on duty as a housekeeper the day Racine and Nagasaka met their demise.

* * *

"The murdering housekeeper from hell," remarked Leila, driving to the cleaning service. "Sounds like a B horror movie."

Seymour chuckled humorlessly beside her. "Yeah, I was thinking the same thing. At the very least, maybe the person saw something or someone before the fact."

"Two bad the dead can't talk."

"But they can in some respects. How they were shot; where and why will speak for them."

"I suppose."

Leila favored him sideways. She liked the deep thinker in Seymour that only came with experience. What else was going on in that head of his? Maybe he would tell her sometime.

They arrived at Ocean View Housekeeping, located in Ka'anapali, and met with the director Tess Kwan.

"We're conducting an investigation into two people murdered at the Crest Creek Condominiums on Tuesday," Leila told her.

"I heard about that." Tess shook her head. "How terrible."

"We understand one of your employees cleaned the condo that day."

"Actually the condo was cleaned on Monday, but we did have a problem with the housekeeper—Melissa Eng."

Seymour gazed at her. "What problem was that?"

Tess hesitated. "I'm afraid Melissa was caught stealing from the residence. Of course, we let her go immediately. We have a zero tolerance policy against any type of inappropriate conduct."

"Who reported it?" he asked.

Tess glanced at her desk. "Larry Nagasaka."

Leila fixed Seymour's face. It appeared Melissa Eng had given them a real reason to pursue this angle further.

* * *

Melissa Eng lived in a house in Ma'alaea. Seymour was familiar with the area not far from Wailea, having worked a case there several years ago in which a disgruntled man shot and killed two co-workers before turning the gun on himself.

Could this be another case of worker rage?

He knocked on the door and waited beside Leila for a response.

It came a moment later. A small boned woman in her late thirties stood there.

"Melissa Eng?"

"Yes..."

He tried to imagine her gunning down two people. Stranger things had happened.

"I'm Detective Seymour and this is Detective Kahana with the Maui Police Department. We'd like to talk to you about the shooting deaths of Larry Nagasaka and Elizabeth Racine at the Crest Creek Condos."

Melissa's eyes grew. "What does it have to do with me?"

"Maybe nothing. Just a routine part of our investigation. Can we come in?"

She waited a beat before nodding.

Seymour took a sweeping glance inside. The faint smell of marijuana crossed his nostrils. He sensed the same from Leila.

He gave Melissa a direct gaze. "Why don't you tell us about being fired for stealing?"

"It wasn't fair." Her brow creased. "I never stole anything from that place."

"Did you explain that to Larry Nagasaka before he reported you?" Leila asked bluntly.

"I tried, but the man took a holier than thou attitude." She sneered.

"So why would he lie about it?"

"How should I know? Maybe it's how he got his kicks. He never proved anything, but they didn't want to listen."

Seymour narrowed an eye. "You've got an audience right now. If there's anything you need to get off your chest, this is the time to do it."

Melissa shot him a cold gaze. "I'm not sure what you're getting at."

"Did you kill Larry Nagasaka and the woman he was with to get back at people who thought they were better than you?"

"No!"

Seymour peered. "Where were you on Tuesday night when the murders occurred?"

"Right here. I never went back there once I turned my key in on Monday."

"Can anyone vouch for that?"

"I was home alone." Her eyes sharpened. "I didn't think I would need to account for where I was."

"Maybe you should rethink that," he said. "Do you own a gun?"

"No. Even if I did, I wouldn't use it to settle a score."

Seymour found it interesting she would consider being fired for what they could only assume was just grounds worthy of settling a score. The question was how far was she prepared to go to carry out her vendetta?

* * *

The autopsies on Elizabeth Racine and Larry Nagasaka were completed by seven p.m. on Thursday.

Seymour and Leila met afterward with the Medical Examiner Patricia Lee to discuss the results.

"Both victims died as a result of massive head trauma and blood loss caused from gunshots," she said. "Based on the powder burns on the skin and contusion rings around the wounds, I'd say the shooter was standing right over the victims toward the left side and shot them at a pointblank range.

"A single bullet entered Mrs. Racine's head from just behind the left ear, exiting from her forehead. Additionally, she was shot twice in the back, ripping though vital organs. Two of the bullets exited her and entered Mr. Nagasaka's body. One lodged in his heart, the other his right thigh. But it was the two shots to the victim's face that proved to be the death blow. They fractured his nose, left cheek, and right eye socket, along with causing extensive brain damage. One bullet was removed from his head while the other exited from the back of Nagasaka's neck."

"Time of death?" asked Seymour, wincing at the description of the victims' violent departure.

"I'd estimate somewhere between eight and eighty-thirty p.m."

This corresponded with the time the gunshots were reported.

"Could there have been more than one shooter?"

Patricia looked at him. "Not likely. The position of the wounds is consistent with a single shooter."

"I don't suppose you can tell if our shooter was a man or woman?" Leila asked.

"I'm afraid that's for you to determine. But if I had to hazard a guess, when looking at all the factors, I'd have to say the killer was probably between five-nine and six feet, so draw your own conclusions."

Seymour already had. Most homicides were committed by adult males, which seemed to be the case this time. Didn't mean women were incapable of such, though, especially when armed with a lethal weapon and the right height. Or there could have been a female accomplice involved the murders.

He rubbed his chin. "One other thing, Doctor. What can you tell us about the type of gun used in the crime?"

She pressed her lips together thoughtfully. "Based on the bullets recovered from the victims, I'd say they likely came from a .25 caliber handgun."

Seymour had guessed as much. Ballistics would confirm, giving them one important piece of the puzzle toward solving this case.

CHAPTER FIVE

Detective Trent Ferguson drove into Honokawai in West Maui. He felt a slight chill thinking about the eighteen-year-old high school senior who was raped and strangled to death two months ago by someone who had been stalking her. Cassandra Woo had a whole life ahead of her, till it was taken away. Ferguson had worked hard to crack the case, motivated at least in part by having lost a cousin the same way twenty years earlier.

Lenny Washburn was finally apprehended this morning after fleeing Maui for the Big Island. If Ferguson had his way, the bastard would get the death penalty. Hawaii was too soft on violent criminals, not having the guts to enact such measures for non federal murder cases.

Ferguson turned onto Lower Honoapiilani Road, where Cassandra's parents lived. He made them a promise that Washburn would not escape justice and wanted to tell them the news in person.

He stopped in front of the bungalow. Yao Woo was mowing the lawn while his wife, Olivia, was sitting on the lanai.

They greeted Ferguson warmly when he approached.

He didn't beat around the bush. "Your daughter's killer was arrested in Hilo an hour ago. Cassandra can rest in peace now."

"Thank you." Olivia wrapped her arms around his waist and wept.

Yao's eyes crinkled. "We only wanted some justice."

Ferguson choked up. "I hope you can move on with your lives now." He doubted they could ever overcome the tragedy. At least there was some sense of closure.

He left them, feeling a little satisfaction, even as Ferguson now had to put his efforts into helping to solve the murder of two doctors. Kahana and Seymour had been handed a case that had all the earmarks of a vendetta.

But against whom?

If he were a betting man, Ferguson would put his money on Larry Nagasaka. He'd read once that the doctor had run into some financial difficulties. Had he been forced to pay the piper?

Ferguson drove to a part of Lahaina that had a known problem with prostitution in recent years, catering to the burgeoning tourism industry. The police department had chosen to focus their efforts primarily on johns, while more or less giving the streetwalkers a free ride.

He brought his official vehicle to a stop not far from a young woman. Ferguson could tell by her body language that she was a hooker.

She walked up to the car and lowered her face to the passenger window. "Hi."

"Hey," he said, noting she wore way too much makeup and had blonde extensions.

"Are you lookin' for some action?"

"Maybe. You offering some?"

She favored him warily. "You a cop?"

He grinned. "Just a guy needing to get off. Can you help me out?"

"You got twenty bucks?"

"Yeah, with your name on it. Why don't you get in the car?"

She looked around as though it were a police sting. Seemingly satisfied, she got in the car.

"What's your name?" he asked.

"Gina."

He was sure it was her street name. Not that he cared one way or the other.

Ferguson stuck a twenty dollar bill inside her top. He unzipped his pants and immediately got an erection.

She bent her head down and gave him a blow job.

It took less than two minutes.

Ferguson said nothing as the prostitute exited the car and took her place again on the street.

He headed home to his wife.

* * *

On Saturday afternoon, Leila met her friend Jan Monroe at a deli in Lahaina. They sat at a corner table by the window.

Jan was just the opposite of Leila in appearance: tall and leggy, blonde and green-eyed. She seemingly had a new man in her life every week and Leila practically needed a scorecard to keep up. But Jan's true passion was her art. She painted beautiful landscapes that Leila could only dream of doing.

"So tell me I can count on you being at my showing Saturday night." Jan batted fake eyelashes.

"Wouldn't miss it for the world." Leila sipped a café latte.

"Good, because even though I invited everyone I know, I wouldn't be surprised if only half of them showed."

"Their loss, which would give the rest of us more room to admire your paintings."

"Good point."

"Just don't forget about us ordinary folks when you hit the big time."

Jan chuckled. "Not sure I want to go there. I'm happy where I am at this point in my life. Besides, you are *anything* but ordinary. Apart from being beautiful, you're one kick ass detective and can out-sketch anyone when push comes to shove."

Leila blushed. "You're good for my ego. Still, my life is far from ideal. I live alone in my late grandfather's house, work too much, date too little, and have the hots for my married, but separated partner, who's only fourteen years my senior. Is that screwed up or what?"

"You're no more screwed up than the rest of us, Leila, if there is such a thing. Who wouldn't want to live mortgage free in a quaint little house within arm's reach of the beach? And we all work too much. It's the world we live in. As for being attracted to your partner, I say let it happen if he feels the same. It's not like you have to marry him or anything, considering his circumstances."

"I'm not opposed to marriage."

"Neither am I. But being a product of divorce, I believe in taking my sweet time before heading down the aisle. Doesn't mean I can't have a lot of fun in the meantime."

Leila wished she could be as carefree. Was Seymour interested in being with anyone other than his wife? Or had he been there, done that one time too many?

Would that lead to a conflict of interest on the job?

* * *

Seymour's rented house was on Kaohu Street in Wailuku. He'd called in a favor to the owner and friend who lived in Hana and offered him a reduced rate to stay there as long as he liked. Seymour only intended for that to be a short while. He had every intention of moving back home once Mele realized they were better together than apart.

But what if that day never came? Could be she was dead serious about this separation becoming permanent and, if so, he would have no one to blame but himself.

Maybe it was time to cut his losses and try someone new. Isn't that what got him into trouble in the first place?

Seymour scanned the channels on TV with the remote. As usual, there was nothing to watch on a Saturday evening in the middle of summer. He sank back into the recliner and grabbed his beer bottle.

He'd met Nikole at a grocery store where a man had been killed during a botched holdup. Nikole was the clerk and witness to the crime. She reminded Seymour of Mele, only she was younger, and without the history that brought routine to a relationship. It hadn't been his intention to get involved with her, but it happened.

Mele walked in on them after he'd been foolish enough to bring Nikole to the house. His wife was supposed to be at the high school where she taught English. It was one of the most embarrassing and frustrating moments of Seymour's life.

If he could do it over again, things would be different. As it was, he had to live with the past.

And the future, too.

Seymour gulped down more beer. He could use some company about now. Mele wasn't in the mood. Might never be again. Didn't mean he would stop trying to win her back.

He wasn't good at fighting what seemed to be a losing battle.

Leila came to mind. She seemed to understand him better than most. There was a sexual attraction between them, though they had refrained from acting on it. Maybe they could get something going.

Was that a smart idea?

He hadn't always made the smartest moves. Why change that now?

* * *

That night Ferguson had dinner with his wife, Brenda. She'd made spaghetti and turkey balls. He felt her staring at him and resisted the temptation to look back. They were ten years into the marriage, but it somehow seemed more like twenty or thirty. Their relationship had grown stale. Especially in bed. The passion that had once kept them hot and heavy at all hours of the night barely registered anymore.

He blamed himself. She deserved better. Yet he couldn't walk away. And go where? Maybe he didn't even want a divorce. They could be messy and expensive.

Instead he preferred to just keep things as they were and see what happened.

Ferguson lifted his head and gazed across the table. "This is good," he said, and rolled more spaghetti onto his fork.

"What's going on with you?" she asked pointblank.

He cocked a brow. "Nothing. Just preoccupied with work."

She frowned. "You never talk to me anymore."

"What do you want me to say?"

"Anything! Just don't shut me out, Trent."

He took a sip of wine. "I don't mean to."

Brenda wiped her mouth with a napkin. "Are you having an affair?"

"No, of course not." Ferguson swallowed, hiding his guilt. "Where is this coming from?" As if he didn't know.

"It's coming from the reality that we don't seem to be on the same page anymore."

"Sure we are." He tried to convince her if not himself. "Sorry if I made you think otherwise."

Brenda leaned forward. "Are you still attracted to me?"

"Yes, of course. After all, you're my wife."

"Then start treating me like it!" She gave him an annoyed look and stood up. "I'm going to bed. You're welcome to join me if you like."

"I'll be there in a minute."

Ferguson finished his wine. He wasn't looking forward to being with his wife tonight. She couldn't give him what he wanted.

So maybe he'd give her time to fall asleep before hitting the bed.

* * *

The doer ate a chicken sandwich while reading the newspaper article about the murders of Doctors Larry Nagasaka and Elizabeth Racine. The police were said to be baffled by the execution style murders and had no suspects, but were following leads.

What leads? Was there reason to be concerned?

Of course not. The police always put a positive spin on every case, if only for morale. Didn't mean they had anything to back it up. The justice had been carefully planned and perfectly executed. Nothing to fear.

The doer's confidence returned.

Let them follow all the leads they wanted. Wouldn't change things any. Those two deserved to die a thousand deaths.

And there was no returning from the dead. They could rot in hell.

The doer sipped wine. It was sweet with just the right amount of tartness.

An image of the shock on Larry's face just before it was blown off was priceless.

And Elizabeth, beautiful in spite of herself, breathed her last breath with Larry wedged inside, before she took a bullet to the head.

More wine was tasted before the doer's rage erupted and the glass was thrown against the wall, shattering.

A deep sigh was let out slowly. Revenge was the great equalizer. The spider caught the two wicked flies when they were most vulnerable and showed them no mercy, biting with the venom of bullets.

As doctors, they couldn't save their own lives when all was said and done. So much for being members of the Medical Association of Maui. Little good it did them. Others should heed the warning or risk being dealt a similar fate.

CHAPTER SIX

On Monday, Leila and Seymour went to the crime lab. The ballistics report had come in on the murder weapon used to kill Elizabeth Racine and Larry Nagasaka.

"The victims were shot with a .25 caliber handgun," said forensic examiner Gil Delfino.

Leila was not surprised, but wanted to have it confirmed. "Were you able to get anything on the bullets used?"

"A couple of them were so mutilated, it was all but impossible to identify markings. But there was one bullet virtually unscathed that spoke in volumes. It was ejected from a gun barrel with six lands and grooves, along with a right hand twist. You find the weapon, you'll find your shooter."

"Is it possible there was more than one shooter?" Seymour asked routinely.

Delfino blinked. "Anything's possible, but probable, no. We also recovered shell casings at the crime scene. The ejection and firing pin marks on them were identical, strongly suggesting a single assailant. Unless the gun was passed from one shooter to another."

"Not likely."

"My thoughts exactly."

Leila envisioned the killer pumping bullets in the victims. It wasn't necessarily the worst way to die, with death by fire coming to mind. It was the way bullets could tear through the body and its vital organs. Nasty.

She didn't want to be the one to set this killer off unsuspectingly. Or had the craving to kill been satisfied with the murders of the doctors?

"Were you able to get any prints?"

Delfino scratched his cheek. "Yeah, lots of them from the victims. There's also plenty of others from people who I assume had nothing to hide in spending time at the condo, except maybe from their spouses or significant others."

"Never assume anything where it concerns murder and murderers," Seymour said. "Killers usually underestimate what we can do with what they leave behind to track them down. We'll see if we can match any of the prints with what we've got on file. Something may show up."

Delfino nodded. "Speaking of fingerprints, it's possible the bullets or fragments could still yield something useful to help identify the assailant. Though prints are typically difficult to obtain from bullets, there are what we call fat molecules or lipids people leave behind on whatever they touch—including the metal surfaces of bullets. We may be able to isolate these by examining the electrochemical reactions caused by the contact, revealing print patterns."

"Sounds complicated." Leila tilted her head.

"It is and may take some time."

"Then we'd better let you get back to it. Anything else?"

"Just the usual DNA evidence found at the scene to sort through: blood—and not all of it from the victims—hair, semen, skin cells. Maybe some of it will come in handy to identify a suspect."

"We can use all the help we get to find our killer," she told him.

Seymour made a grim face. "Yeah, before they nail someone else."

* * *

Officer Kelly Long was doing his standard patrol around the park, which had seen an up tick in juvenile vandalism lately and some drug use. Obviously they had nothing better to do in the dead of summer. Not on his watch.

He drove slowly, not wanting to miss anything that would come back at him later. Yeah, this was grunt work. Whatever it took to make detective.

Long's thoughts drifted to the woman he was living with, Carol Fleisher. She was pregnant. But was it his? They'd been involved for just over a year and had shared the same house for the last four months. That didn't include the two weeks she disappeared after they had a big fight, before coming back.

Had she gotten pregnant then?

He wasn't the least bit interested in supporting another man's baby. Long wasn't even sure he was ready for his own kid at this stage of his life. He could barely stay above water on a cop's salary with two mouths to feed. Three might really put him in a crunch.

He would demand a paternity test.

Long spotted a man hanging around a trash can. He looked familiar. Long picked up the sketch of a mugger.

It was him.

Slowing down, he called it in. Fearing the man would get away if he didn't act immediately, Long decided it would look good on his record if he brought the son of a bitch into custody himself.

He pulled the car to the curb, checked his firearm, and got out. Surprisingly, the suspect was so fixated on the trash, he didn't notice Long approaching with his gun drawn.

By the time he did, Long was practically on him. "Put your hands up."

The man tossed garbage his way that never came close to hitting him and made a run for it.

"Stop!" Long's voice raised a couple of octaves. The man ignored his command. Damn. His first thought was to shoot him, which was well within his right in the line of duty. But

Long had no desire to possibly kill a man who gave no indication of possessing a weapon and was not directly threatening his own life.

The next best thing was to remember he ran track in high school and should have no problem outrunning the suspect.

Putting on the burners, Long caught up to the man and tackled him to the ground. Acting quickly and decisively, he handcuffed him.

"Don't move!" Long had a knee firmly planted in the middle of his back, so he didn't imagine the suspect was going anywhere. "You're under arrest."

* * *

"I'll have my contact on the street ask around to see if anyone has purchased a hot .25 caliber gun," Seymour told Leila as they headed down the hall. "It's a long shot, no pun intended, but our killer may not be the brightest bulb in the chandelier."

"The unsub was bright enough to penetrate a multimillion dollar condo complex and execute two people before making a clean escape." Leila scratched her nose. "But anything's worth a try. At least we know the type of gun used and have the ballistic fingerprints to try and match."

"Now all we need is to find that murder weapon. Why don't you call the local gun shops and see if any .25 caliber guns or ammo has been sold recently and, if so, to whom."

"Will do. Might also be a good idea to look back and see if a .25 caliber gun was used in any other recent homicides. Could be this wasn't the first time our killer struck."

"And may not be the last," feared Seymour. "Since this very likely wasn't a random act, the killer might just be getting started."

"What would the motive be?"

"Maybe he just hates doctors the way I do dentists."

"But you're not murdering them."

"That's because I know where to draw the line. The killer obviously already stepped over it and there's no going back.

But there's plenty of potential to move forward for further bloodshed."

Leila made a face. "A scary thought."

"Tell me about it."

"You like art?"

Seymour fixed her. "As in Rembrandt or Picasso?"

"Contemporary art."

"Yeah, sure. Can't afford to buy any, but it's nice to look at." He wondered where this was going.

Leila met his eyes. "My artist friend's having a showing Saturday night. I thought if you weren't busy..."

"I'd love to go." He smiled.

"Cool."

"My social schedule's not exactly overflowing these days."

"Neither is mine."

"Then it's a date." Seymour regretted saying that, hoping it didn't make her uncomfortable. Or should he make that assumption?

She batted her lashes. "I suppose it is."

* * *

Leila had done it. She'd invited Seymour to accompany her to the showing. She didn't know if that would lead to anything, but at least it would give them a chance to step outside the official box that had defined their relationship for so long.

She wouldn't dare look beyond that.

"Hey, Kahana." Detective Fujimoto caught up to her.

Leila saw a half grin on his face. "Hey back."

"Just wanted you to know your composite sketch worked. We arrested the mugger. Turns out he's a meth addict named Jeremy Irwin. Been in and out of jail half his life. Time to go back in again, hopefully for a long stretch this time."

She smiled. "Glad you got him."

"Couldn't have done it without you."

"I just got lucky this time. Maybe the next composite will end up leading the search in the wrong direction."

"I doubt that. Personally, I'd trust your skills far more than some computer generated sketches."

Was he actually coming onto her? Leila had known Fujimoto since joining the force. She saw them as nothing more than acquaintances.

"Try telling that to the top brass," she said, downplaying it even if she agreed. "It's only a matter of time before sketch artists like me become a thing of the past. Good thing I have my day job to fall back on."

His cell phone rang and he looked disappointed. "I've gotta get that."

Leila was happy for the intrusion. "No problem. See you later."

She was still thinking about her art show date with Seymour when Leila noticed a thirty-something, dark haired Asian woman standing at her desk.

"May I help you?"

"I'd like to know when you plan to arrest the person who murdered my brother."

Leila assessed her. "You're Larry Nagasaka's sister?"

"My name is Rita Nagasaka."

Leila could see the resemblance, though the image that stuck most in her mind was of Nagasaka with much of his face missing.

"Ms. Nagasaka, the investigation is still ongoing..."

"She killed him!"

Leila lifted a brow. "Who?"

"That bitch my brother married. Connie..."

CHAPTER SEVEN

Seymour joined Leila in listening to the accusation Rita Nagasaka was making against her sister-in-law Connie. It was normal for relatives of murder victims to blame a spouse when no other suspects were named. But each such instance had to be taken seriously until proven otherwise.

"Why do you believe she murdered your brother?" he asked curiously.

"For one thing, Connie only married Larry for his money. She couldn't get enough of it and spent every penny she could."

Leila glanced at Seymour. "I'm sure you may resent that, but I'm afraid it isn't a motive for murder."

"How about life insurance?"

"We know Nagasaka was insured for half a million," Seymour said. "Not unusual for a man in his position."

"Connie insisted that he get a second policy for one million dollars about a month ago." Rita's lips pursed. "Larry wasn't happy about it, but he agreed. He often bent over backwards to appease her for some reason."

They had missed this other insurance policy. Both policies created a million and a half reasons why Connie might want to see her husband dead.

Seymour gazed at Rita. "We'll look into it."

She sneered. "So what, in the meantime, Connie just gets to live in that house doing whatever she wants?"

Leila leaned forward. "Ms. Nagasaka, whatever you may think of your sister-in-law, she was married to your brother and is innocent till proven guilty. That means we can't just kick her out on the street or make an arrest without probable cause."

"Well I hope you get it soon. She doesn't deserve to profit from Larry's death."

"She won't if it turns out she's responsible for his death," Seymour assured her. "Did your brother ever express any concern that Connie might try to hurt him due to his affair with Elizabeth Racine?"

Rita rolled her eyes. "He knew it pissed her off. If he'd realized just how dangerous she could be, I think he would have left her a long time ago."

Seymour doubted that. When it came to domestic homicides, the victim often chose to stay for one reason or another. Till it was too late. It remained to be seen if that was the case here.

"We'll be in touch with you," he told Rita.

* * *

"You think the wife followed her cheating husband and shot him to death with his lover?" Leila was thinking out loud as she sat on a corner of Seymour's desk, looking down at him.

"Can't rule it out, especially now that we know she stands to get a windfall from his death."

"People get life insurance policies all the time for different reasons, even when they can't stand each other. If she did kill them, I think it was more about the infidelity than the money she stood to gain."

"You really think so?" Seymour asked.

Leila had second thoughts about opening up this can of worms. Since Seymour had cheated on his own wife and could be headed that way with her, it was unfair to put him on the spot.

"I'm only saying that she struck me as a woman who was more interested in seeing her husband's lover dead than him."

Seymour scratched his pate. "You might be right about that. I think we need to get Connie Nagasaka in here and see what she has to say outside her comfort zone."

Leila was not about to disagree. She wanted to solve this case before the killer decided it was so easy, why not find some other targets.

Maybe Connie could shed some light on this notion.

* * *

Ferguson walked into the day spa in Ma'alaea. He ignored the hot bodies that came into view, remembering he was on the job.

"Can I help you?" asked a shapely strawberry blonde in her thirties.

"I'm looking for Suzanne Darby."

"Look no further. I'm Suzanne."

He showed his identification. "I'm investigating the murder of Elizabeth Racine. I understand you were her best friend."

"Yes, that's right. I still can't believe Liz is gone."

"I'd like to ask you a few questions about her."

Suzanne blinked. "Sure. Why don't we go to my office?"

Ferguson followed, wishing he could have a piece of her. "Nice place you've got here."

"That's what I'm told." She offered him a seat and took one herself. "What would you like to know?"

"Why don't you start by telling me what type of person Elizabeth was?"

"That's easy. She was smart, funny, gifted, and always there for the people she cared about."

"Did that include her husband?"

Suzanne's brow furrowed. "It wasn't easy being married to Kenneth. He could be a real bastard sometimes."

"Can you be more specific?"

"He was possessive and treated her like a trophy wife rather than an equal as a physician and wife."

"Do you think that's why she had an affair with Larry Nagasaka?"

"Liz liked the way Larry made her feel. And not just in bed. He treated her with respect. She never felt anything long term would come out of the relationship, but was just willing to go with the flow."

"Did Racine know about his wife's affair?"

Suzanne rolled fingers through her hair. "She tried hard to keep it from him. Don't know if she succeeded. But I do know Liz had planned to ask Kenneth for a divorce and was afraid of how he might react."

Ferguson's brows knitted. "Like he might try to hurt her?"

"I wouldn't put it past him. Once Kenneth had his hooks in you, he didn't want to give up easily."

* * *

Seymour stepped inside the Wailuku tavern on 31st Street. He found just the person he was looking for sitting at a table all by his lonesome, nursing a scotch on the rocks.

Marty Mendoza had grown up on the island and gotten involved with the wrong elements. It led to a confrontation that cost him his eyesight ten years ago. For half that time he had supplemented an insurance settlement by being a listening ear on the streets of Maui for information that might prove useful to Seymour that was normally out of his reach.

Once again he was counting on Marty earning a few bucks.

"Can smell you a mile away, Seymour," Marty claimed and showed his teeth.

"Didn't know my cologne was that strong."

"It isn't." Marty laughed. He wore dark shades.

Seymour sat across from him. "Can I buy you another drink?"

"Only if you join me."

Seymour tossed aside the no drinking on duty policy. "Sure." He ordered two scotches.

"So to what do I owe the pleasure?" Marty asked. "Or do you want me to guess?"

"Two people were shot execution-style at a condo last week."

"Yeah, I heard. Hope they got their groove on in time."

"Wouldn't know." Seymour left that one alone. "The murder weapon was a .25 caliber gun. I'd like to find out if the perp bought it off the street. And, if so, from who?"

"What's in it for me, aside from a cheap drink?"

Seymour slid three bills across the table so they touched Marty's hands. "That's fifty dollars. I'll double it if you give me anything useful."

"You've got yourself a deal." Marty squeezed the money between thick fingers. "I'll see if there's anything on the grapevine."

"I was hoping you'd say that."

"You make it easy to do my civic duty."

The drinks came and Seymour held up his end of the bargain and looked for a greater return down the line.

* * *

That night Leila's mother, Rena, phoned. As always, Leila tried to remain respectful, even when it could be trying at times dealing with a mother large on tradition and being a good Hawaiian girl. This meant not working outside the house unless in an approved field such as teaching and nursing. A career in law enforcement was frowned upon. Even if Leila was following the footsteps of her father and grandfather.

"It's not the life I envisioned for my only daughter," Rena complained.

"I didn't envision it for myself either." Leila bit her lip. "But it's my job and I'm trying to make the best of it."

"No reason to settle for something that isn't right for you and could get you killed."

"This is the right thing for me at this time in my life, Mom. And I could die anywhere, no matter my profession."

"You could move back home."

"This is my home now. It has been for a few years."

Rena made a snorting noise. "Must you always be so stubborn like your Makuakane?"

"I'm proud to be like dad and Kapuna," Leila point out, adding her grandfather as though it would make difference in trying to appeal to his daughter. "Why can't you just be happy for me?"

"Are you eating right? You're way too thin these days. It's not good for you."

As always Rena changed the subject when things got heated. Leila considered this to be safer ground for debate.

"My eating is just fine. You taught me how to cook and I haven't forgotten. Being fit is necessary for my work, so I have to show restraint in what I eat."

"I just hope that job doesn't make you anorexic. Heaven knows how awful that would be."

Leila's nostrils flared. Would this ever end? Of course not, so long as she continued to dance to a different drummer.

"I've been at this for a while, Mom, and I haven't turned into a stick yet. Don't worry so much about me."

"I'm your mother," Rena said unapologetically. "Worrying comes with the territory."

Leila got that and had no basis for argument. "I have to go now."

"Are you going out?"

Leila wished that were the case. Instead, she was once again spending the night with her own company.

Maybe that would soon change if things between her and Seymour panned out.

Or maybe it was just her destiny to be a failure in all meaningful relationships.

CHAPTER EIGHT

On Tuesday morning, Gabe Devane walked into Maui General Hospital. He had been told the elderly mugging victim, Roslyn O'Shea, was being kept under observation for a couple of days. Gabe decided to pay her a visit since she reminded him of his own grandmother who passed away at ninety-two. He hoped longevity was in his genes, as there was still a lot he wanted to do in life.

For the moment, he would settle for checking up on the woman he'd rescued from an attacker. Now that the asshole was in police custody, it made things easier all the way around. Gabe still wasn't sure how the man had managed to evade Sal, unless his dog was losing his touch.

Roslyn O'Shea was in room 461 and, according to a nurse, had good vital signs, along with a couple of cracked ribs and some minor bruising. Apparently she was still a bit disoriented from the mugging.

Gabe stepped into the room, observing a woman in her fifties who bore some resemblance to Roslyn. He assumed she was her daughter.

She shot him a cold look. "Who are you?"

"Gabe Devane. I was there when your—"

"You—" Roslyn spoke in a hoarse voice.

Gabe faced her. She looked every bit her age, but tried to smile.

The other woman didn't see it that way. "Look, Mr. Devane, you're upsetting my mother, so if you could just—"

"Thank you for coming to my rescue, young man," Roslyn said forcefully.

"I wasn't sure if you would remember." Gabe recalled the police saying that she had been unable to identify her attacker to support his eyewitness account.

"Of course I remember," she snapped. "I don't have Alzheimer's disease. Not yet anyway."

He cracked an amused smile. "Sorry about what happened. I wanted to make sure you were all right."

"I'll be fine. Just a little winded, that's all."

"Well, I'm sure you were told they caught the man, so you won't have to worry about him attacking you again."

She sighed. "I'm happy he's behind bars. Maybe that will do him some good."

Gabe doubted that. He was of the opinion most criminals left incarceration worse than when they went in.

He didn't want to upset the woman. "One can only hope."

"It's nice to know there are still people in the world willing to get involved by helping others in need."

Gabe grinned. He wanted no part of being a hero. He was anything but that. As long as it made Roslyn feel better, he could deal with it.

Now if only this good feeling could cross over into the rest of his life.

* * *

Leila stood outside the interview room next to Rachel, Seymour, Ferguson, and Lt. Ortega. They watched through the one-way window as the suspect, Connie Nagasaka, sat quietly. It was decided that Leila and Rachel would question her, believing Connie would be more likely to open up to them.

"I'd say we've let her sweat it out long enough," Leila said.

"Agreed. Go talk to her."

"It will be interesting to see how the widow responds," Ferguson said. "There's no doubt there was some bad blood between her and the husband's mistress. Could've spilled over into murder."

Rachel curled her lip. "Money's always a strong motivator for getting rid of your husband. But it's also a reason to keep him around, even if he is unfaithful."

"Just remember she's here as the widow of a victim and not a suspect, per se," Ortega made clear. "The moment she asks for a lawyer, the questioning stops."

Leila nodded. "Got it."

The two detectives went in the room. It was Leila's job to be the soft-spoken one, while Rachel played the tough cop. Sometimes it was the other way around, depending on the case.

Leila had no problem either way, so long as there were results.

"Sorry to keep you waiting," she told Connie Nagasaka.

"No problem. Did you speak to Kenneth Racine?"

"We did, and he has an alibi for the time of his wife's murder."

Connie looked disappointed. "Maybe you should double check that."

"Actually, we'd like to know more about what you were doing at the time your husband was killed," Rachel said bluntly.

Connie's lashes fluttered. "I already made clear I was at home."

"But, you see, the problem is no one can verify that."

"Am I a suspect in Larry's death?"

The detectives exchanged glances before Leila answered. "This is just a routine part of the investigation. We need to eliminate everyone close to the victims so we can focus on the perpetrator."

Connie sighed. "I understand."

Leila took a moment, eyeing her. "Why don't you tell us about the million dollar insurance policy you insisted Larry get a month before he died?"

Connie looked caught off guard. "It was Larry's idea, not mine."

"You're sure about that?" Rachel regarded her with skepticism. "Seems to me it was more money than necessary on top of the other policy. Especially for a man who had his eye on another woman."

"Most men think from below the waist." Connie maintained her composure. "Larry still loved me and would never have left me for her. He wanted me to be taken care of in case something happened to him."

Leila arched a brow. "Are you saying your husband feared for his life?"

"There were some concerns he may have made some enemies. Larry had a gambling problem. He liked to bet on baseball and basketball games. He wasn't always able to cover what he owed his bookie. Larry usually managed to work something out, but feared what could happen if he fell short."

Leila caught Rachel's gaze. "Do you know the name of his bookie?"

"I only know him as Art," Connie said.

It didn't surprise Leila that Nagasaka was a gambling addict. She'd read that many professionals got into gambling as a way to relieve the pressures of the job, only to find themselves hooked. Was that what had happened to Nagasaka?

Or was it a clever attempt by Connie to divert attention from herself as a suspect?

"We'll certainly look into this," Leila promised.

Rachel leaned toward Connie. "Do you own a gun?"

"No. I'm afraid of guns."

"Lots of people are. But it doesn't stop them from using one to kill somebody they hated."

Connie's eyes narrowed. "I loved my husband and felt sorry for Elizabeth Racine. Because her own marriage failed, she went after my husband. And now I'm paying the price."

Leila looked at the one-way mirror, imagining what they were thinking on the other side in assessing the twists and turns of this case.

She favored Connie. "Whoever killed your husband and Elizabeth Racine will pay a far worse price."

* * *

Though Connie Nagasaka was hardly in the clear, her assertions about her dead husband's gambling problem was something Seymour and Leila could hardly ignore. Particularly when it gave someone else a motive to murder Larry Nagasaka, with Elizabeth Racine possibly killed simply because she'd chosen the wrong man to have an affair with.

Seymour was willing to go along with this theory for the time being, among other possibilities.

It didn't take long to figure out the bookie known as Art was in fact Arthur Zachias. He ran a small bookmaking operation in Lahaina.

Seymour headed over there with Leila to have a chat with him.

"Did you buy the bit about it being Nagasaka's idea to make his wife a millionaire upon his death?" Seymour asked.

Leila blinked. "Not sure. They certainly had a strange relationship. My gut feeling tells me it was more about Connie looking out for number one."

"Yeah, same here," Seymour said. "Not that I could blame her any, since Nagasaka was definitely more focused on himself."

"For her sake, I hope Connie didn't play the wrong hand here. If it turns out she's responsible for her husband's death, she won't get to spend a dime of that insurance money. Not where she'll be headed."

Seymour turned onto Front Street. "Too bad most killers only think about the present and not the effect it will have on their future."

"Honestly, I'm not sure they think at all," Leila said. "Otherwise they might want to rethink things before there's no turning back."

"True."

"It's scary how easy it is for some to take another's life."

"Scarier is when you're the one being targeted," Seymour said. "The laws do an adequate job of putting the bad guys away eventually. But usually it's too little, too late for the victim."

"Tell me about it."

Seymour glanced her way. He wanted to get to know the woman outside the detective. Would she let down that barrier? Or should he not go there, unsure what he could offer in return?

"So is the art show a black tie affair or what?"

"No. Business casual is good." Leila smiled. "Bet you'd look great in a black tie, though."

"Oh you think so, do you?" Seymour felt flattered.

"Yeah. You should try it sometime."

He would do just that. For her.

* * *

Leila was still thinking about Seymour in a black tie till they entered the building. A climb up steep stairs took them to a small office open for business.

A forty-something, deeply tanned man with grayish blond hair was yapping on the phone. He hung up before they could ask him to.

"What can I do for you?" He eyed them warily.

"You must be Art," Leila said.

"Yeah, that's me. So what."

She showed her badge, as did Seymour. "We're investigating a homicide. The victim is—was—one of your clients."

"I have lots of clients. Who are we talking about?"

"Larry Nagasaka," said Seymour.

Zachias licked his lips. "Yeah, heard about his death. What's that got to do with me?"

"We understand you took bets for him."

He tensed. "Hey, I run a strictly legit operation here. I'm a business man."

"That's not what we hear." Seymour gave him a hard look. "But that's not our concern."

"Oh? So what is?"

Leila peered at him. "Whether or not you went from placing bets to murder."

His eyes bulged. "You're asking if I killed Larry?"

"Maybe when he couldn't cover his debts, you decided to take his life instead."

"I never laid a hand on him." Zachias sat back uneasily. "Yeah, he owed me money and I hate when people don't pay up on time. But murder—no way. Not only is it bad for business, I'd be a fool to knock off an addict doctor who had a ready source of income and risk spending the rest of my life in prison."

This made sense to Leila, except that murder was typically a crime of impulse.

And often greed.

"Do you happen to own a .25 caliber handgun?" she asked.

"No. I've got a .38 revolver. Bought it legally for protection. That's all."

Seymour's brows touched. "Hope you've got a good alibi for the time Larry Nagasaka was shot to death."

"Try me."

CHAPTER NINE

On Wednesday evening, Ferguson drove from Maui General Hospital to the Crest Creek Condominiums and back. Going slightly above the speed limit, he was able to cover the distance in less than half an hour. Word from the hospital staff was that there were approximately forty-five minutes around the time of the murders where Kenneth Racine could not be accounted for, leaving him more than enough time to slip away, kill his wife and lover, and return with no one being the wiser.

But did the doctor actually commit a double homicide?

Ferguson wouldn't rule it out. He'd seen firsthand the lengths some men went to when it came to intimate matters and betrayal. And some women, too.

Racine had agreed to come in on Thursday morning for an informal talk. If he came with his lawyer, it would suggest Racine was covering his bases as a guilty man. Ferguson hoped he came by himself so he could trip him up more easily if he had something to hide.

Ferguson drove to the part of Lahaina where he expected to find Gina plying her trade. He spotted her leaning against the side of a building, smoking a cigarette.

She must have recognized his car, for Gina approached him, her large breasts bouncing with each step. He let the window down in anticipation.

"Hi," she said.

"Hi. You think we can get together?"

"In your car?"

"No, this time I want to go inside. Maybe a hotel."

Gina smiled. "I've got a place right around the corner."

"That works for me."

She hesitated like before, as though he were a cop or killer, but got in.

"So what's your name?"

"Trent."

"Trent's a nice name."

"So is Gina." Ferguson meant it as he thought of a girl he knew in high school named Gina. They had dated for a year.

Gina's place turned out to be a motel room. Ferguson wasn't sure if the whole place was a front for prostitution or if the manager turned a blind eye as long as you were a paying customer.

"How much?" Ferguson asked without prelude.

"Fifty, and we can do anything."

He liked the sound of anything, setting two twenties and a ten on the dresser. Gina grabbed the money and stuffed it in her purse.

"Get naked," he ordered.

Ferguson admired her body as she peeled off what little clothing she wore. He guessed she was about twenty-five or even a bit younger, but looked older because of life on the streets. He could feel himself getting hard. He removed his own clothes and grabbed a condom from the pocket of his pants.

"I just want straight sex with you on top."

She licked glossy lips. "That's cool with me."

Ferguson watched her glide onto him before closing his eyes and imagining she was his wife. Then he realized that wasn't what he wanted. He preferred Gina for who she was.

* * *

Officer Long took a detour from making his rounds for an unplanned trip home. Ever since his girlfriend had sprung the big news about the baby, it had eaten away at him. He'd kept his thoughts to himself long enough.

He lived in a fixer-upper on the South Shore. It was affordable and gave him the opportunity to use his hands.

Carol was on the living room sofa, holding a glass of wine. Was it smart to drink alcohol when pregnant?

She smiled. "You're home early."

"Just tell me one thing: is it my child you're carrying?"

Carol stiffened. "Do you even have to ask?"

Long didn't back down. "How the hell do I know what you were doing when you left?"

"I wasn't with another man," she insisted. "I stayed at my sister's. It hurts that you're bringing this up now."

He wished he had from the very start. "So sue me. I have a right to question this, especially since it wasn't supposed to happen."

"No birth control is foolproof." She sneered. "Do you want me to have an abortion? Is that what this is about?"

Long had asked himself that very thing. The reality was he'd never want to get rid of his kid that way. So long as it really was his.

"I don't want you to do that." He hated to see her cry. "Come here."

Carol got up and stepped into his arms. Long held her close. He hoped they could hang in there long enough for him to take the detective's exam and make enough money to support them more comfortably.

* * *

At ten a.m. on Thursday, Leila conferred with Lt. Ortega, Seymour, and Detective Ferguson as Kenneth Racine waited in the interview room.

"The man is as cool as ice," she said. "Not even breaking a sweat. Is it all a façade? Or is he just empty inside when he's not doctoring his patients?"

Ortega ran a hand across his chin. "Could be Racine's trying hard not to look guilty of murdering his wife and her lover and hoping we'll buy it."

"Or the man is wondering what the hell he's doing here while the real killer is still out there," Seymour said.

Ferguson frowned. "As far as the wife's best friend is concerned, we're looking at the one who murdered Elizabeth Racine. She could be onto something. He had the time to get the job done and make it back to the hospital without missing a beat."

Leila blinked. "Sounds like the stuff a TV movie is made of."

"Yeah. Except this is real life and there are no cameras to document the crime."

"I wish there had been," she said sadly, as it would make their job easier if they were armed with hard evidence. She regarded the suspect through the one-way window.

"Let's see what the good—or bad—doctor has to say for himself," Ortega said.

Leila sneered. "I can hardly wait."

She went into the room with Ferguson. Seymour would watch the whole thing and see if he picked up anything they missed.

"Thanks for coming in, Dr. Racine," Leila spoke in a friendly voice.

Kenneth's forehead creased. "It sounded more like a demand to me."

"You're under no obligation to stay. This is strictly routine, to cover our bases while trying to find out who killed your wife."

She hoped he didn't call her bluff.

He sighed. "So what is it you want from me?"

Ferguson peered at him. "Did you know your wife was planning to ask for a divorce?"

"What?" Kenneth hoisted a brow.

"She'd had enough of a domineering husband and wanted out."

Kenneth's lip curled. "Who the hell told you that?"

"Doesn't matter."

"Liz and I never talked about a divorce. This is the first I've heard of it."

Ferguson's chin jutted. "Just like you never knew about her affair with Larry Nagasaka. Do you really expect us to believe you've been in the dark about your wife's secret life and plans to go it alone?"

Kenneth wiped his mouth. "All right, so I knew Liz was fooling around on me. What I didn't know was that she'd become so damned good at lying."

"Maybe she had a very good teacher," Leila said, favoring him with a stern look.

"I didn't mention knowing about the affair earlier precisely for this reason."

"What reason would that be?"

"So you could point the finger in the wrong direction in your investigation into who killed Liz and Larry."

"No one's doing any finger pointing. Not yet anyway."

Leila peeked at the window, wondering what Seymour and the lieutenant were thinking.

Could Racine be guilty of this brutal crime? Or were they heading down the wrong road?

"Let's talk about your alibi," Ferguson said.

Kenneth stared. "I already told you that I was—"

"I know and we checked it out. Problem is, there was a window around the time of the murders when no one seemed to know where you were. You could easily have gone to that condo with your own key and rid yourself of two problems and been back at the helm of the Behavioral Health Unit with time to spare."

Kenneth chuckled without humor. "You must think I'm quite a calculating bastard."

"Are you?" Leila tilted her head. "Did you kill your wife and her lover, Doctor?"

"No!" He made a straight face. "I sometimes like to be by myself as a way to relieve stress. If I'd known I needed to be amongst a crowd while my wife was being shot to death, I wouldn't have hesitated to do just that."

"Do you own a gun?"

"Yes, a nine millimeter automatic. I've had the gun for years and never had a reason to use it. You're welcome to test it if you like."

Leila looked at Ferguson and back to Kenneth Racine. She had a feeling he knew they were looking for a .25 caliber gun, thereby testing his 9 mm pistol would be a waste of time.

Admittedly, they had nothing to hold him on even if his story was shaky.

Which may have been what he was banking on.

* * *

Gabe held Sal's leash as they crossed the street and approached a red house. It was where Gabe's girlfriend, or ex, Linda Waverly lived. This was his last ditch effort to try and salvage what they had.

Moving up the walkway, he sensed that even Sal knew there were no more tomorrows in this relationship.

Before Gabe could ring the bell, the door opened. Linda stepped onto the lanai.

"What are you doing here?"

"I came to see you." He looked her in the eye. "I was hoping we could talk."

"There's nothing more to talk about."

Gabe tightened his grip on the leash. "You're sure you want to do this?"

"It's already done," Linda replied curtly. "I'm sorry, but I just don't think we're right for each other."

Gabe wasn't certain he disagreed. It didn't make this any less painful. "Why did I even bother?"

She rolled her eyes. "Maybe you should ask yourself that question."

His jaw tightened and he considered a comeback when someone else came to the door.

The man, only half dressed, put his arm around Linda while glaring at Gabe. "Is there a problem?"

Gabe restrained Sal from taking a bite out of the asshole. He met Linda's empty eyes and finally got it loud and clear, as if he hadn't before.

"Not anymore," he said, and walked away, while taking a deep breath and pondering his next move.

CHAPTER TEN

After work, Seymour paid a visit to his estranged wife. He hadn't bothered to call first and ask if it was okay, knowing she would likely say no. There was something developing between him and Leila and before it went any further, it was time he and Mele had a talk. If their relationship was over, he wanted to hear it from her and move on, though with regrets.

Since Akela was spending the night with her best friend Katie, Seymour didn't have to worry about putting her in the middle of something she had nothing to do with.

Mele opened the door and gave him a wide-eyed look. "What are you doing here?"

"I came to see you."

"Not sure this is a good idea."

"Probably not, but I'm here anyway. Just give me a few minutes."

She stepped aside and allowed him to walk through. He could smell her lilac fragrance, reminding him of happier times.

"Just say what you have to and leave."

She wasn't going to make this easy for him. Not that he deserved such.

"I think we need to talk about what happened."

Mele wrinkled her nose. "What is there to say?"

"Say anything. Hell, hit me if it'll make you feel better. But this silent treatment from you is killing me."

"Maybe you should have thought about that before you killed our relationship."

He looked into her eyes. "Are you saying it's over between us for good?"

Mele turned her back to him. "It was over when you decided to screw around on me."

"I did a stupid thing and I'm sorry. I never stopped loving you."

She rounded on him. "Don't say that."

"It's true. I went looking for something I already had. If I could do it over again—"

"You'd do the same thing!" Mele narrowed her eyes. "People only regret things after they're out in the open."

"My regrets are sincere."

She scoffed. "That's what they all say. Too little, too late."

"It doesn't have to be."

"You think you're any different from those murdered doctors?"

He cocked a brow. "Excuse me?"

"The case you're working on. They were married people having an affair. Look what it cost them."

Seymour bit his tongue. "Their affair may have had nothing to do with their deaths."

"If they hadn't chosen to forsake their marriage vows, they wouldn't have both been in that condo for a killer to come after. Maybe it was punishment for what they were doing with each other, no matter why the crime was committed."

He frowned, feeling guilty, but refusing to believe adultery in and of itself should be punishable by murder. Even if some individuals took this act upon themselves. In his book sex between consenting adults, married or not, didn't rise to such a level by a higher authority.

"So what is it you want—a divorce?"

Mele paused. "I think I do."

Seymour hadn't wanted to hear those words. "We could try counseling."

"It won't change what I saw."

He winced. "What about Akela?"

"She understands there are consequences when you do bad things."

Seymour was beginning to realize there was no such thing as second chances.

* * *

Across Kahului on South Puunene Avenue, Rachel sat in a bar called Tides. She was nursing her second martini. It was how she often spent her evenings, alone and bitter, having little reason to go home. After all, with Greg dead, all she had was a cold bed instead of his muscular body to warm up to. If only they had been given more time to do the things couples did: make love till the wee hours of the morning, travel, and grow old together. Instead it had all been taken away from her.

And for what? A war that had done more harm than good by taking lives that deserved to be lived rather than buried in some wooden box and forgotten by most of the world.

Rachel's eyes watered. Maybe she should have been more supportive of Greg's commitment to serving his country. Instead she'd made clear her steadfast opposition to war and it had been a source of friction between them. She had hoped her love would be strong enough to get Greg to see things her way, but it had only put more distance between them. He had come from a military family and could no more extricate himself from it than Rachel could a family that had turned its back on her.

Now she would give anything to take back the hurtful things she'd said to Greg. Even keep more of an open mind on his career path as he had hers. If only he were still alive so she could show him just how much she loved him. But he wasn't and she would never again feel the touch of Greg's lips on her face or his gentle hands on her body.

"How are we doing here?" Rachel heard the bartender ask.

"Don't ask."

"That bad, huh?"

"Yeah," she muttered.

"I'm a good listener."

Rachel looked up at the fifty-something man. "Not much in the mood to talk right now."

"Maybe some other time."

She doubted that, sure he wasn't really interested in what she had to say. Probably no one was, which made it all the more painful.

She downed the rest of the drink, tempted to have another, but passed it up. There was more of where this came from at home.

Rachel got up and headed to her empty house even as she dreaded it.

CHAPTER ELEVEN

On Friday, Leila rode with Seymour to Honokowai to interview a physician assistant and member of the Medical Association of Maui who reportedly had spent time at the condo before she was fired six months ago for substance abuse. As with every case, they had to follow all roads in pursuit of a killer, even if it led nowhere.

"Hope our killer isn't getting restless," Leila remarked. "At least not before we make an arrest."

"I don't think you have to worry about that. It's only been a week, and my hunch is our killer is laying low, hoping this will all disappear."

"But what if that isn't the case?"

"Then we keep digging, waiting for the break that will crack the case."

Leila would have preferred that to be yesterday instead of tomorrow. Patience was never her strongest suit, especially where it concerned murderers running free.

Maybe the woman they were going to see would end her misery and Leila could turn her attention elsewhere. Like going to her friend's art show in two days with her partner.

Adrianne Pompeo lived in an apartment on Lower Honoapiilani Road. Seymour knocked on the door twice and for a moment Leila thought she might not be home.

Then the door was opened by a tall, slender woman in her thirties with curly brunette hair. A cigarette dangled from the corner of her mouth.

"Adrianne Pompeo?" Seymour asked.

"Yeah, that's me."

"We're detectives from the Maui P.D. Wonder if we could ask you a few questions?"

"About what?"

"The murder of Larry Nagasaka and Elizabeth Racine."

Adrianne nodded. "I wondered what took you so long to come my way."

"We're here now," Leila told her. "Mind if we come inside?"

"Why not? I don't have anything to hide."

They stepped into a small, sparsely furnished living room. There was what smelled like meth in the air, telling Leila she was still doing drugs. Had it escalated to murder?

"Why were you expecting a visit from us?" Leila gazed at her.

Adrianne drew coolly on the cigarette. "It's no secret I didn't get along well with Larry or Elizabeth. He was a control freak and she could be a real bitch. But I didn't kill them."

"So you say." Seymour bristled. "You don't deny being given access to the condo where they were killed?"

"Yeah, I bribed Larry to stay there for a few days when I was between residences. But I wasn't the only one in the association not amongst the privileged who got a freebie there every now and then. That doesn't make me a killer."

"Tell us about being fired from your job for using drugs," Leila said.

Adrianne stiffened. "What do you want me to say? I screwed up. It was just a recreational thing and never a problem. Probably half the doctors and nurses there take something to get through the day. I shouldn't have been made a scapegoat."

"Maybe you figured you would make someone else pay," Seymour voiced sharply. "And why not two doctors who happened to make your life hell?"

"Because it would only make my life worse. I don't even own a gun, in case you're wondering. Feel free to look around if you want."

Leila was tempted to take her up on that, but didn't want to run into problems later should they find something incriminating.

"We'd like to know what you were doing when Doctors Racine and Nagasaka were killed."

"I was here all by myself." Adrianne took a last drag on the cigarette and squashed it in an ashtray. "If you're looking for someone who had it in for Larry, why don't you try Douglas Brennan? He divorced his wife after she was rumored to have had an affair with Larry. From what I understood, Mr. CEO didn't take it very well."

Leila eyed Seymour thoughtfully.

* * *

"This Nagasaka was a real character," remarked Seymour behind the wheel.

"Sure looks that way."

"Brennan never bothered to mention that wrinkle involving his ex."

"Maybe he didn't think it was relevant."

"Or maybe he thought it was." Seymour slowed down as traffic had stopped at the light. "Could be an O.J. wannabe, only in reverse. That is, unable to deal with the jealousy and betrayal of a cheating wife, even though no longer married, Brennan decides to take his rage out on Nagasaka and the latest cheating spouse he's bedding."

Leila rolled her eyes. "Don't you think that's a bit of a stretch?"

"Probably. But he had motive and means for being at the scene of the crime. We'll see if it's got any legs."

She waited a beat. "Didn't know you were a leg man, Seymour."

He grinned. "You don't know me very well."

"Who's fault is that?"

"Point taken." He would like them to get to know each other better.

Leila turned his way. "So tell me something else I don't know about you?"

Seymour swallowed, deciding he might as well be up front about this. "My wife wants a divorce."

"Oh. Sorry."

"You don't have to be. I saw it coming." Even if he'd tried to block its path.

"That doesn't make it any better for you."

He winced. "You're right, it doesn't." Somehow she made him feel better. "I'll be fine. People break up all the time, right?"

"Yeah, it seems like it." Leila looked out the window. "Sometimes they get back together."

"I doubt that'll be the case this time." Seymour wondered if Mele had really thought this through. Had they truly reached the end of the line? Maybe it was time to let go and focus on someone who did seem to want to be with him.

"Can't say my own love life has been all that great either," Leila said sourly. "I've made some mistakes and avoided others."

Seymour recalled her last relationship. She hadn't spoken much about it, but seemed to have trouble finding someone who understood what she was all about. He hoped they would never end up each other's mistake, while fearing it may be unavoidable.

"We're only human," he said as if she thought otherwise. "Better to fail than not try at all, as they say."

"I agree."

Another reason why Seymour liked her.

CHAPTER TWELVE

Leila felt like really getting dressed up for the art show. Or was it more to impress Seymour? Maybe a little of both. She slid into a black silk ruffle dress and matching slingbacks, adding some simple pearls around her neck for effect.

She felt nervous. After all, this was their first date. And it was Seymour's first since his wife asked for a divorce.

How would that affect their relationship? Would Seymour be on a guilt trip now, so why bother?

Leila put those thoughts behind her, wanting only to get through this evening for starters.

By the time Seymour came to pick her up, Leila had regained control of her nerves.

"You look nice," she told him. He wore one of his better suits. "Especially the black tie."

"I'm a man of my word." He smiled. "I like your dress."

She blushed. "Gave me a good excuse to wear it."

"Maybe your friend needs to have more showings."

"I'll tell her." Leila looked up at him. For the first time, she noted the tiny mole on his cheek. "Are you ready?"

"Let's do it."

* * *

The gallery was not far from Leila's house on Dickenson Street. Seymour grabbed them both a flute of champagne being offered and took a chocolate truffle for himself. This type of thing was normally outside of his league, but he was happy to attend.

Especially with Leila looking as appealing as he'd ever seen her.

"There you are," he heard the spirited voice. Looking to his right, Seymour saw the artist briskly approaching.

Leila hugged her. "Hi, Jan."

"Hi, back at you." She turned to Seymour. "Why you must be the partner I've heard so much about?"

Seymour half grinned. "Yeah, that would be me. Blake Seymour. Hope she only told you the good things."

Jan chuckled. "You mean there are bad things?"

"My lips are sealed."

"Then we won't go there." She smiled. "Thank you both for coming."

"You think you could have stopped me?" Leila grinned.

"Not if you valued our friendship."

"I do."

"In that case, let's show Blake around and see what he thinks of my artwork."

"From what I've already seen, you clearly know what you're doing," Seymour told her.

Jan crinkled her eyes at Leila. "Better hold onto this one. He's a real charmer."

Leila colored. "We'll see about that."

Seymour liked how she opened the door to whatever happened, while leaving them both some wiggle room. At the moment, he couldn't think of a better place to be than in her company.

Except for maybe in her bed.

* * *

The showing was a success by any measure and Leila envied Jan for using her artistic talents in a way she could only dream about. Maybe in another lifetime when there were no more bad guys to go after.

If only.

When Seymour took her home, all Leila could think of was jumping his bones. He had been one of the nicest looking men at the show, even if in an unassuming way. They hit it off well together in a social setting that didn't involve the police department. Seymour seemed to enjoy her company as much as Leila enjoyed his.

She believed the real test would come later. Was he ready to move beyond his failed marriage? Was the sour taste left in Leila's mouth after her last involvement with a man ready to turn sweet again on someone?

"Do you want to come in for a nightcap?" she asked tentatively.

Seymour met her eyes. "Yeah, that works for me."

"Good."

Just how good remained to be seen.

* * *

The moment Seymour stepped inside the house, he only wanted to kiss Leila and be inside her. Were they on the same wavelength? He needed to be sure. Once that line had been crossed there was no turning back.

"I have beer, wine, cognac," she said. "Sorry, no champagne."

"What I really want is you."

"I want that, too."

He put his arms around her slender waist. "Yeah?"

Leila raised her face and kissed him. "Does that answer your question?"

Seymour licked his lips, becoming instantly aroused. "Loud and clear."

This time he kissed her. Then they went to the bedroom, where each undressed till they were naked.

Seymour liked what he saw. Leila's breasts were high and small, stomach flat, and her legs nicely toned. She kissed him again, and then lay on the bed in wait.

After putting on a condom, he joined her lustfully. Their mouths kissed some more and bodies touched. Seymour put his hand between Leila's legs. She was wet and wanting.

So was he.

Unable to hold back anymore, Seymour inserted himself inside Leila. It was a tight fit, stimulating him all the more.

Now it was time to make this new sexual relationship everything it could be.

* * *

Leila clutched his buttocks, pulling Seymour deeper inside, needing the feel of his erection, the closeness of his hard frame.

She climaxed almost instantly as expected. He followed shortly thereafter, both breathing heavily and bodies trembling till settling down.

Leila gave a little chuckle, with Seymour slumped half atop her. "Looks like we both had no staying power whatsoever."

He rolled off her. "Can we work on that the next time?"

She gazed at him. "So there will be a next time?"

"I hope so."

"So do I." Leila touched his shoulder. "I don't want this to affect us on the job."

"No reason it has to." Seymour kissed her chin. "What we do in our private lives stays here."

Leila smiled, though unsure if it was possible to totally separate the two. But she was willing to try, as he was worth treading the line.

She put her hand between his legs. He still had an erection. "Maybe we could make that next time right now?"

He grinned, hungry for her and no one else, including his wife.

"Maybe we could," he said.

CHAPTER THIRTEEN

On Monday, Leila focused on the black and white photograph. The eight-year-old Polynesian girl in the picture had been missing for seven years now, abducted by her own father after a bitter custody battle with the girl's mother, Ingrid Mumea. It was thought that Jordan Mumea had fled from Oahu to Maui with his daughter, Iolana, hiding amongst relatives there.

"Can you do an age progression sketch of the girl?" Lt. Tanji of the Kidnapping and Parental Abduction Unit asked.

"I think so," Leila answered. "Do you have any other pictures of her?"

"Afraid not. Apparently Jordan Mumea confiscated all the photos of the girl before he abducted her, except that one."

"Then this will have to do." Leila looked at the picture again. "I'll get right to work on it."

Tanji made a tiny smile. "Thanks. Whatever you come up with will be more than we have to go on now. We may never find the creep who stole his own daughter and broke her mother's heart, but you never know. With the sketch, we could get lucky and everyone ends up happy."

"Everyone except the father," she said. "But that's his problem."

Hers was giving the police another important tool to work with. Leila would have to rely largely on her own insight and imagination to draw the age progression sketch as to how the girl might look today.

She left his office and went to get her supplies. Tony Fujimoto was at the end of the hall. He came toward her.

"Where are you off to in such a hurry?"

"Have to do a sketch of a missing girl."

He made a face. "As in presumed dead?"

"As in taken by her father years ago. The mother wants her daughter back."

"Better late than never."

"You're preaching to the choir, Fujimoto."

He laughed. "So you sing, too? What else am I missing?"

"More than you'll ever know." Leila gave a teasing laugh and moved on lest he get any ideas.

Her mind was still fresh on the sex with Seymour two days ago. She didn't know how long this would last, but planned to go along for the ride as long as he wanted the same thing.

* * *

Seymour took Akela to the mall for ice cream. He watched with joy and a bit of uneasiness as his soon to be nine-year-old little girl was growing up right before his very eyes. In less than a decade she would turn eighteen. Adulthood, and likely even sooner, meant everything from her own cell phone to a car, college, and boys. He didn't even want to think about Akela dating or getting married and having her own children. Not yet anyway.

Seymour hated to think that Akela would one day no longer be as dependent on her parents and have to make her own choices in life, good or bad.

One choice he figured she would one day make was to try and meet her birth mother. As far as Seymour was concerned, she had the only parents who mattered—even if no longer together. But who was he to say Akela shouldn't satisfy her curiosity, should it to come to that?

They knew little about her birth mother. Only that she'd had a tough life and wanted to do right by Akela by giving her a chance for a better life. That was good enough for Seymour and Mele who loved Akela as much as any child they might have conceived on their own.

But would that suffice for Akela at the end of the day?

Right now, Seymour intended to enjoy her sweet innocence and making a mess of a brownie sundae she could eat with her hands.

"Sure that's not more than you can handle?" he asked, biting off his dipped cone.

Akela giggled. "It's not too much."

"Just asking." He wondered how much Mele had told her about their situation. Maybe more than she should have. Or not enough. "Next week, we can take in a movie. How does that sound?"

"Okay."

"And if you want extra butter, you can have it. Just be sure not to tell your mom."

"I won't." She wiped her mouth with a napkin. "What's going to happen with you and Makuahine?"

Seymour was caught off guard with the question. He didn't want to sugar coat an answer. "I'm not sure."

"Do you still love each other?"

He could only speak for himself. "We do. But sometimes adults don't get along well enough to stay together, even if they love each other. Does that make sense?"

"Yeah, kinda."

Seymour left it at that, while wondering if there was any chance Mele might reconsider her decision to end the marriage.

* * *

Two hours later Leila had completed the sketch of what Iolana Mumea might look like today.

"Pretty young lady," commented Rachel.

Leila agreed, careful not to sound too sure of herself for a girl who might not even still be alive. "We have to find her and see just how good an age progression artist I really am."

Rachel tasted her coffee. "You're the best. Around here anyway."

"Not saying too much when my competition is a computer."

"Doesn't that say it all?"

Leila smiled. "I suppose so."

"Hope the guys can find her. I know if it were my daughter, just knowing she was out there somewhere, maybe even right under my nose, would drive me crazy."

"I know what you mean." Leila thought about Rachel losing her husband. The one good thing about it was his death was confirmed. Meaning she wasn't left wondering like with some soldiers who were MIA.

Or a mother not knowing if her daughter was alive or dead.

"I'd better get this to Lt. Tanji."

Rachel put the cup to her mouth. "And I've got another person to interview."

Leila nodded. "You mean the kid who supposedly overheard another kid bragging about killing the doctors?"

"Yeah. Probably a wild goose chase."

"You never know. The ones we overlook sometimes come back to haunt us."

CHAPTER FOURTEEN

Rachel took the drive down Haleakala Highway to Makawao in the Upcountry part of Maui. She admired the views it afforded of the North and South Shores. Once upon a time she and Greg had shared a romantic getaway there, escaping the hustle and bustle of central Maui. Now Rachel would give anything to relive those days instead of having to go it alone.

She turned onto Makawao Highway and soon made her way through downtown, where Makawao's legacy as a paniolo or cowboy town was very much evident in the old west architecture. Past this, Rachel came to the address on Baldwin Avenue for Emily Hofmeister.

The front door opened before Rachel could ring the bell. A fortyish woman with short gray hair stood there.

"Are you Emily?"

She nodded. "You're the detective I spoke to on the phone?"

"Yes. Detective Lancaster." Rachel flashed her ID.

"Please come in."

Rachel stepped inside the small house. The stench of stale cigarettes crossed her nostrils.

"Is your son Donnie home?"

Emily nodded. "He's in his room. I'll tell him you're here."

Rachel suspected he already knew that. After all, it was his allegations that had brought her there.

A moment later she saw the tall, lanky sixteen-year-old walk into the room. His head had been shaved, but he had a goatee.

"Donnie, this is Detective Lancaster," his mother said.

"Hi." He stuck his hands in his pockets nervously.

"Hello, Donnie." Rachel looked at Emily. "Why don't we all sit down?"

"You heard her." Emily eyed her son and the two sat on a worn sofa.

Rachel took a chair. She directed her attention to Donnie. "I understand you have information pertinent to a murder investigation?"

He didn't respond, as if having second thoughts.

"Go on. Tell her what you heard," Emily instructed.

Rachel tried to make the boy feel at ease. "Whatever you say, I promise it won't get back to anyone you're accusing of a crime." Not unless he was called upon to testify, should his story lead to an arrest and trial.

Donnie wrung his hands. "Okay, I was just hanging out at the playground when I heard this guy I go to school with, Travis Takamori, talking on his cell phone. He said he was responsible for killing those doctors."

Rachel lifted a brow. "What exactly did you hear him say?"

He paused, glancing at his mother.

"It's okay. Tell her," she said, holding his hand.

Donnie looked down. "Well, he said, 'I took care of them doctors and it was easy. I knew right where the key was. I liked watching them die, choking on their own blood.'"

Rachel frowned. "That's quite a bit to remember." Maybe too much. "You're positive that's what you heard?"

"Yeah. Kinda freaked me out, you know. I just wanted to forget about it. But I had to tell somebody, so I told my mom. She said I should repeat it to the police."

"I'm glad you did." Rachel wondered if Travis Takamori could be their killer. "Is he the type of person prone to practical jokes?"

Donnie shrugged. "Don't really know him that well."

"Travis is a crack head," Emily said. "And a little crazy. I wouldn't put anything past him, including murder just for kicks."

Rachel kept that in mind with Takamori being someone they definitely needed to have a talk with.

* * *

Ferguson managed to track down Travis Takamori at his aunt's house in Ma'alaea. Turned out the aunt was none other than Melissa Eng, the housekeeper who cleaned the condo where Nagasaka and Racine were killed. She'd been fired when Nagasaka caught her stealing.

"I already spoke to the cops," Melissa said nervously at the door. "I don't know anything."

"So I've heard." Maybe she knew more than the she was letting on. "I'd like to ask your nephew, Travis Takamori, a few questions."

Her eyes bulged. "Travis ain't here."

Ferguson frowned. "I watched him walk in that door not two minutes ago." He made a quick identification after a background check determined Takamori already had a long rap sheet at seventeen. "And unless he or both of you have something to hide, I suggest you tell him to get his ass out here right now!"

Before Melissa could react, some shuffling noise behind her got louder and the door opened wider.

Travis Takamori stood there. He was tall and slim with a flattop. "It's all right, Anake Mel. I'll talk to him."

"You don't have to," she insisted.

"No big deal." He eyed Ferguson. "Let's talk out here."

"That's fine." Ferguson watched the suspect carefully as he closed the door on his aunt.

"So what do we have to talk about?"

"Why don't we start with your telling someone on the phone that you took care of those doctors and enjoyed watching them choke on their own blood?"

Travis looked uneasy. "Where'd you hear that?"

Ferguson never took his eyes off of him. "You know I hate when people answer a question with a question."

"I never said that!"

"Why is it I don't believe you?"

"Maybe it's cause you'd rather believe lies being told about me."

"Why would someone want to lie about you?" asked Ferguson.

"How do I know?" Travis shrugged. "Probably just to give you cops something to do."

"I'm afraid that won't cut it." Ferguson got in his face. "I think you'd better give me a good reason for not hauling your ass down to the station where I promise it won't be pretty."

"Okay, okay. So I said it. Don't mean any of it was true. I was just messin' around."

Ferguson frowned. "You call taking credit for murdering two people messing around?"

Travis rubbed his nose. "Whatever. It seemed like a good idea at the time."

"Maybe you decided to exact a little payback because your aunt lost her job to those rich doctors by shooting them to death."

"I didn't kill anybody."

Ferguson wasn't convinced. "Are you still using?"

Travis blinked. "I'm clean, man."

"I doubt that. I can see the crack in your eyes. But that's your problem. My only concern is whether or not it helped you get a little cuckoo in doing something really stupid."

Travis fidgeted. "I told you I had nothing to do with that!"

Ferguson backed off just slightly. If he'd thought for one minute the punk was carrying a piece, he would already have him in handcuffs.

"Where were you the night the doctors were murdered?"

Travis smoothed an eyebrow. "Hanging out with my girlfriend."

"Does your girlfriend have a name?"

"Yeah, Jocelyn Dandridge."

Ferguson set his jaw. "She'd better back up your story."

"She will."

That sounded a bit too pat for Ferguson, as if the alibi had already been manufactured. Time would tell.

"Be seeing you around," he told Travis, sure it was more than just empty words.

* * *

Gina knew he was a cop, even if Trent wouldn't admit it. She could smell the cop in him as sure as if it were the cheap cologne he wore. Not that it mattered to her. No chance she would be busted for prostitution by the john paying for her services.

As business was slow these days, Gina wasn't in a position to pick and choose who she gave a blow job to.

Gina put his erection deep into her mouth till it tickled her throat. Once he took care of his business, she stopped and got off her knees.

"Why do you do this?" he asked, surprising her.

"Why do you come to me instead of being with your wife?"

He cocked a brow. "Who said anything about me being married?"

She laughed. "I can see on your finger where you usually wear a ring. No tan in that spot. It's okay. Most of my customers are married. To answer your question, I've been turning tricks off and on since I ran away from home at fifteen."

"You were being abused?"

"Not sexually, but my step dad beat the hell out of me and my mom. She chose to keep being a punching bag, I didn't."

"There was no one you could stay with?"

Gina wasn't used to johns asking her these types of questions like they cared. Did he actually care about her?

"I've always been independent. I didn't want to lay my problems on someone else. It hasn't been so bad for me. I don't do drugs and try to stay away from the creeps."

"I'm glad."

"Don't your wife like to give you blow jobs?" she asked curiously. "Or would you rather not say?"

"She'll do anything I want. Guess I'm just not feeling it with her these days."

"Sorry. I was with someone once, but it didn't work out. I didn't see any reason to stay where I wasn't wanted."

"Are you saying my wife should leave me?" His brows stitched.

Gina bit her tongue. The last thing she needed was to alienate a regular customer.

"No, but maybe you should leave her and find someone you want to come home to."

"Right now I'm happy to come and see you."

Gina doubted he meant anything other than to get his rocks off. It was nice to hear anyhow.

"If you want to fool around some more as a freebie, we can."

"I'd like that. But not as a freebie. You deserve to get paid for your services."

She couldn't disagree with him.

CHAPTER FIFTEEN

On Tuesday afternoon, Seymour headed to the Medical Association of Maui's West Maui office with Leila for a chat with Douglas Brennan, the group's CEO. They needed to check out Adrianne Pompeo's story that Brennan may have had reason to want Larry Nagasaka dead, with Elizabeth Racine a victim by happenstance.

Seymour glanced at Leila. He wondered if she thought about their times in bed as much as he did. Maybe it was exactly what he shouldn't be thinking about. At least not on the job. They were both professionals and had a case to solve.

There would be time later to explore their newfound relationship and where it was headed. Or not.

He gazed over the wheel. "Should be interesting to see how Brennan responds to having the finger pointed at him as the possible shooter."

Leila faced his profile. "Don't be surprised if he denies it," she quipped. "CEO's rarely ever take responsibility for anything that's bad."

"I think murder would fall under that category."

"Yeah, it would."

Seymour turned into the parking lot. "I think many killers want to be caught, especially when it involves love triangles, but they lack the guts to show up at the police station."

"And make our job easier? I don't think so. I doubt this killer wants to be caught. That would mean facing up to a double homicide and the consequences."

"Our doer may just need a little nudging in the right direction."

"You mean like Douglas Brennan?" Leila voiced.

"Why not?" Seymour brought the car to a stop.

* * *

"Do you have some news on the shootings?" Douglas looked from Leila to Seymour in his office.

"Not exactly." Leila met his eyes. "We're actually here hoping you can answer a few questions for us."

"Oh?" He arched a brow. "No problem, though I don't know what I can tell you that I haven't already said."

"How about you knew your ex-wife had an affair with Larry Nagasaka?" She watched his reaction carefully, deciding to take a chance it was more than mere innuendo.

Douglas turned away. "Where did you hear that?"

"Then it's true?"

He ran a hand across his mouth. "Yes."

Seymour narrowed his eyes. "Why didn't you tell us before?"

"I didn't think it was relevant."

"Think again, Doctor. When two people are shot to death in a condo where you not only had access but motive to kill at least one victim, I'd say it's damned relevant."

Douglas drew a breath. "My wife—ex—was involved with Larry over a year ago. We've been divorced for six months and are barely on speaking terms. If I had wanted to kill Larry, I would've done so when I actually still loved Courtney."

Leila sensed the love hadn't gone away. Perhaps not the bitterness either. "It couldn't have been very easy to work with someone who had been sleeping with your wife."

He frowned. "Of course it was difficult. The man was a bastard and everyone knew it. But he was also a good doctor. As the CEO of this organization, I was obligated to put aside our personal differences and maintain a cordial working relationship."

"And did you?"

"We never came to blows, if that's what you're asking."

Seymour batted his eyes. "All the same, clearly the big happy family and supportive work environment you indicated earlier was somewhat exaggerated."

Douglas stiffened. "As you said, detective, even families can have their problems. Doesn't mean they don't still care for each other at the end of the day."

"Someone didn't care much for Nagasaka or Racine. That person may be part of your association. Indeed, it could be you."

"I didn't kill Larry or Elizabeth."

"You'd better hope that's more than just words, doctor," warned Seymour.

Leila moved her feet. "We're going to need to know your whereabouts at the time your colleagues were killed."

Douglas flinched. "I believe I was home."

"Can someone verify that?"

"I doubt it, unless you figure out a way to communicate with my cat."

Leila put him down as another strong suspect to contend with.

* * *

It had been a while since Leila cooked for anyone other than herself. But inviting Seymour to dinner seemed like a good idea. They were both tired after a long day on the job and she could use the casual company, apart from their sexual relationship.

She made a typical Hawaiian meal of macaroni salad, teriyaki beef, poi dinner rolls, and fresh pineapple. Dessert would be coconut cake.

For his part, Seymour brought the wine and wasn't late.

"This is great," he told her.

Leila tasted the wine. "You can thank my mother the next time she comes to visit. I learned how to cook from her."

"She taught you well."

Leila knew her mother would not approve of Seymour as her boyfriend. Not that he was at this point. She would say he was too old. Too white. Too married. Too ensconced in his career.

The only one that concerned Leila mildly was that he was married. She didn't make a habit of dating married men, estranged or not. But with Seymour things were different. She happened to be attracted to the man and couldn't help that.

And he obviously felt the same.

Why look for ways to ruin a good thing?

"So how well did you know your grandfather?" Seymour bit into a roll.

"Not too well. We used to come and visit him every summer, but he was too busy with work to spend much time with me."

"Think he would approve of your joining the force?"

Leila considered the question. "Probably not. I think he'd feel I could do better."

"Maybe you could."

She looked at him with surprise. "Are you suggesting I should retire and do something more feminine?"

"Not at all." He wiped his mouth. "I just think you're a hell of a lot smarter than I am and could probably be anything you wanted."

"I'm happy with what I'm doing."

"Then keep doing it. I certainly wouldn't want anyone else as my partner."

Leila blushed while admiring the way he covered his tracks. "Neither would I."

"I'm not going anywhere."

She wasn't so sure of that. Word had it he was next in line for lieutenant when Ortega retired.

She hoped that wouldn't be at least for a few more years.

* * *

"I like kissing you," Seymour spoke between their open mouths moving in harmony. "But I'd rather save some of those kisses to enjoy the rest of you..."

"Don't let me stop you," Leila murmured.

Seymour pulled away from her lips and began kissing Leila's neckline and down to her small, but firm breasts. He teased one nipple then the other with his tongue.

"Hmm..." she cooed.

He met his lover's eyes for an instant, detecting slight abashment, but even more desire, before spreading her legs and kissing between them.

Leila ran her fingers through his hair and breathed heavily till her orgasm came. Only then did Seymour raise his head, eager to be inside her.

"I need you," he spoke huskily.

She widened her thighs. "I'm all yours."

After sliding on protection, Seymour began to make love to his partner. With her legs wrapped high across his back, he propelled himself into Leila, enjoying every moment. He was able to extend the passion through willpower, before the urge caught up to him and he let it happen.

They clung to each other and kissed when the moment came before Seymour rolled off.

He caught his breath. "You were great."

"So were you," Leila said. "Guess that makes us great together."

"You'll get no argument from me there."

"Didn't think so."

Seymour kissed her again and held her close. He could hear her heart beating. Or was it his?

He agreed they had chemistry. But so did he and Mele, along with history. If he had things his way, Seymour would rather be with his estranged wife at the moment. But she had made her choice and it didn't include him.

So he had to move on. Leila was doing a nice job to make him forget he was still married.

He hoped it lasted for a little while.

CHAPTER SIXTEEN

Douglas Brennan drove his BMW home while listening to classical music. Weighing heavily on his mind was the earlier visit from the detectives. He doubted he'd satisfied them as far as his alibi, but unless they were prepared to arrest him for murder, to hell with them.

He thought about his ex in bed with Larry Nagasaka, filling him with fury. How could she have humiliated him like that?

Douglas hated that Larry destroyed his marriage and also put unwanted attention on the association because of his philandering. The bastard deserved everything he got and then some. And so did Elizabeth for her poor judgment in getting involved with him.

Douglas pulled into the driveway of his house, wishing he had more than his cat Tully to share it with.

He left the car with his briefcase and headed down the walkway when he heard rustling in the bushes. His first thought was that Tully had gotten out.

But the sound grew louder and was clearly not a cat. Before he could react, someone emerged from the shadows.

Douglas cocked a brow. "What are you doing here?"

Without a response, a gun was pointed at him. Douglas tried to shield himself with the briefcase as multiple shots rang out, hitting their mark.

Douglas fell to the ground. In great pain, he managed to look into the eyes of the killer before a final shot slammed into his face, shattering it.

* * *

The doer watched with satisfaction as the last bullet went into Douglas Brennan's head. It was a fitting end to a pathetic life of privilege and excess.

Stuffing the gun in a pocket, the doer made haste in fleeing the scene. Through patches of darkness and around the block, an escape vehicle awaited.

The drive went without a hitch and soon the doer breathed a deep sigh of satisfaction over the latest revenge killing and focused on the future. It was sure to be brighter with one less burdensome asshole.

Passing a police cruiser, the doer instinctively slowed down, though well within the speed limit, and was careful not to even look their way. No need to give the officer the slightest reason to be suspicious, which could spell doom.

The fears proved unfounded, as the police cruiser continued on its merry way, unaware it had just passed a killer.

One who was not quite through righting some wrongs.

* * *

Officer Kelly Long took the call at 9:45 p.m. Shots had been reported fired in front of a home at 17806 Palms View Road.

So much for a peaceful night.

Not that he wanted to earn his keep by driving around for nothing. All that did was give him more time to think about the fact he was soon to be a dad.

A paternity test had proven the child his girlfriend was carrying belonged to him and not another man.

Long considered it a mixed blessing. Having a kid meant he had to think about someone other than himself. And a girlfriend Long wasn't sure he could count on to be there in the long run.

He was scared as hell this would wreak havoc on a life that, up to this point, had pretty much revolved around a career in law enforcement. The last thing he wanted was to get in over his head. Or end up on the other side of a bullet, leaving his kid without a father.

Long pulled up to the house that was way outside his income level and immediately spotted the body. It appeared to be a man in a suit, lying on his back on the walkway. A briefcase was nearby.

After radioing it in, Long got out of the car. Though seeing no other person in sight, he removed his weapon and proceeded toward the downed man with caution.

It took only one look at his shattered remains to know they were likely dealing with a homicide.

* * *

Leila was given a start as she was awakened by the phone ringing. Recognizing her ring tone, she untangled herself from Seymour's hard body and stretched an arm to grab the cell phone from the nightstand.

The Caller ID told her it was Lt. Ortega.

"Hi, Lieutenant." She glanced at Seymour who was beginning to stir.

"Sorry to wake you, Kahana, but we've got another murder on our hands."

"Who?"

"Douglas Brennan, CEO of the Medical Association of Maui. He was shot to death in front of his home."

Leila hummed with surprise.

"Haven't been able to reach Seymour," Ortega said.

Leila eyed her lover. "I'll make sure he gets the message." She hung up, wondering if Ortega knew about them.

Seymour sat up. "What is it?" he asked, propping on one elbow.

"Brennan is dead. Looks like our unsub may have struck again."

Seymour belted out an expletive and hopped out of bed. Leila admired his naked body only long enough for him to admire hers before turning into homicide detective mode.

Within twenty minutes they arrived at the Makena residence. The crime scene had already been secured and cordoned off from the public. Leila and Seymour identified themselves and made their way through.

They were met halfway by Officer Kelly Long. "I was the first one to arrive at the scene," he said. "The victim was dead by that time. Apparently he was just coming home when ambushed by someone."

Leila winced. "Bad timing." She suspected it wouldn't have mattered what time Brennan had arrived home. Someone wanted him dead. Quite possibly the same person who had killed Elizabeth Racine and Larry Nagasaka. "Did you see anyone else?"

"Wish I had. Whoever did it got away."

Leila stifled a yawn. "Hopefully not for long."

She kept walking till she stood over the body. A nighttime photographer, Sheila Walker, was busy capturing images of the decedent.

"Tough way to go," she said.

"What way isn't?" Leila rolled her eyes and studied the victim. If she hadn't remembered the suit Douglas Brennan had worn, she might not believe it was him, since half his face had been blown off. He had also been shot at least once in the chest.

She noted the briefcase on the grass had bullet holes in it and nodded at Seymour.

"I'm guessing Brennan somehow thought that might protect him," he said.

"He guessed wrong." Leila looked at Long. "Has the house been searched?"

"Yeah. We had to use the victim's key to get inside. Brennan left behind a cat. It was unharmed. No sign anything was disturbed or missing. And Brennan's wallet was still in his pocket, so it doesn't look like a robbery."

"Not surprised. The M.O. suggests this had nothing to do with robbing the victim. The murder was personal."

She watched Seymour head toward the bushes in front of the house, following him.

"What do you see?"

He pointed toward a slight indentation. "My guess is the killer hid inside the bushes, waiting for Brennan to show his face."

"You think?"

Seymour used gloved hands to separate the bushes. "It's a long shot, but the unsub may have left behind DNA, a footprint, or other clues."

He instructed the CSI team to see what evidence they could gather there.

"Brennan must have seen the killer's face before losing half his own." Leila gave Seymour a sour look as they headed away from the crime scene.

He scratched his jaw. "Yeah. Too bad he's not in a position to share that knowledge."

It was something Leila was painfully aware of as they searched for the person who murdered Douglas Brennan.

* * *

Seymour wanted only to get away from the scene and digest the latest murder investigation. But no sooner had they stepped outside the crime scene tape when he spotted Renee Bradley weaving her way to get to them. The twenty-something pesky reporter was never far from a news story.

And this certainly had the makings of one whether Seymour liked it or not.

"Don't look now," he told Leila, "but I think we're about to be cornered."

Leila sniffled. "I wondered how long it would take her to show up. You want to handle this? Or shall I?"

"We can both take her on. Ms. Bradley doesn't intimidate easily."

"Neither do I."

He grinned, as this was part of what attracted him to Leila. "Ah, Renee, funny we should run into you. Or is it the other way around?"

Renee was not amused. "Why don't you tell me about the latest murder to hit Maui?"

"I'm sure you realize we can't comment on an ongoing investigation." Unless it benefited them to speak to the press.

She wrinkled her nose. "Can you at least confirm the deceased is Douglas Brennan, CEO of the Medical Association of Maui?"

Seymour wondered who her source was. Could be anyone on the force, other than himself or Leila.

"We'd rather not. At least not until the next of kin is notified."

This didn't seem to faze her. "From what I understand, the victim was shot to death in a manner similar to the deaths of Elizabeth Racine and Larry Nagasaka. Is this hunting season against doctors or what?"

"It's premature to speculate on any relationship between the current victim and others," Leila said with an edge to her voice.

"Premature for who, Detective? I think the public has a right to know if we've got a serial killer in our midst."

"Right now there's no indication we're dealing with a serial killer. Whether these murders are linked or not remains to be seen."

In Seymour's mind there was little doubt the connection was there—whether the same killer or a copycat. The real questions were who should they be looking for and could they find the person before another doctor was shot to death?

"Well, can you at least tell me if you have any suspects in either investigation?" Renee eyed him.

Seymour had no intention of baiting the bait only to have it blow up in their faces. Yes, they had at least one person of interest on the radar. Until they had him in custody, there was no reason to spill the beans and draw the ire of Lt. Ortega for one. Not to mention, being a suspect was not the same thing as being guilty.

Except in the eyes of the press.

"There's no one in custody right now," he told her. "But we're doing everything we can to change that. Now if you'll excuse us, we have a job to do."

Seymour gave her a hard look and Renee got the message. He fully expected to go through this again soon. Hopefully by then they would have something useful to say.

CHAPTER SEVENTEEN

Ferguson squeezed his eyes shut and clutched Gina's shoulders as she held his erection in her mouth, teasing the shaft with her tongue and teeth till he exploded.

He pulled himself out and wished he could stay longer. But duty called.

"I have to go," he told her.

"So what else is new?"

He grinned, zipping his pants. "Don't be like that."

Gina got off her knees. "Going back to the wife and pretending things are fine?"

"They are fine. We have an understanding." Or he did. "Anyway, I'm still on duty."

"When will I see you again?"

"Whenever." He ran a hand along the side of her soft face. "I can see myself out."

"Whatever."

Ferguson thought it was sexy when she pouted. Whereas when Brenda pouted, it was plain old unappealing.

In his car, he heard the latest on the murder of CEO Douglas Brennan. Gunned down in front of his home. So far no suspects named. Ferguson couldn't help but think about Travis Takamori. His alibi had held up for the murders of Racine and Nagasaka, insofar as giving Takamori someone who supported his story. That didn't mean he wasn't still a suspect. As far as Ferguson was concerned, no one could be ruled out till the actual killer was in custody.

Same was true for the killer of Douglas Brennan, assuming they weren't one and the same.

Ferguson called his wife, not particularly wanting to talk to her, but feeling obliged to tell her he would be later than expected.

"Hey," he said nonchalantly.

"Hi."

"What are you doing?"

"Waiting for you." Brenda paused. "Or shouldn't I?"

Ferguson sighed. "You probably shouldn't. There's been a murder. I have to do my part in the investigation. I'll get home as soon as I can."

"I'm sure you will." Her voice was thick with sarcasm.

Ferguson gripped the steering wheel. "I'll make it up to you."

"How many times have I heard that?"

"Probably too many," he conceded. "I'm sorry. I have to go."

"Then go. I'm sure you can heat up your own food when you get here. I'm going to bed."

He heard the phone disconnect and Ferguson felt a strange sense of relief that the issues between them could be put off for at least another day.

* * *

Rachel rang the bell of a house across the street from Douglas Brennan's. They were hoping someone saw something. From experience, she'd learned most people were reluctant to get involved where it concerned homicides. Especially when the killer was still at large, as though they might be targeted next as a result of speaking out.

A thirty-something woman came to the door.

"Hi. I'm Detective Lancaster of the Maui P.D. I'm investigating—"

"I know. The death of Doug Brennan. I saw the shooter. I'm Jessie Cortez. Please come in."

Rachel lifted a brow. Inside the home, she could tell immediately that Jessie was part of a military family. There were photographs of her and a young man in uniform, ribbon magnets, and decals decorating the place. It made Rachel think of Greg and what they were missing.

"I can't believe this happened." Jessie rolled her eyes. "I didn't know Doug very well, but he seemed like a nice man who pretty much kept to himself since his divorce. He didn't deserve to die like that."

"No, he didn't." Rachel agreed. And Larry Nagasaka and Elizabeth Racine should still be alive. Someone obviously felt otherwise. "So tell me what you saw, Ms. Cortez."

"I was just putting my baby to sleep when I heard the pops. I knew it was the sound of gunfire." Jessie touched her lips. "When I looked out the window, that's when I saw Doug lying in his driveway. Then I turned and saw someone running down the street like their pants were on fire."

Rachel took notes. "So you didn't actually see the shooting take place?"

Jessie shook her head. "It probably would've given me nightmares."

"Was the person you saw male or female?"

"It was dark and I only saw them from the back, but I think it was a man."

"How tall would you say he was?"

Jessie shrugged. "I'm not sure. Maybe six feet or less."

"Can you describe his clothes?"

"No, not really. Just that they were dark. I was too freaked out to think anything like this could happen in our neighborhood."

"I understand." Rachel spoke softly. "Unfortunately no area is safe when someone is determined to kill you."

Jessie arched a brow. "Does this have anything to do with those other two doctors who were killed?"

"That's yet to be determined." At least officially. Unofficially Rachel was sure the shootings were more than mere coincidence. Now they needed to prove it.

"My husband's a medic in the Army, serving in Afghanistan," Jessie said. "I wish he were home now, but the last thing I'd ever want is to see someone go after him here."

Rachel wished she could be so fortunate to have Greg still serving his country. Unfortunately his luck had run out.

"You're right," she told her. "You wouldn't want to see that."

* * *

"I'm sure it was a woman I saw running away from the house after Dr. Brennan was shot," said Albert Shuri, the neighbor who called 911.

Ferguson favored the sixty-something man with narrowed eyes. "What makes you so sure? Earlier you said it was too dark to make out much other than the sounds."

Albert touched his glasses. "I heard the pop, pop, pop," he said. "When I went to the window, the first thing I did was look in the direction I thought it was coming from. I saw what looked like someone on the ground...Dr. Brennan, turns out. It took a moment before I stepped outside. That's when I saw the person on the move. Sure it was dark, but there were street lights."

"Describe the person for me."

"Tall, thin, wore dark clothes."

Ferguson took this down. "Could you tell if the hair was long or short?"

Albert slouched. "Neither. Probably shoulder length."

"Hair color?"

"Not sure. Maybe brown."

"Did you see her face?"

"She never looked back."

Ferguson leaned toward him. "Did she get into a car?"

"Can't say. She disappeared into the darkness."

"Did you see anyone else?" Ferguson asked.

Albert shook his head. "Not till the officer showed up."

"Guess that's all for now."

"So was it a robbery or what?"

Ferguson put his pad away. From what he understood there was no evidence of forced entry or burglary.

"I don't think you have to worry about that," he told him. "Whoever killed Douglas Brennan had a different agenda."

* * *

Officer Natalie Yuen was cruising around Pukalani and thinking about the hot sex with her lover this morning when she spotted the BMW weaving dangerously in and out of traffic. Either the driver was in a hurry to go nowhere or, more likely, was inebriated.

She went in pursuit and hoped the person was cooperative for everyone's sake.

The driver obeyed her command to pull over. A good first step. After stopping behind the vehicle, she approached.

Under the beam of her flashlight, Natalie observed a white male at the wheel. He appeared to be in his mid to late thirties, dressed casually, and was calm.

Maybe too calm.

"Can I see your driver's license, sir?"

He hesitated. "Did I do something wrong, officer?"

"You were driving erratically."

"Didn't mean to. Guess I was a little impatient. Sorry about that."

"License," she said again while scanning the interior of vehicle. There was a closed bag on the passenger side of the front seat and some CDs strewn on the back seat.

"Sure." He pulled the license from his wallet and handed it to her.

Natalie studied it. Jeremy Lockhart of 4189 Aapueo Parkway. She compared the photo with his face.

"Have you been drinking, Mr. Lockhart?"

"I had a couple of drinks, but I'm not drunk."

She shone the light on his eyes. "I think maybe you are. What's in the bag?"

He turned away. "Nothing."

Natalie knew a lie when she heard it. Her first thought was that he had a gun.

"I'd like you to step out of the car."

When he hesitated, she drew her own weapon, not taking any chances.

CHAPTER EIGHTEEN

The next morning, Leila entered the conference room with Seymour, separating before taking chairs amongst the detectives. Though they had not talked about keeping their relationship under wraps, neither saw the need to advertise it either. Certainly not in the middle of a homicide investigation.

"As everyone here knows, Douglas Brennan was gunned down last night," Lt. Ortega said grimly. "That makes three doctors killed in the past two weeks—all members of the Medical Association of Maui. We won't know if we're dealing with the same shooter till ballistics compares the bullets. But it's reasonable to assume that's the case under the circumstances."

Leila leaned forward. "What about the suspect brought in last night?"

"Had to let him go. Though he tested positive for gunshot residue, there was no weapon found and Jeremy Lockhart's alibi of being at work as an X-ray technician around the time Brennan was shot held up. Also, his clothing didn't match what witnesses described the shooter wearing. We were able to get him for DUI, though. He's still a suspect, but we don't have enough to hold him."

Leila concurred, even if it would have been so nice if a simple traffic stop had brought this nightmare to an end. "How did he explain the GSR?"

"He didn't. Basically suggested it must have been from cross contamination. We couldn't dispute it, given the number of particles he tested positive for."

"Our perp could still be a woman," Rachel said. "Witnesses have made conflicting statements over whether a person seen running from the scene of the latest homicide was a male or female. This seems to fall in step with the unsub in the murders of Racine and Nagasaka."

"Maybe we're looking at a male and female working together," Ferguson stated. "I say we haul in Melissa Eng and Travis Takamori. Both their alibis were shaky and I wouldn't put it past Eng to get her drug crazed nephew to do her dirty work."

"I think you're right." Ortega nodded. "Let's bring them in and see what they have to say."

"Might be a good idea to talk to Brennan's ex-wife, too," Seymour said. "There obviously was no love lost between them. And she probably wasn't a big fan of Larry Nagasaka either, since he dumped her for Elizabeth Racine. Maybe Courtney Brennan decided to make some people pay for getting on her bad side."

"Makes sense. Do it." Ortega looked at Leila. "Any other suggestions for trying to find a killer?"

Leila felt put on the spot. As one of the lead investigators, she didn't want to overlook something or someone who could make a difference.

"We interview everyone again who might have been involved with the victims, personally and professionally, or by association."

Ortega pursed his lips. "Fine. Whatever it takes. Anyone else have something to say?"

Rachel raised her hand. "If it turns out we're headed in the wrong direction, we may need to step outside the box and see if there's someone out there gunning for doctors with a different agenda."

"Such as?" Seymour regarded her.

"Revenge for a medical procedure gone wrong. Or maybe some other vendetta against the association itself."

"I agree," Leila said. "The more doctors killed, the more likely the unsub is a disgruntled person out to right some perceived wrongs in targeting the group."

Ortega's brow furrowed. "The point is we don't want any more doctors killed if we can help it. Let's stop whoever is responsible, whatever the motivation is!"

Leila was sure they were all on the same page there. Now if only the killer or killers would step forward and take responsibility, they could turn their attention elsewhere.

She wasn't holding her breath.

* * *

"Akela's birthday is next week," Seymour told Leila en route to pay a visit to Courtney Brennan. "Got any idea what to buy a nine-year-old these days?" He used to talk about this with Mele, but since she had decided to shut him out, Leila was the next best thing.

"Have you tried asking her what she likes?"

"Wouldn't that sort of defeat the purpose of surprising her?"

"Not really. My dad used to ask me that all the time. I usually had a long wish list, so whatever he decided to get was a surprise."

Seymour grinned. "You're a genius."

"You don't have to be Einstein to figure out kids. Just a little ingenuity."

"I knew I liked you for some reason."

Leila chuckled. "And I thought it was my sex appeal all this time."

"That, too." He warmed at the thought of making love to her before forcing himself to focus on the investigation. "Seems like being in the medical profession is becoming pretty risky these days."

"Only if you're marked for death. Brennan surely never expected his days as the CEO of the Medical Association of Maui would end so suddenly."

"Wonder who his replacement will be?" Seymour dribbled his fingers on the steering wheel.

"Maybe someone who would do anything to be at the top—including commit murder..."

* * *

Courtney Brennan lived in a condo on Ka'anapali Beach. Leila was sure she'd gotten her fair share of what her ex had when they divorced. But was it enough?

The door was opened by a twenty-something man, muscular and tanned.

"Yes?"

"Detective Kahana and Detective Seymour with the police department," Leila said. "We'd like to speak to Courtney."

He gave her the once over. "C'mon in."

They waited in a large foyer while the man went upstairs.

"Looks like the former Mrs. has moved on," remarked Seymour.

Leila chuckled. "More like a boy toy. And just the type of person who might do anything for you."

"A frightening thought."

They watched as an attractive woman in her mid forties bounded down the stairs, followed by the man.

"I'm Courtney. How can I help you?"

"We'd like to talk to you about your ex-husband," Leila said.

"What about him?"

"Can we speak alone?"

Courtney favored her companion. "Why don't you go make us a drink? I'm sure this won't take long."

He nodded obediently. "Whatever you say."

She waited a beat and then met Seymour's eyes. "I'm listening..."

"Douglas Brennan was shot and killed last night." Seymour held her gaze.

Courtney flinched. "Douglas...dead?"

"I'm afraid so."

"Who shot him?"

Leila got her attention. "We don't know yet. Maybe you can help us with that."

"Not sure how I could." Courtney hand brushed platinum hair from her face. "Douglas and I haven't kept in touch much since our divorce."

"We understand your husband left you because you had an affair with Larry Nagasaka."

Courtney's mouth furrowed. "I made a mistake with Larry and paid the price."

Leila glanced at the expensive condo. "Looks like you came out pretty well after the divorce."

"I got what I deserved after a ten year marriage. I'm not ashamed of that."

"No one's asking you to be. Unfortunately the bad blood between you and Brennan makes you a suspect in his murder."

Courtney widened her eyes. "You think I killed Douglas?"

"Did you?" Seymour's voice was blunt. "Wouldn't be the first time an embittered ex-wife got her ultimate revenge after losing more than what she gained in a divorce settlement."

Courtney flashed him a wicked look. "You're barking up the wrong tree. I had nothing to do with what happened to Douglas. I spent the entire night with my boyfriend, Henri."

"I'm sure he'll vouch for that," Leila said.

"Yes." Courtney wrung her hands. "No matter our differences, I never wanted Douglas dead."

"How about Larry Nagasaka?" Seymour asked. "Did you want him dead? Maybe losing to Elizabeth Racine was enough to send you over the edge."

"It was never serious with Larry. We both agreed that when the time came to move on, we would with no questions asked. The fact he chose to be with Elizabeth was not my concern." Courtney licked her lips. "I've moved on from my past relationships and am happy with Henri. There's no room for bitterness in my heart."

Leila saw Henri approaching them with two drinks. She gave Courtney the benefit of the doubt till proven otherwise.

CHAPTER NINETEEN

When Seymour suggested they bypass lunch for sex at his place, Leila was quick to agree. Each stripped the other naked and fell onto the bed, kissing and touching all the way.

Leila felt free with Seymour to express her sexuality and enjoy his. She put him in her mouth and teased with her tongue. For an instant she imagined his wife doing this and felt a twinge of jealousy before it passed. She wouldn't let his past lessen their present.

Seymour grunted and twirled strands of her hair with his fingers. "Feels damn good," he said.

"Then just lie back and let it happen."

"I'd rather not, especially when it would be even nicer being inside you."

"If that's what you want."

"Yeah, badly!"

Leila lifted and grabbed a condom packet, tearing it open with her teeth. She covered Seymour's erection, straddled him, and slid on.

She liked the feel of him impaling her as she slowly moved up and down. Her face lowered to his and she attacked his mouth in whole.

He attacked back, gripping the back of her head and sucking Leila's lips. Their bodies were in perpetual motion, perspiring and moist, hot and bothered. The sounds of sex and erratic breaths filled the air like a melody.

Leila heard herself cry out Seymour's name as an orgasm ripped through her. A few moments later he climaxed with a shudder.

Leila climbed off him. "What a fun way to take a break."

"Beats fighting crime anytime," Seymour said.

She looked at him. "Anytime?"

"Yeah. Especially with you."

Leila smiled, feeling the same way. Was that really smart? At the moment she could care less.

* * *

Rachel sat across from Melissa Eng, while Ferguson hovered over them. The object was to see if she knew anything about the murder of Douglas Brennan. Though Melissa's beef seemed to be directed toward Larry Nagasaka, the similar M.O. in both cases made her a suspect.

"We'd just like to clear up a few things and then you should be on your way," Rachel said, knowing her nephew, Travis Takamori was being grilled in another interview room. "Any time you'd like to have counsel present, just let us know."

Melissa sneered. "I didn't do anything so I don't need a lawyer."

"Fine." Rachel glanced at the one-way mirror where Lt. Ortega and maybe Detective Seymour were observing. "Why don't we start by asking where you were last night between 9:30 and 9:45?"

"At home where I always am at that time."

"Can anyone verify that?"

Melissa sighed. "If you want to know if I killed that CEO, the answer is no!"

"What CEO would that be?" Ferguson asked.

"The one shot in front of his house. You think I don't know what this is all about?"

"Good for you that you've got a brain in there somewhere. Too bad you only choose to use it selectively. Otherwise you wouldn't have gotten canned for stealing."

Melissa scowled. "It was a lie," she reiterated. "I had no desire to take any of their precious items out of the condo."

Ferguson narrowed his eyes. "Maybe you got yourself a gun and decided you could take something even better from rich people like Larry Nagasaka and Douglas Brennan—like their lives."

"That's ridiculous. You can't pin these murders on me."

"No one's trying to pin anything on you." Rachel's tone was friendly. "We only want to make sure a killer doesn't slip through the net. If it wasn't you, maybe Travis was acting on your behalf...perhaps without your knowledge?"

"No way!" Melissa tensed. "Travis has his problems, but he's a good kid deep down inside. He couldn't kill anyone any more than I could."

Rachel wanted to believe her. Except for the fact that anyone was capable of murder if provoked enough, real or imaginary.

Including Travis Takamori.

* * *

Seymour let Leila take the lead in questioning Travis Takamori. The jury was still out on whether or not they were looking at a murderer. At the very least, he seemed unpredictable.

Leila sat close to the suspect. "Your story about being with your girlfriend the night Elizabeth Racine and Larry Nagasaka were killed didn't exactly hold up."

Travis cocked a brow. "I told you the truth."

"That's not what I heard. According to Jocelyn Dandridge's statement, there was a period in there were you and she were separated. Maybe that's when you made your move against the doctors."

"I didn't kill them. I don't care what Jocelyn told you, we were together!"

"So how do you explain the discrepancy?" asked Seymour.

Travis hunched his shoulders. "I can't."

"Just like you can't adequately explain why you would brag about killing two people you didn't even know."

"It was stupid." Travis frowned. "I didn't really shoot them."

"How about Douglas Brennan?"

"Huh?"

Leila took over. "He was shot to death last night the same way as the doctors. Do you know anything about that?"

"No. Why would I?"

"You tell me. Could be you simply did what Melissa told you to."

Travis rubbed his nose. "She'd never tell me to kill anybody."

"What if she had? Would you have done it, damn the consequences for you and her?"

"No way. I'm not a killer."

"So prove it to us."

"How?"

"By giving us an alibi that will stick for your whereabouts last night around nine-thirty."

He sniffed. "Yeah, I can do that. I was with my girlfriend...having sex. There was no time when she let me out of her sight."

Leila met Seymour's eyes. He cracked a smile and she colored as images of their afternoon romp danced in her head.

"We'll check out your story," she told Travis.

* * *

Leila met with Jan that night for drinks at a Lahaina watering hole.

"So tell me more about this new guy." Leila looked across the table. Jan had text messaged her about him a day earlier.

"Well, he's good looking, charming, and loaded. Not to say I'm looking for a sugar daddy. In fact, I wasn't really even looking, per se. But there he was at the art supply shop."

"So he's an artist?"

"More of an art connoisseur."

"What happened to the last guy?" Leila tried to remember which one it was.

"Turned out to be a total flake." Jan wrinkled her nose. "Maybe this one will be different."

"When do I get to meet him?"

"After I get to know him better. Patience has never been my thing, but I'd really like to give it a try this time and see if things work out."

"Good luck!" Leila lifted her cocktail.

"To us both." Jan touched her glass to Leila's. "Looks like things between you and Blake are heating up."

"Yes, in bed. Still too soon to know if there's a future."

"Is that what you want?"

"Not sure it's what he wants." Leila sat back. "We're just starting to get comfortable with each other as lovers. I don't want to push and scare him away."

"Then don't," Jan said. "Just be careful to keep things in a proper perspective. I'm sure he's a great catch, hot in bed and all, but at the end of the day, the man's still married and may only be in this for the short run."

"His marriage is over." Or so Leila had been told.

"In that case, I say have your fun and let nature take its course, just as I intend to. What happens will happen."

Leila sipped her drink. Jan was right. No reason to rock the boat or try to predict a future she couldn't control. Best to enjoy the delicate balance she had with Seymour between work and play without having any expectations, realistic or not.

CHAPTER TWENTY

Seymour was up at six a.m. on Thursday. He was in his own bed, though wishing it had been Leila's bed, if not Mele's.

He did fifty pushups and rode an exercise bike for half an hour. Every now and then he went to the gym. The truth was he was too damned busy to dedicate a regular program to strength training and the other benefits of a fully equipped gym. Maybe if he was lucky he'd get to retire with enough time left to smell the roses.

He drove to work, contemplating everything from picking out Akela's birthday gift to hoping to solve three murders before things really got out of hand. Problem was, they hadn't reached that stage, and the clock was ticking.

At his desk, Seymour worked on a little unfinished paperwork. He looked for Leila, but she wasn't at her desk. He might have thought she wasn't coming in today, except that Leila never missed work.

He doubted that would change as the nature of their relationship had.

"Blake Seymour...?"

Startled to hear his own name in full, Seymour looked at the man standing over him. He was holding an envelope.

"Yeah, I'm Seymour."

"I've got a delivery for you. If you'd just sign here..."

He grabbed the pen from man's hand and gave his signature.

"You have a good day," the man said with a smirk and walked away.

Seymour opened the envelope and pulled out a document. His heart skipped a beat when he realized it was divorce papers. He'd just been served, meaning there truly was no turning back in the glimmer of hope he could still salvage his marriage.

Hadn't he expected this? Yes, he just didn't expect it to hurt so much.

"Are you awake?"

Seymour saw Leila and realized he'd been so caught up in his thoughts he must have missed what she'd said. "Yeah, I'm awake."

"Why so gloomy?"

He pondered whether to share the news with his lover before handing her the papers. "Mele's made it official."

Leila flashed a sad look. "I'm sorry."

Seymour believed her, even if it was awkward for both of them.

"It's not like I didn't expect this. Mele made it perfectly clear that what we had is over. I have to accept it."

"Do you think you can?"

He met her probing eyes and didn't want to disappoint. "I don't have any choice. Life goes on."

A tiny smile played on her lips. "Glad you feel that way."

He touched her in a non sexual way. "Are you ready to head over to the M.E.'s office?"

"I am if you are."

"Let's go."

* * *

Leila felt a bit odd learning Mele had actually filed for divorce. She had met Seymour's wife a couple of times at police functions. Though cordial, Mele had also seemed distant with little desire for friendship. Leila imagined it might have been a reflection of her feelings about Seymour being in law enforcement.

Or had Mele's disposition really been a defense mechanism against being hurt?

Leila refused to feel guilty about sleeping with Seymour as though she had been the cause of his marital breakup. That was his own doing, along with perhaps Mele and whatever issues had come between them.

As far as Leila was concerned, Seymour was a grown man more than capable of choosing who he wanted to be with post Mele. And he'd chosen to be with her for now. Leila got what she wanted, too—an experienced lover and great person to hang out with. She had no intention of allowing herself to fall in love with him.

Only to end up being hurt, like Mele was.

Or was Seymour hurting even more right now?

Leila switched her thoughts to something more morbid as the medical examiner welcomed them.

"Did I ever tell you how nice it is to talk to living people?" Patricia Lee quipped, standing over the covered remains of Douglas Brennan.

"You're not telling us you talk to the corpses, are you?" Leila joked.

"Hey, it's great therapy. I can tell them everything and they'll never reveal it to a soul."

Seymour laughed. "Maybe you need a break from cutting up bodies."

"Tell me about it." Patricia made a face.

"Before you head for the hills, give us the rundown on Brennan's cause of death, etc."

"It would be my pleasure, Detective." Patricia put on her glasses. "The victim died as the result of shock from his wounds after being shot multiple times—four to be exact—at close range as indicated by powder burns. The manner of death is homicide and mechanism, a small caliber firearm. I was able to retrieve bullets and bullet fragments from the deceased.

"Two of the bullets went through the victim's briefcase, which Dr. Brennan apparently hoped might deflect them. Unfortunately that didn't work. These bullets punctured vital organs. A third bullet lodged in his left femur, shattering it. The last bullet struck the right side of the decedent's face, causing massive damage externally and to his brain.

"In short, the victim's brutal death was reminiscent of the way Elizabeth Racine and Larry Nagasaka met their end," Patricia concluded.

"So you're saying we're looking at the same shooter?" Leila faced her.

"Based on the entry and exit wounds, yes, I'd have to say that's a strong likelihood."

Leila expected forensic ballistics to confirm this after examining the bullets. It still didn't put them any closer to the killer's identity.

"Is there anything else you can tell us about the unsub?" Seymour asked.

Patricia removed her glasses. "Well, only that he or she wants to get close enough to the victims to inflict maximum damage. Always the scariest kind of killer, since that means the person is willing to take serious risks for the rewards."

Leila swallowed at the notion while wondering who else might be one step closer to execution without being the wiser.

* * *

"Hey, Ferguson, you gotta minute?"

Ferguson was just about to get out of there early when Detective Jonny Chung from the vice squad blocked his path.

"Yeah, what's up?"

"When you look at me what do you see?" Chung stepped back.

Ferguson studied him. He was Chinese-American with short black hair, probably five-nine, and reasonably fit. Was that what he wanted to hear?

"I see someone who wouldn't have a place on my dance card."

Chung laughed. "Ditto. Do I look like a john?"

Ferguson's pulse skipped a beat as if his secret had been discovered. But how? He'd been careful.

"No more than I do," he said tentatively.

Chung frowned and muttered an expletive. "Guess I need to work on my appearance more."

"I don't follow."

"Got a sting going down tomorrow. We're hoping to nab as many hookers as possible. Not that it's as bad here as Honolulu. We just want to keep it that way."

"Makes sense." Ferguson took a breath. "Where's this sting taking place?"

Chung tilted his head. "You looking to find out where the action is or what?"

Ferguson chuckled. "The only action for me is with my wife. Just wondered where the problem area is for streetwalkers since I never see any."

"You wouldn't, unless they were dead. Most only come out when we're not looking. We're targeting Wailuku and Lahaina this round."

Ferguson looked nonchalant. "Good luck."

"I'm not the one who'll need it."

"I meant playing your part."

"Oh yeah, well practice makes perfect, as they say."

Ferguson watched him walk away, relieved they weren't onto him. But they could be arresting Gina for solicitation. And what if she should run into him as a police detective and start talking to save her own neck? It could ruin his career. Not to mention his marriage.

He needed to warn Gina for both their sakes.

* * *

"I want you to do something for me." Gina listened as Trent whispered in her ear while in bed. She assumed he wanted to try a new sexual position. She was game so long as it didn't hurt.

"What?"

"Stay off the streets tomorrow."

"Why?"

"The vice squad is doing a sting and anyone caught soliciting will be arrested."

Gina was no stranger to arrest. It was no big deal. They usually let her out after a day. But obviously it meant something to Trent. Did he really care that much about her?

She looked at him. "You a cop or something?"

"Something." He kissed between her breasts. "Let's just leave it at that."

"Okay, whatever you say." Gina didn't care if he was a cop. She'd already figured that out. Everyone had their secrets, including her.

The most important thing was that he treated her a hell of a lot better than most, if not all, johns and his frequent business put food on the table. It would hurt when Trent decided to go back to his wife for sex. Many men eventually did when their guilt consumed them.

Until then, Gina intended to milk this for all it was worth. Something told her he intended to do the same.

* * *

Seymour stood in Paul Ortega's Great Room while his boss and friend made them drinks.

"So Mele really did it, huh?" Ortega handed him a glass of scotch.

"Yeah. It's official now." Seymour thought about the moment he received the divorce papers. "On my way to being a free man, whether I like it or not."

"That's not what I heard."

"Oh yeah? What did you hear?" Seymour suspected what was coming next.

"That things are heating up between you and Kahana."

Seymour tasted the drink, seeing no reason to deny it. "We've been spending some time together. She seems to accept me, flaws and all. That's a comforting thing at this time in my life."

Ortega nodded. "When my ex decided to call it quits, I looked for anyone who could make me feel like a man again. After a while I realized I was the only one who could do that."

"Not sure that's what it's all about with Leila."

"What you do in your personal life is none of my business," Ortega said. "You're good cop and so is Kahana. I just don't want to see either of you mess that up."

Seymour was thoughtful. "It probably won't last very long. We're at different stages of our lives, but the job still comes first." Or so it did with him, which may have been part of the problem in his failed marriage.

Ortega put a hand on his shoulder. "Glad to hear that."

Seymour put down more scotch.

CHAPTER TWENTY-ONE

The next morning, Leila went to get the ballistics report. "So what's it say?" she asked, standing between Seymour and Gil Delfino, the forensic examiner.

Delfino handed her the report. "Your latest murder victim was shot with the same .25 caliber weapon as the other victims."

"You're sure about that?" Seymour favored him.

"Oh yeah. The bullets retrieved from Douglas Brennan and one lodged in the briefcase had six lands and grooves with right hand twist marks—a perfect match for the ones recovered from the Racine and Nagasaka murders. Same is true for the shell casings. Their ejection and firing pin marks are identical to the others. You've clearly got yourself a single shooter here."

"Why am I not surprised?" Leila rolled her eyes. "It's been obvious since Brennan's murder that one person has chosen doctors to target for reasons we're still trying to uncover."

"I suggest you do it fast. Otherwise you just may have me working overtime. Not that I can't use the extra money."

"We'll do our best to not let your bank account overflow, Delfino," Seymour said. "I don't suppose you were able to get any prints from the bullets?"

"Sorry." Delfino shook his head. "But don't give up. I still may be able to help you out there. I'm working on it."

"Maybe you could work a little harder. There's a good chance our unsub is in the system. Trouble is, we don't have what we need to track him or her down."

"You'll help yourself by locating the murder weapon, which the shooter is apparently keeping for now. That would be even better than fingerprints, since we could match the bullets to the gun they came from."

Leila narrowed her eyes. "Tell us something we don't know."

"Actually I can do that." Delfino drew a breath. "CSI also recovered some DNA from hair strands. Not saying they belong to the killer. But they were pulled from the bushes in front of Brennan's house and didn't come from him."

"I'm guessing the hair doesn't belong to the gardener," Seymour said.

"That's for you to figure out."

Leila saw this as another potentially important piece of the puzzle. But it still meant little till they could corner their killer and seal the case by corroborating the evidence.

* * *

At three p.m., Gabe sat at the bar sipping a margarita and wondering how his personal life had gotten so screwed up. It hadn't affected his profession, per se, but his patients had noticed a change in his demeanor. He would have to work on that. It was time he faced up to the fact there was no going back.

Linda wasn't worth the effort.

It was time he found someone who was.

"Hi."

Gabe turned to lay eyes on a gorgeous blonde. "Hi."

"You look like you could use some company."

"Does it show that much?"

"Afraid so." She smiled softly. "Buy a lady a drink?"

He wasn't used to women hitting on him outside the office. Is that what she was doing?

It made him feel good.

"Sure. Why not?"

She ordered a strawberry cosmopolitan. "I'm Brenda."

"Gabe."

"Nice to meet you."

She held her hand out and he shook it, enjoying the feel of her soft fingers. He wondered what reason she had for being there alone.

"You tell me your story and I'll tell you mine." Brenda eyed him as though reading his mind.

Gabe twisted his lips. "Not that much to tell, really."

"In that case, it should definitely hold my attention."

He couldn't help but smile, liking her already. "I just broke up with my girlfriend after two years together. And she's already seeing someone else. It sucks."

"Have you considered that maybe she did you a favor?"

"How? By telling me she didn't give a damn about our history?"

"By not sticking with something that obviously wasn't working. It would've only been more painful later."

"I suppose." Gabe tasted his drink as hers came. "What about you?"

Brenda frowned. "I think my husband's having an affair."

The fact she was married disappointed Gabe. He recovered quickly, realizing that most of the good ones were.

"What makes you think so?"

"He hasn't touched me in weeks. Even before then it was like he wasn't there."

"Ouch." Gabe wondered if her husband was insane. Or blind. "Have you confronted him?"

"Yes, sort of. Of course, he denied it."

"Maybe he's telling the truth."

"At this point I don't think I care anymore. I just want to feel like a healthy, sexual woman again."

"I think I understand where you're coming from."

Brenda gazed at him. "Maybe we can help each other out."

"What did you have in mind?" Gabe wanted to be sure they truly were on the same wavelength.

"Take me to your place," she said. "Then take me."

He met the hunger in her eyes, matching his own, and found himself unable to turn down the invitation.

"Let's go."

* * *

Brenda Ferguson hadn't planned to seduce anyone when she walked into that bar. But feeling as low as she was and meeting a good looking guy who seemed equally in need of a quick, if not temporary, fix was too much to resist.

She followed him down Piilani Highway to a condo in Makena. For an instant Brenda had second thoughts about doing this. That disappeared with the reality her husband was no longer attracted to her sexually. But Gabe was.

And that was good enough for her.

They wasted little time talking, barely making it to the bedroom before each stripped naked and attacked one another with a sense of urgency.

Brenda came instantly. And again when Gabe climaxed inside her.

Afterwards she had to catch her breath. "You were great."

Gabe nibbled on her chin. "So were you."

She felt a tingle and found herself wishing it had come as the result of her husband's romantic affections.

As it was, she had to take a man's desire when it came.

She kissed his nose. "Care to go another round?"

His actions spoke for him.

When they were done, Brenda dressed quickly. She wasn't sure how Gabe would take the news that she was married to a cop.

Who said he had to know? She didn't want to scare him off. Not when Gabe had given her a whole new reason to want to spend time with someone.

* * *

Ferguson arrived home, feeling exhausted after another day of investigating the murders of Brennan, Racine, and Nagasaka. Everyone was feeling the stress of not having anyone in custody at the moment. Worse would be to arrest the wrong person, only to have the real unsub kill again.

He looked for Brenda, but didn't see her in the home office where she ran a web design business, or the kitchen.

Where the hell was she?

He went upstairs and saw her standing in the bathroom. She was wearing a robe, clearly having just taken a shower.

"Hey," he said.

She turned around. "Hi."

"What's up?"

"Nothing much. Did my workout. You hungry?"

"No, I grabbed a bite earlier with some people at work. I think I'm just going to go to bed."

He expected her to want to join him, but hoped she wouldn't. Gina was all he could handle for one night.

Brenda smiled. "Fine. I'm going to go work in my office for a little bit. I'll be up soon."

She gave him a kiss on the cheek and he inhaled her perfume. Was it new?

Ferguson felt a strange sense of disappointment that Brenda wasn't on his back about giving her more attention in the bedroom. Maybe he'd better leave well enough alone.

CHAPTER TWENTY-TWO

Douglas Brennan's body was released to his next of kin, a sister, who flew in from Oregon. The funeral was held on a hot and humid Saturday afternoon in Maui. Leila attended along with Seymour and other members of the police force, less to pay their respects than to see who showed up from the Medical Association of Maui.

In Leila's experience, some killers got a thrill out of showing their face while hidden behind a façade of remorse. Was that the case here?

She looked amongst the mourners, recognizing many who were still suspects in the death of Brennan and/or Elizabeth Racine and Larry Nagasaka. Kenneth Racine stood next to Adrianne Pompeo, while Courtney Brennan looked out of place with her companion, Henri.

Connie Nagasaka seemed to be taking Brennan's death hard, as though more than just an acquaintance. Or was it a reflection of losing her husband so recently?

Leila honed in on a familiar face that took her a moment to recognize. It was the man who had scared off a mugger and provided her a description to sketch.

Gabe Devane, if memory served her correctly. What was he doing here? Did he know the victim?

"What is it?" Seymour asked over her shoulder.

"Just curious. That man behind Connie Nagasaka—I know him."

"Know him how?"

She told him. "Strange, huh?"

"Not necessarily. Maui isn't exactly New York City. Doesn't take much to connect one person to another."

"True. Still I'm not too big on coincidences. Not where it concerns a serial killer at large."

"Was Devane checked out?" Seymour brushed against her.

Leila reacted. "We ran a criminal background check on him as we would anyone under similar circumstances. He was clean. There was no reason at the time to suspect he could have anything to do with this case."

"Maybe he doesn't."

"There's only one way to find out," she said.

"If you need a hand, just wave."

An erotic thought entered her head. "I might need a hand later—but not here."

He grinned and Leila walked away on that note for an unanticipated reunion with Gabe Devane.

* * *

Gabe had seen enough. After the urn containing Douglas Brennan's cremated remains was lowered into the ground, he decided it was time to exit. It was doubtful anyone would miss him, considering he wasn't expected to be there in the first place. He had just made it past the other mourners when someone called his name from behind.

He turned and immediately recognized the woman. "Detective Kahana!"

"Hello, Gabe." Leila gave him an unsmiling look. "I'm surprised to see you here."

Gabe considered the nature of Brennan's death and the investigation into it, along with two other doctors killed recently.

"Douglas and I were friends."

"Small world, huh?"

"I suppose so."

"Since you knew the victim, I'd like to ask you a few questions. Do you mind?"

He wondered what would happen if he were to refuse. Would she think him guilty of a crime?

"Not at all."

Leila raised her head. "Why don't we step over there?"

Gabe glanced at a patch of grass where someone else was buried. He nodded and let her lead the way till they were again face to face.

"I understand you got your mugger," he said.

She smiled slightly. "Yes, thanks to your help."

"I'd hope someone would do the same were my own grandmother being attacked by a thug."

"Good way to think." Leila paused. "How did you know Douglas Brennan?"

Gabe gazed down at her. "We were colleagues."

She raised a brow. "Are you a doctor?"

"An ER trauma surgeon."

"I see." Leila met his eyes. "Would you happen to be member of the Medical Association of Maui?"

He had already anticipated the question. "I was once, but quit the group."

"May I ask why?"

"Professional differences."

"With Douglas Brennan?"

"With the organization as a whole."

Leila flashed a thoughtful look. "Well, I think that will be all for now."

That told Gabe there could be more questions later. Did she consider him a suspect in Brennan's murder? He wasn't averse to seeing her again, per se, except he was kind of involved with someone else.

But how long would that last?

He gave Leila a crooked smile. "If you have any more questions, you can reach me at Maui General or my home number, which you already have."

Gabe walked away and had a feeling he was being watched by more than just the lady detective.

* * *

Seymour studied Gabe Devane as he separated from Leila and moved back amongst the mourners. There was no outward sign the man was nervous or otherwise hiding a dark secret. But most serial killers were as cool as ice. Some also liked to taunt the police during their reign of terror. Or through reporting another crime incognito, while laughing inside at being hidden in plain view.

Was this the case with Devane?

Seymour would dig deeper to see if they might have missed something about the man. Unless Leila had decided his presence at Brennan's funeral was totally plausible.

Turning his attention elsewhere, Seymour looked for anything that might suggest someone was out of place. Or perhaps too comfortable in showing up to pay respects. Aside from Devane, no one in particular stood out.

This hardly meant to Seymour that previous suspects were off the hook. Or that others weren't waiting to be discovered.

He had a suspicion their killer was present and may actually be surveying other potential targets.

Seymour choked back the thought. The last thing anyone wanted was to see another doctor shot to death because they couldn't identify the shooter beforehand.

He left his spot to confer with others on the case and what they may or may not have seen.

* * *

The doer coolly took in the surroundings as mourners began to break up. Douglas Brennan's death had brought out those who hated and loved him, as if to see and be seen. It also had the police out in force. Some pretended to be paying their respects. Others were more blatant in the hopes of spotting a killer in their midst.

But the doer was too smart for all of them. Making it easy for the detectives wasn't in the cards. There would be no slip up. No graveyard confession. No smoking gun.

Vengeance was sweet just like fine wine. Douglas Brennan got exactly what was coming to him. Just as Elizabeth Racine and Larry Nagasaka had found themselves on the front end of bullets.

That none of them lived to see another day was the ultimate justice for bastards who were self-serving in their poor choices.

The doer showed the appropriate remorse and well wishes for all encountered, as to be expected. Anything less might have made them suspicious. Even the police were hesitant to name the doer as a serious suspect, so careful were they not to focus on the wrong person in their pursuit of justice.

That was their mistake.

The doer was happy to be underestimated. Just as Douglas, Elizabeth, and Larry had done. It made the job so much easier and satisfying.

Passing by Brennan's sister, the doer gave her a gentle pat on the hand and insincere smile, before moving on and away from a scene that would soon be repeated.

CHAPTER TWENTY-THREE

"Have you found it?" Leila's mother asked impatiently over the phone on Sunday afternoon. "I have other things to do, you know."

Leila gritted her teeth. As if she didn't have more to do than get a book her mother requested—no, ordered—she buy and send to her.

She switched the cell phone to her other ear. "Not yet."

"Do you need the title again?"

"I wrote it down." Leila walked down the bookstore aisle that held Hawaiian history titles. She found the book on ancient Hawaii. "Got it."

"I'm glad you found it." Rena sighed. "You could deliver it in person, you know."

"I can't."

"You wouldn't have to stay long."

"I'm in the middle of an investigation."

"Aren't you always? Everyone needs a break, including you."

"Cops don't always have that luxury." Leila had no doubt her mother knew this since she was the daughter and wife of a cop herself. Yet she still liked to push Leila's buttons.

"That's why they run out of steam far too early in life," Rena stated tersely.

Leila believed there may be some merit to that. But there were no guarantees the result wouldn't be the same no matter her profession. But she wasn't about to debate the issue with her mother while standing in the aisle of the bookstore.

Leila couldn't help but notice the girl sitting on a chair holding a Harry Potter book. She was maybe fifteen with long black hair off to one side. There was something strangely familiar about her.

Leila recalled the age progression sketch she'd done of Iolana Mumea, the eight-year-old who had been abducted by her father seven years ago and was believed to be in Maui.

Could this be her?

Or had Leila merely sketched an image that looked more like a different girl?

"Are you still there?" Rena's irritation was apparent.

"I have to go," Leila did not mind saying.

"Why?"

"Something's come up. I'll call you later."

Leila disconnected before her mother could protest. She focused again on the girl who looked more as if she were daydreaming than reading. Where were her parents?

Or had she come alone?

Leila glanced around. She saw no parental figure in sight before deciding to go with her instincts. She approached the girl.

"Iolana...?"

The girl looked up immediately. "Are you talking to me?"

"What's your name?"

Before she could answer, Leila heard a deep voice say from behind, "Mily, are you ready to go?"

Leila turned to see a forty-something, dark haired man with a solid build. He glared at her before walking up to the girl.

"Yeah." The girl sprung to her feet. She was tall and pretty.

After flashing Leila a tentative look, she went with the man.

Leila sensed that Mily was apprehensive. Or was it just her imagination?

She certainly wasn't imagining that the man suddenly seemed in a hurry to leave the bookstore. He grabbed the Harry Potter book from her and tossed it on a table before shuffling Mily toward the door.

Though off duty and not exactly having probable cause, Leila thought about detaining the man and girl as a possible child abductor and abductee. But with so little to go on other than a vague image in her head, she opted against acting rashly.

Yet fearing the girl could be crying out for help and not wanting to be left wondering, possibly forever, Leila went against protocol and decided to follow them. She set aside the book for her mother, promising to come back for it.

* * *

Leila saw the girl named Mily and the man she believed could be Jordan Mumea get into a Ford Bronco. Hurrying to her car, Leila ducked down as the Bronco drove by. She started the ignition and waited a moment before pursuing.

She got close enough to see the license plate number. Getting on her cell phone, Leila rang Lt. Tanji.

"Kahana, what can I do for you?"

"I think it's more the other way around." Leila tensed. "I may have spotted Iolana Mumea, the little girl taken by her father seven years ago."

"Really? Where?"

She told him. "The man called the girl Mily, but she seemed to respond when I asked if her name was Iolana."

"Maybe she was only curious," he said.

"She's about the same age Iolana would be now and comes pretty close to the age progression composite."

"Where is she now?"

"In a Bronco just ahead of me. I can give you the license plate number."

"Do it."

Leila moved a little closer. "SKN 259"

She waited while he ran the number. Would it be nothing more than a wild goose chase? Or might she be on the verge of reuniting a mother and daughter?

It made Leila think about the relationship she had with her own mother. Would they ever truly be on the same page? Or was micromanaging her life something Leila would have to learn to live with?

"The vehicle is registered to a Kent Mumea," Tanji said. "I think you may be onto something."

"I hope so. If it is Iolana, she deserves to be with the person who has legal custody of her."

"You won't get any disagreement there. Give me your location and I'll take over from here."

Leila was reluctant to let the car out of her sight. If somehow Jordan were onto her, he could bolt and leave the island with the girl.

"I'll stick with them till someone can take over."

"Not sure that's a good idea."

"Why not? I don't have anything better to do right now and unless you want to risk them vanishing again."

Tanji checked her. "All right. Keep a visual on the suspect. We'll put out an APB on Jordan Mumea."

Leila hung up, getting an adrenalin rush in pursuing something other than her normal killers. At least Iolana was alive, unlike many missing people by the time they were found.

She thought about calling Seymour and apprising him of the situation. But since he was also off duty and planning to attend his daughter's birthday party, Leila chose not to use the needy card or play on Seymour's affections. She even understood why she wasn't invited. Being in the same space as Mele would only make things awkward for everyone under the circumstances.

It would be difficult enough for Seymour. Or so she wanted to believe.

The Bronco made a right turn onto Papalaua Street. Leila followed and slowed down when the car pulled into a driveway. The man and girl got out and hurried inside the house.

Leila phoned it in. She suspected Jordan Mumea was ready to flee again.

Not this time, if she could help it.

* * *

Carrying several gifts he'd wrapped himself, Seymour walked across the park toward his daughter's birthday party that was in full swing. He considered that Mele might not want him there, but that was her problem. He had as much right to celebrate Akela's ninth birthday as she did, in spite of their pending divorce.

Though it still bothered him, especially being blindsided with the papers, Seymour would not let that take away from what Akela had come to mean to them.

Mele intercepted him just as he was about to join Akela and her friends gathered around a picnic table.

"I didn't expect you to come," she said.

"I don't know why the hell not. Believe it or not, I still love our daughter, even if you've stopped loving me."

It hurt to even draw that conclusion. Seymour had no choice but to live with it.

Mele's brow furrowed. "I thought we agreed that while we're going through a divorce, it was best not to spend too much time together pretending to be a happy family, only confusing her more."

"Maybe you should give Akela a bit more credit than that." Seymour took a breath. "She knows things aren't right between us, considering we now live in separate houses. I'm sure she has friends from broken homes."

"So that's supposed to make it all right?"

His nostrils grew. "Hey, I'm not the one who kicked you out and served divorce papers."

"This isn't the time or place."

"There's never a time or place to air one's dirty laundry. What do you want me to say?"

She rested a hand on her hip. "Please don't make a scene."

"I don't intend to. All I want is to wish my daughter a happy birthday and I'll be on my way."

"Fine." Mele glanced at the girls. "Just try not to make her any promises you can't or won't keep."

That stung, but Seymour shrugged it off. He wished he had the type of job that wasn't often 24/7. It was what it was, though, and all he could do was give his best shot to do right by Akela, even if too late for Mele.

* * *

"How's my birthday girl?" Seymour scooped Akela into his arms.

"You remembered," she said jubilantly.

"Of course. My favorite girl in the whole world doesn't turn nine every year."

She giggled. "Can I open my gifts now?"

"Don't let me stop you."

He glanced at Mele, who stayed a safe distance from him, but close enough to present a façade for their daughter, before watching Akela's friends gather around her. Akela eagerly opened the gift-wrapped packages to reveal a jewelry making kit, a scroll with her name on it, and a child's sewing machine.

Akela flashed a thousand watt smile. "Thank you, Daddy. I love everything!"

"I'm glad to hear that, honey."

She looked to her mother for a reaction.

Mele forced a smile. "They're great gifts," she conceded, meeting Seymour's eyes.

He took some solace in that while silently thanking Leila for pointing him in the right direction in making sure he couldn't lose buying Akela's birthday presents. He wished Leila could be there with him. Especially since Mele apparently had no interest in his company anymore. But this was all about Akela today.

He hoped she and Leila might have the opportunity to become friends one day.

* * *

Gina stood among the kiawe trees in the park, hidden from view of those gathered nearby at the picnic table. They were having a birthday party. She honed in on the birthday girl, pretty as could be and seemingly enjoying the attention.

It was all Gina could do not to cry. The one they called Akela was in fact her little girl. She had made the painful choice to give her up for adoption after carelessly getting pregnant from a john. What kind of life would that have been for her as the daughter of a whore? And since Gina had no real working skills, how else would she have raised her daughter?

She'd never considered having an abortion because it went against everything Gina believed in. So she had the child and gave her up in the hope she would be placed with a decent family and have a good life.

By all accounts, that seemed to have come true. Three years ago, overcome with guilt and curiosity, Gina had hired a private detective to help locate her daughter. Ever since then she had tried to check in on her secretly from time to time to make sure Akela was being well cared for.

Maybe someday her daughter would want to meet her.

By then, maybe Gina would have long gotten out of the sex business. Until then she was content to keep her little secret all to herself.

* * *

The knock on the driver's side window nearly gave Leila a heart attack. For an instant she thought it might be Jordan Mumea, having slipped out the back door and prepared to do whatever was necessary to keep his daughter separated from her mother.

Instead Leila saw Lt. Tanji. She took a breath and rolled down the window.

"They still in there?" he asked.

"As far as I know."

"Good. Hope you're right about this, Kahana."

She gave him a faint smile. "You and me both."

Tanji made eye contact with others who had taken positions. "Wait here."

"I'd rather be in on it, if you don't mind."

"Do you have your weapon?"

"No, but everyone else does, so I can live with that."

He considered this and nodded. "With any luck, no one has to get hurt."

Leila approached the residence beside Tanji, flanked by detectives and uniformed officers with weapons drawn.

Tanji knocked on the door while shouting, "Police!"

It was opened by the man Leila saw at the bookstore.

"Are you Jordan Mumea?" asked Tanji.

"Yeah, that's me." His head slumped down.

"You're under arrest for abducting your daughter."

As he was handcuffed, Leila made her way inside, hoping the girl hadn't been harmed. There was no one else downstairs.

She slowly emerged from an upstairs bedroom, looking scared, but in good condition.

"Iolana?" Leila asked.

She remained mute. "I'm Detective Kahana. We're here to take you back to your mother, Ingrid Mumea."

Iolana did not move for a moment, then she ran into Leila's arms and she knew the good guys had won this battle. Her one wish was that Iolana did not come to regret the major changes this was about to bring to the life she had known for the past seven years.

Now if only they could slap the handcuffs on a serial killer, everyone in the department could breathe a little easier.

* * *

That evening Seymour showed up at Leila's door. He probably should have called first, but here he was. Maybe she would send him away.

He hoped Leila would invite him to stay for a while.

She opened the door, wearing a bathrobe. He guessed there was nothing beneath it.

"Hi," he said.

She smiled. "How was the party?"

"Probably not half as exciting as yours."

"You heard about that?"

"Who hasn't? Your perception is remarkable. Not to mention you've got damned good detective skills."

Leila batted her lashes. "Maybe you're beginning to rub off on me a little."

"Then I guess I'm doing my job." He met her eyes. She still hadn't invited him in. Could that be a bad sign? "Hope you weren't busy."

"Actually I was—busy waiting for you."

"I like the sound of that." Seymour grinned as he went inside, closing the door behind him.

Leila dropped her robe to the floor, revealing her nakedness. "Hope you like what you see?"

He felt aroused. "How could I not?"

She licked her lips then kissed him, putting her tongue into his mouth.

That was more than enough to get him going. Seymour lifted her in his arms and headed for the bedroom.

There would be plenty of time later to talk about her heroics, Akela's party, and even how Seymour was really starting to feel comfortable with someone who got turned on rather than repelled by him.

CHAPTER TWENTY-FOUR

On Monday morning, Detective Tony Fujimoto from the Property Crimes and Robbery Unit sat at his desk analyzing the information they had on a series of home burglaries. The thieves had thus far struck at least five homes, mostly in the Lahaina and Honokowai areas. In at least one instance the homeowner was present and beaten before the unsubs took what they wanted and got away.

Fujimoto feared it was only a matter of time before these burglaries escalated in violence and someone ended up dead. He couldn't allow this to happen. Not when it was his investigation and ass on the line.

"We can assume the thieves live within their target zone," he told his partner, Detective Ronald Dailey.

"Yeah, so?"

"So we need to track down every known thief in that radius till they're either eliminated as a suspect or apprehended."

"That shouldn't be too hard."

Fujimoto bit his lip. Seemed like Dailey was more interested in being lazy than doing his job.

"Then get on it. I'll go interview some witnesses, then we can compare notes."

He watched Dailey shuffle away before Fujimoto went down to the coffee room. Leila was in there for her usual decaf. He'd heard she was banging Seymour while he was on the outs with his wife. Admittedly Fujimoto would rather it was him in her bed. But obviously she didn't feel the same way and he had to accept it.

"Hey," he said from behind.

She turned swiftly, obviously startled. "Hey Fujimoto."

"You getting any closer to catching this Doc Killer, as the press has dubbed the unsub?"

Leila frowned. "If you mean is an arrest imminent, the answer is no. But we are working every angle to solve the case."

"Yeah, I hear you." He went to the coffee pot. "I've got my own problems."

"You mean the home burglaries?"

He nodded. "Crime never takes a holiday, not even in paradise."

She half grinned. "Don't you know by now it's because we live in paradise that criminals find it so attractive? Especially the ones you go after. They live for rich tourists who come here with their guard down."

"Maybe they'd be better off coming with guards," Fujimoto said, and thought about her doing the nasty with Seymour.

Leila rolled her eyes. "Right and scare them into going elsewhere with their money? The best bet would be to keep putting the thieves in jail."

"Right alongside the murderers."

"Ouch."

"Sorry, couldn't resist." Maybe if he were on homicide detail she would take him more seriously as a man worthy of sexual attraction.

"Knock yourself out," she said stiffly. "I'll keep doing my job and let the chips fall where they may."

"Same here."

She smiled. "Enjoy your coffee."

Fujimoto watched Leila walk away, before realizing he was spilling coffee. He spat an expletive and wondered if it was her, his present case, or too much coffee that had made him a bit jittery.

* * *

Leila walked through security at Maui Community Correctional Center in Wailuku right behind Rachel. They were to interview a man who had threatened to kill members of the Medical Association of Maui nine months ago after a botched extortion attempt. Since Guillermo Garcia had been locked up for the last two months while awaiting trial, he couldn't have possibly killed Racine, Nagasaka, or Brennan.

But the insistence by Lt. Ortega that they cover all bases, meant Leila had to either eliminate Garcia as a viable suspect or consider him with a reach long enough to commit three murders.

They waited in an interrogation room for the prisoner to be brought in.

Leila thought briefly about the hot sex with Seymour last night. She'd never realized just how bold and demanding she could be. He must have brought out this side of her.

She glanced at Rachel and felt a little guilty she was not getting any action in the bedroom, apparently disinterested in men since the death of her husband. Leila had gone out with her for drinks every now and then, but they had never gotten too close. Maybe that would change in the future as they got to know each other better.

"I said we needed to step outside the box," Rachel said. "Well, this is it. Garcia was certainly into some shady business when out. It's not too much of a stretch to think he could've had someone do his dirty work for him."

"You're right. If that's the case, can we get him to talk?"

"Guess we're about to find out."

Guillermo Garcia was brought into the room in handcuffs, waist chain, and leg irons. He was a heavy man and had a gray beard.

He grinned. "If I'd known some pretty ladies were coming to visit, I'd have dressed up."

Leila frowned. "This isn't a social call."

"Too bad, since I don't know any other reason I'd be talkin' to you."

"Just consider it a break from your normal routine," Rachel said.

He scratched his face. "What do you want?"

Leila looked him in the eye. "Suppose you start by telling us about the threats you made against the Medical Association of Maui."

"Oh that," he said, as though sensing where this was going.

"Yes, that. We take threats to kill very seriously."

"People say a lot of things in the heat of the moment."

"Others say exactly what they mean," countered Rachel. "Three doctors—all members of the Medical Association of Maui—were recently murdered. Maybe you had something to do with it?"

Garcia grinned.

Leila's brows knitted. "You think this is funny?"

He lost the grin. "Look, I had nothing to do with any murders. If someone decided to waste them, that's their business."

"That's not what you thought when you tried to extort three hundred thousand dollars from an undercover cop pretending to represent the sales arm of the organization. According to his statement, you said, 'You're dead and so is everyone else belonging to this group that I can take out.' Sounds to me like you were determined to settle a score."

Garcia looked uncomfortable. "So maybe I was at the time. But that was before I ended up in here. Unless you think I get passes to go out and do whatever I like?"

Rachel batted her eyes. "We know there were people you worked with. Could be someone decided to get revenge on your behalf."

He shook his head. "There's no one out there willing to kill someone for me. I wouldn't ask. Not if it meant ending up in here."

"Maybe you should have thought of that before you decided to put the squeeze on the Medical Association of Maui."

"Tell me something I don't already know."

Leila took a step closer, thankful he was in no position to attack. "If we find out you had anything to do with these murders, you can kiss goodbye any chance you have of ever getting out of here."

Garcia flinched. "If I went after anyone, it would be the asshole cop who set me up. Only I don't know who he is. Again, these are only words..."

Leila was relieved the detective had since been reassigned to another unit. She didn't doubt Garcia's words might have carried more weight if he weren't in prison.

She nodded to the guard to take him away.

* * *

Gabe was glad to get away from the ER for a while and its assortment of injuries sustained by locals and tourists alike. All he wanted now was a hot bath, a drink, and some sleep. He unlocked the door to his condo and went inside.

Sal greeted him as usual, slobbering all over his face.

"Nice to see you, too, boy," he said, "even though it's only been a few hours."

The dog seemed a bit restless for some reason. Gabe imagined he just needed to get out for some fresh air.

Then Gabe heard a noise upstairs.

He first thought it might be an intruder. He'd heard there was a problem with break-ins in the area. Well, he'd be damned if someone took his stuff without a fight.

Never mind that Sal had apparently chosen to stay out of harm's way.

Sal followed him to the den where Gabe kept a loaded pistol. After releasing the safety, he crept back into the hall and looked up the stairs, seeing nothing.

But there was clearly someone up there.

"We'll check this out together," he whispered to the dog.

The noise seemed to be coming from his bedroom. Gabe sucked in a deep breath and prepared himself for whoever he might confront, before Sal suddenly got courageous and took the lead in leaping into the room.

Gabe followed, gun out in front of him.

He looked his ex-girlfriend, Linda, right in the eye. "What the hell are you doing here?"

She petted Sal, who jumped on her playfully; then favored Gabe, her face flushed. "Why are you pointing a gun at me?"

He lowered it. "I thought you were a burglar. Or worse. Guess I should've figured out why Sal wasn't in a biting mood."

"Sorry to disappoint you."

Actually he was glad to see her. "You still haven't answered my question."

Linda ran a hand through dark hair. "I just came to pick up the rest of my things."

So much for any hope he'd had that she wanted to get back together.

"You could have called." He did not see her car outside.

"I figured it would be best if I slipped in and out. I didn't think you would be home."

He curled his lip. "Well, you thought wrong."

She grabbed some lingerie out of a drawer and tossed it in a bag on the floor.

"Don't make a scene, okay?"

"Maybe you should have thought about that before breaking and entering."

Her eyes widened. "I still have my key."

"You should leave it on your way out."

"Fine." Linda took a key from her purse and threw it on the dresser.

The last thing Gabe wanted was to shut her out of his life. But clinging to someone who had obviously turned her attention elsewhere was not a smart thing.

He was still holding the gun at his side. "It doesn't have to be this way."

"I think it does." She zipped the bag and met his eyes coldly. "Have a good life."

She walked past him and Sal, hurrying down the stairs.

Gabe followed and thought how easy it would be to shoot her in the back. Maybe too easy.

The thought was quickly dismissed and he called out her name just before Linda reached the door. She faced him.

"Same to you," he told her, and meant it at some level.

Once she had gone, Gabe put the gun away and decided he needed that drink more than ever now.

The bell rang.

He was hopeful that Linda had a change of heart. He opened the door to find Brenda standing there.

"Thought you might want some company."

All things considered, Gabe couldn't disagree. "Come in."

* * *

Brenda had watched the attractive woman leave the condo just as she was arriving. Must have been the ex. A touch of jealousy sliced through Brenda, though she had no right to feel that way. After all, she was married to a man who no longer loved her. Expecting any more from Gabe than he offered was unrealistic.

But she was still human and was not big on sharing a man. From the look on his ex-girlfriend's face, she couldn't get away from him fast enough. Which was just fine with Brenda.

She wasn't sure Gabe agreed.

He wasn't complaining either. She took that as an invitation to continue things between them as they were.

She spread her legs wide and waited till he was deep inside her before Brenda started making love to him. All the while she couldn't help but wish it was her husband lusting after her.

With that not being the case, Brenda was content to be in the company of a man who seemed happy enough to be with her.

CHAPTER TWENTY-FIVE

Ferguson sat across from Adrianne Pompeo in the interrogation room. He wondered if the physician assistant had it in her to gun down Douglas Brennan, along with Elizabeth Racine and Larry Nagasaka. She had no verifiable alibi for the latter murders. What about the former?

"Thanks for coming," he said in a friendly voice.

She sneered. "No one told me I could say no to this."

"I just need to ask you a few questions and someone will drive you home."

"When will you people get off my back? No, I didn't have anything to do with Douglas's death or Larry's or Elizabeth's."

Ferguson hadn't really expected her to cave in, were she guilty.

"Perhaps you could start by telling me where you were the night Douglas Brennan was shot to death?"

Adrianne scratched the side of her nose. "Out taking a walk."

"By yourself?"

"That's usually the case."

"Did anyone see you?"

She shrugged. "Yeah, I passed by some people. But I can't give you any names, if that's what you're asking."

"Too bad. That would've been helpful." Ferguson gazed at her, thinking briefly about Gina; then Brenda. "What time did you get home?"

"I don't know. I wasn't keeping track of time."

"Take a wild guess."

"Maybe eleven."

"And what time did you begin this walk?"

"Nine-thirty."

Ferguson mused. The timeline was right for her to have had the opportunity to snuff out Brennan, short of anyone who could vouch for Adrianne's whereabouts. He had a feeling that wouldn't happen.

"How would you feel about taking a lie detector test?"

Her eyes popped wide. "I won't do it," she declared.

"Do you have something to hide like killing Douglas Brennan, who helped get you fired?"

"I'm not hiding anything. I didn't shoot anyone. Why should I let you trap me into being made a scapegoat?"

Ferguson glanced at the mirror with Ortega and Seymour on the other side.

It was time to let this suspect go. For now.

* * *

Seymour and Leila were paying another visit to Connie Nagasaka. Cell phone records indicated Douglas Brennan had called her number around an hour before his death.

"What do you think those two had to talk about?" Seymour turned away from the road.

"Good question." Leila faced him. "Maybe they were lovers?"

"You think?"

"Why not? Both were single again."

Seymour realized that being single applied to him as well, now that Mele had filed for divorce. Leila had stepped right into her shoes and filled that spot nicely for the moment.

"Or maybe Brennan knew something Connie didn't want revealed and she killed him as a result."

"You mean like murdering her husband and his lover?"

"Exactly."

Leila made a humming sound. "We shall see."

There was a Lexus and Mercedes in the driveway when they arrived.

"Looks like the lady has company," Seymour said, wishing that either vehicle was in his price range.

"Hope they don't mind if we crash the party." Leila unfastened her seatbelt.

Seymour followed her up the walkway. They rang the bell once and Connie opened the door.

She flashed a surprised look. "Detectives! I thought I already answered all your questions?"

"You did," Leila said. "But I'm afraid we have a few more for you."

"Can't they wait? I'm not really able to talk at the moment."

Seymour's brows touched. "No they can't wait. You can either talk to us here or we can take you to the station to continue this."

Connie cocked a brow, but remained speechless.

A voice behind her said authoritatively, "Let them in."

Seymour recognized the voice before he saw the person. Kenneth Racine.

What the hell was he doing here? Seymour imagined the same words rang in Leila's head. Two spouses of dead lovers in cahoots?

Where did this figure into Brennan calling Connie?

"Detective Seymour. Detective Kahana." Kenneth greeted them smoothly.

"Racine." Seymour favored him with a straight look. "Didn't expect to find you of all people visiting Larry Nagasaka's widow."

"To tell you the truth, I didn't expect to be here. Connie asked me to drop by to go over some issues related to Liz and Larry."

"What issues?"

"Apparently Liz invested in some real estate owned by Larry. We're putting our heads together to if it's in our best interests to keep it or sell. I hope there aren't any laws against that?"

"None that involve homicide cops," Seymour said glibly. "Unless, of course, that proves to be the case."

"I can assure you it doesn't." Kenneth set his jaw. "The fact we know each other shouldn't come across as a surprise to either of you, all things considered. That hardly means we conspired to kill the people we loved."

"No one's suggesting anything of the sort," Leila said right on cue. "In fact, we're not here about your late spouses."

Connie wrung her hands. "Then why are you here?"

"Douglas Brennan called you shortly before his death and we'd like to know why."

Connie hesitated, glancing at Kenneth.

Leila caught this. "If you'd rather talk about it in private—"

Connie met her eyes. "Douglas called to see if I wanted to go to a movie."

Leila glanced at Seymour and back. "Are you telling us you were involved with Douglas Brennan?"

"No, but he was hoping that might change. I told him, as I did when Larry was alive, that I wasn't interested in a relationship with him."

Seymour wondered if that was because she was already involved with someone, such as Kenneth Racine.

"Was that all you talked about?" He recalled the cell phone records showed the call lasted fifteen minutes.

"He wanted to know how I was holding up after Larry's death. I told him I was just trying to move on with my life."

"And have you?" Seymour asked with an eye on Kenneth.

"I don't think I like what you're suggesting," he said. "Connie and I are just friends, nothing more. If you can't respect that..."

"We have no problem with your friendship," Leila interceded. "Our only interest is in solving three murders that are clearly connected. I'm sure you both have alibis for the time Douglas Brennan was killed."

Kenneth moved closer to Connie. "I'm sure we do, Detective. I'm also sure that whoever killed my colleagues is still out there hoping to stay under the radar while you go around in circles interrogating innocent people like us."

Seymour held off lecturing him on how a homicide investigation was conducted. He hoped for both their sakes this issue was not revisited under circumstances neither were likely to enjoy.

* * *

At six p.m., Rachel was at her desk clearing up some paperwork and thinking about how nice it would be if Greg were still alive and they could be out doing something fun.

But that wasn't meant to be, no matter how unfair.

"You're still here?"

Rachel looked up at Lt. Ortega. "That makes two of us."

"It's what I get paid to do. What's your excuse?"

"Just doing a little catch up work."

"Seems like you've been doing a little too much of that lately."

She sniffed. "Has to be done some time."

"Just not so often on your own time," he said.

"It's not like I have that much to do outside the job."

He favored her with a sympathetic look. "That's what concerns me. Why don't we step into my office?"

Rachel wasn't really in the mood for any fatherly advice. But she couldn't exactly turn down his request. Could she?

"Sure."

She followed him into the corner office.

"Have a seat," Ortega said.

Rachel sat in one of two chairs behind his desk and watched him remove a bottle of scotch from a drawer.

"I keep this for special occasions. Will you join me for a drink?"

With her taste buds sorely in need of some alcohol, she didn't have to think about it twice. "I'd be happy to."

"Good." He poured the amber liquid into two glasses, handing Rachel one. "So how have you been doing?"

"I'm fine," she pretended.

"I don't doubt that, as far as being able to do your job. But what about inside?"

Rachel sipped the scotch, allowing it to drain down her throat. "If you're asking how I'm coping with Greg's death—it has been two years."

"Yeah and you've never really talked about it."

"What's there to say?"

"How you feel would be a good place to start."

She fought back tears. "I feel like it should've happened to someone else, not Greg."

"It did happen to others," Ortega said gently. "Greg just happened to be one of many unfortunate soldiers who left here before their time."

"So what am I supposed to do?"

"Deal with it. There's no other choice."

Rachel tasted more alcohol. "I know. But it's just so...hard."

"You've got a good support team here. If you need help, all you have to do is ask."

She recalled her therapist spouting the same words. Problem was, Rachel wasn't sure what to ask for, other than the impossible. Bringing Greg back to life.

"Thanks for the talk." She resisted finishing off the drink in Ortega's presence.

"Anytime."

She got up. "Think I'll head home now."

Ortega sipped scotch. "Yeah, it's about that time. I'll walk you out. Maybe you've got a new angle on our elusive doctor killer that Kahana and Seymour somehow overlooked."

Rachel wasn't sure about that. They seemed to be doing a good job taking the lead in this investigation. She sensed it wouldn't be long before they had someone in custody.

For now she was glad to have the job to focus on, instead of Greg and what they were missing.

CHAPTER TWENTY-SIX

Leila watched Seymour for a moment while he slept in her bed. He was snoring slightly. She had a mind to wake him to join her on her morning run, but since that wasn't his thing he would only slow her down.

Leila was still adjusting to having a man in her life again, though she wasn't sure how long it would last. Seymour seemed to like her well enough, and they got along on the job and in the bedroom. But since Seymour was soon to be divorced and older than her, she was realistic enough to know they may not be in sync forever.

But so what?

She was happy with the way things were right now. When Seymour felt otherwise, Leila was sure he would clue her in.

After tying her running shoes, she headed out. If Seymour was still asleep when she got back, maybe she would join him in bed for some morning sex after a shower.

It was a cool morning by Maui standards and Leila enjoyed having the wind at her back as she ran on the beach. Though she tried to be just another early riser getting her exercise, the current case was never far from Leila's mind.

Three people dead and a killer at large. Obviously the unsub was out for blood and had no qualms about spilling as much as necessary to achieve the objective behind the killings. Leila had yet to figure out exactly what that was. But something told her this wasn't over yet.

Someone else likely had an X on his or her back, just waiting to be pummeled with bullets when least expecting it.

Unless they could stop the killer before it was too late.

As Leila began her cool down, she thought about Gabe Devane. She hadn't pegged him as a killer. But those were the types to be most concerned about. With some other suspects either cleared or on hold, it was time to dig a little further into Gabe's background in relation to the Medical Association of Maui to see if there was more there than met the eye.

When Leila entered her house, the aroma of coffee hit her nostrils. She found Seymour in the kitchen, dressed and making breakfast.

So much for morning sex. Maybe this afternoon.

"You're up," she said.

"It was hard to sleep while you were out working up a sweat."

"Remind me to bring you with me next time."

He grinned. "I can think of better ways to work out."

"You would." She had a mind to put that to the test, but resisted the challenge. "I'm going to jump in the shower."

"Don't take too long, or I might have to join you."

She gave him a sexy smile. "Be my guest."

"I already am." Seymour favored her. "I'll take a rain check on that for when we have more time to do it right."

Leila accepted that at face value rather than as a brush off. They did have something a little more important on the agenda this morning than another round of sex.

Like trying to get the bead on a killer.

* * *

Seymour drove toward the Medical Association of Maui offices, trying to keep his mind off his personal life. As much as he wished to be back with Mele, that didn't seem to be in the cards. Leila, on the other hand, was very much in the picture. She kept him feeling young and energetic.

Could they keep it up? Did she want more than he could possibly give her out of this relationship?

He turned his attention to Gabe Devane. So far they had nothing on him that rose to the level of serial murderer. What didn't they know? Did he own a gun?

Seymour eyed Leila. She was wearing glasses and studying a folder containing information on the case.

"Anything interesting in there?" he asked.

"Well, there's a lot of interesting stuff about Gabe. He graduated from Harvard Med School, was a member of Sigma Alpha Epsilon, is a well-regarded surgeon, and was the medical director of the Medical Association of Maui until six months ago. That's when the trail gets thin. All that's known publicly is he resigned."

"So he's a disgruntled ex member of an exclusive organization?" Seymour turned into the parking lot.

"Sure looks that way. We'll have to find out if it gets any worse than that."

He agreed. "Hope they're forthcoming inside, even if it means breaking the code of silence against one of their own."

* * *

"We just need a few minutes of your time," Leila told the most recent medical director turned CEO, Agnes Piimauna, as they walked into her office. Unless it took longer.

"It's quite all right." Agnes shook back thick crimson hair. "Everyone is stunned over Douglas's death, especially coming so soon after Larry and Elizabeth were killed."

"We have reason to believe they were all killed by the same person." Leila doubted this came as a shock to her, given the press had covered the serial killer angle almost nonstop ever since Brennan's death.

Agnes furrowed her brow. "Why on earth would anyone want to do this?"

"That's what we're trying to find out," Seymour said. "At this point, we think it's a good possibility the killer may have come from within your ranks."

"Douglas and I speculated on that before his death. Neither of us could come up with anyone who seemed capable of committing cold-blooded murder. Especially with all our members abiding by the Hippocratic Oath in doing what we can to preserve life, not take it away willfully."

"Even with the best of intentions, I'm sure you realize that some in your profession can fall off the wagon, so to speak, and decide it's not so bad to kill people for their own purposes."

"I suppose, but I think you may be going down the wrong path."

Leila looked at her. "What can you tell us about Gabe Devane?"

Agnes arched a brow. "He's a fine surgeon and former member of our association." She paused. "Surely you don't think Gabe has anything to do with this?"

"He probably doesn't," Leila said, though far from certain on that. "We still need to cover all our bases and he happened to come into view. Can you tell us if he and Douglas Brennan were close?"

Agnes swallowed. "I wouldn't exactly say they were bosom buddies. They had their differences."

"What kind of differences?"

She hesitated. "Well, both were vying for CEO of the association earlier this year before Douglas received the appointment."

"I take it that didn't set too well with Devane?" Seymour met her eyes.

"No one likes to lose, Detective. Even if there were no real losers insofar as both were practicing doctors first and foremost."

"I'd say there was one real loser here, since Brennan is dead and Devane very much alive to maybe take another crack at the top spot. I imagine you might have something to say about that?"

She smiled thinly. "I certainly wouldn't kill Gabe or anyone else for this job. It's not worth it."

"Too bad everyone doesn't think as you do when it comes to getting ahead—sometimes at all costs."

Leila stood between the two. "Maybe you could tell us how Douglas ended up as CEO? Was he considered the more qualified candidate for the job?"

Agnes sighed. "Basically it came down to a power play. Douglas had the right people on his side and won."

"Does that include you?" Seymour asked.

She blinked. "If you must know, I was pulling for Gabe. I felt he had the leadership qualities this organization needed."

"Too bad that view wasn't shared by everyone."

"Isn't that usually the case?" She gazed at him.

"Whose side of the fence were Larry Nagasaka and Elizabeth Racine on?" Leila asked with more than curiosity.

Agnes looked away. "Actually they backed Douglas."

"How did Gabe take it?" Leila asked, glancing at Seymour.

Agnes faced her. "Well, obviously he was upset. Who wouldn't be? That hardly meant he went after Liz and Larry."

"But he did resign as medical director afterward?"

Agnes nodded. "Gabe thought he might be able to form a rival organization for medical practitioners. Unfortunately this town isn't big enough to support two such groups."

Seymour took a step forward. "So Devane not only lost a heated battle to his rivals in the organization, he came up short as well in a bid to compete with it. Sounds to me like he had some scores to settle."

Agnes shook her head. "You're wrong. Gabe's not a killer."

Leila wanted to believe that. If only because most killers could care less about stopping muggers. There was always a first time to go against the grain.

"Did he make a veiled threat against any of them?" she asked the CEO.

Agnes chewed her lip thoughtfully. "Maybe Gabe did accuse them of collusion and threaten to get back at them, but I'm sure he was just caught up in the moment."

Leila wasn't so sure about that and by the look in Seymour's eyes, it was clear he felt the same.

Suddenly Gabe Devane had moved to the head of their suspect list.

CHAPTER TWENTY-SEVEN

Ferguson ran his hands through Gina's hair as she held him steadily in her mouth, slowly building to an orgasm. He marveled at how she had the ability to arouse him more than his wife did. What was it about paid sex that got him up? He couldn't explain it, other than maybe feeling relieved of the pressure to perform or seeing it as a way to escape the boredom of routine sex.

When the surge came, Ferguson closed his eyes tightly and grabbed Gina's head, holding her in place till the climax had come and gone.

He stepped away and pulled up his slacks. "You were great, as always."

She wiped her mouth, rising. "It's my job to be great."

Removing money from his wallet, Ferguson slid it down her cleavage. "There's a little something extra there. Why don't you buy yourself something nice?"

Her eyes crinkled. "Maybe I will."

"I have to go."

"To your wife?"

"To my job."

Gina gave him a direct look. "What's her name?"

Ferguson paused. He preferred to keep his personal life out of this. But what the hell. "Brenda."

"What does Brenda think about your being a cop?"

"Not much most of the time," he admitted.

"You should tell her there are worse things to be."

Ferguson cocked a brow, assuming she was referring to her own way of making a living. "I doubt that would make any difference to her. Being a cop's wife isn't right for everyone."

"So why not quit?" Gina batted her eyes.

"And do what?"

"Whatever you want."

"Wish it were that simple."

She touched his cheek. "Nothing is ever simple. But it doesn't mean it can't be done."

"I'll make you a deal. You stop turning tricks and maybe I'll retire from the force." He didn't think for one minute she would take him up on that.

She ran a hand down his chest. "Is that what you really want? Who would take care of your special needs?"

Ferguson felt turned on. "Good point. So we'll keep things as they are for both of us and make the most of it."

"Does that mean you'd like a little something extra?"

He grinned. "Maybe some other time."

"You know where to find me."

Did he ever, which was part of the problem.

* * *

Gabe went jogging and thought briefly about how he and Linda used to do this together till things went sour. It was just another piece of bad luck that had turned his year upside down. If he could change history, he would. Since that wasn't possible, he had to live with the consequences for better or worse.

The one good thing to come his way lately was Brenda. She was fun and kept him going in bed. But while sleeping with a married woman had its advantages for a busy surgeon with little interest in playing the dating game, it was also a dead end street. Little chance Brenda would ever leave her husband for him. Gabe wasn't sure he'd ever want her to.

Still, it would be nice to just be able to call her anytime. Only she hadn't given him her number, preferring not to take any chances on the husband finding out.

And so Gabe was left to see Brenda only when it was convenient for her. Fortunately she had thus far made it more than worth his while in the absence of Linda in his life.

When he got back to the condo, Gabe was approached by a group of police officers. Leading the way was none other than Detective Kahana.

* * *

Leila could see the startled look on Gabe's face, as if she were the last person he expected to see again under less than sociable circumstances. But now that their case had unexpectedly pointed in his direction, there was no other choice in the matter.

"What can I do for you, Detective?" he asked.

She met his eyes. "We have a warrant to search your place."

"What on earth for?"

"We'll know when we find it."

"Am I a suspect or something?" He wrinkled his nose. "You don't think I had anything to do with Douglas's death?"

Leila took a small breath. "Let's just say you're a person of interest."

"That's absurd."

"In that case, you have nothing to worry about. Right now, we simply want your cooperation. We don't need it."

She handed him the warrant, which hadn't been too hard to get, given the heat generated by the case. No judge wanted to pass on any possibility that a serial killer might be within their grasp.

Gabe barely glanced at the warrant before flashing Leila a hard look. "Of course I'll cooperate. But whatever you're looking for, you're not going to find it here."

"I hope that's the case."

Seymour stepped forward. "I understand you have a dog?"

"Yeah, Sal," Gabe said.

"If he's in there, you'd better make sure Sal is on his best behavior. Otherwise there could be trouble."

"I'll take care of my dog. Just try and leave things the way you found them."

Gabe unlocked the door and was immediately met by his dog. He quickly restrained Sal while the police came in and fanned out.

* * *

"Why didn't you tell me there was bad blood between you and Douglas Brennan?" Leila favored Gabe with narrowed eyes.

Gabe cocked a brow. "I don't know what you're talking about."

"I think you do."

His gaze lowered. "We weren't enemies—not really."

"That's not what we heard," Seymour said, getting his attention. "It pissed you off when Brennan, along with the backing of influential players Larry Nagasaka and Elizabeth Racine, ended up as CEO instead of you."

Gabe blinked. "Who have you been talking to?"

"What difference does it make? It's all in the public record, other than hearing your side of the story."

"So maybe I'm a sore loser. That didn't mean I respected Douglas any less as a professional. And it certainly doesn't make me a killer."

"Maybe this does..." Seymour heard the voice.

An officer approached them. Wearing latex gloves, he held up a gun and box of shells. "We found these tucked away inside a drawer in the den. Looks like we've got ourselves a .25 caliber gun and some of the shells are missing from the box."

Seymour regarded Gabe. "That your gun?"

"Yeah, so what? It's registered."

"Have you used it recently?"

"Just for target practice."

Seymour widened his eyes skeptically. "Wonder just who the targets were?"

He turned to Leila, giving her the honor of bringing her Good Samaritan into custody for much more than witnessing a mugging.

Leila's jaw set. "Gabe Devane, I'm placing you under arrest for suspicion of murder in the deaths of Douglas Brennan, Elizabeth Racine, and Larry Nagasaka."

She stepped behind the suspect and handcuffed him before reading him his rights.

CHAPTER TWENTY-EIGHT

Brenda was standing in front of her TV channel surfing when she came upon the breaking news.

"Dr. Gabe Devane, a thirty-eight-year-old ER surgeon at Maui General, has been arrested in connection with the deaths of fellow Doctors Douglas Brennan, Elizabeth Racine, and Larry Nagasaka. All three victims were shot to death in two separate instances. Authorities believe one person was responsible for all three murders. They're not saying right now if that person was Devane, who recently lost his bid to become the CEO of the Medical Association of Maui to Brennan."

Brenda felt her legs grow wobbly and she sat down. Gabe a murderer? Or an accomplice to murder? There had to be a mistake. Though she hadn't known him very long, and really only knew his sexual tastes, he didn't strike her as someone who could do such a thing. Especially when he made a living saving lives.

But what did she really know about him?

Maybe he had a dark side she hadn't seen. Much like the part of her husband that Brenda didn't know. She hesitated to think Gabe could have been planning to murder her at some point.

When she felt something on her shoulder, Brenda nearly jumped out of her skin. She whipped her head around and saw Trent staring at her.

"You scared me!"

"Sorry about that."

"How long have you been standing there?" She tried to steady her nerves.

"Long enough to catch that report on the doctor."

Brenda swallowed. "Do they really think he did it?"

"It's too soon to say for sure. But there's compelling evidence to suggest he may be our guy."

"But he's a surgeon, for heaven's sake," she found herself defending the man who was her lover.

"So was Jack the Ripper, some believe. Doesn't mean Devane isn't guilty of the murders."

Brenda clung to the hope this wasn't the case. Being with him had filled the void in her marriage. She hated to think it was all over.

She raised her eyes. "What are you doing home?"

"Just stopped by for a few minutes to see what you were up to and if you needed anything."

"What if I said I needed you?"

He grinned. "I was hoping you'd say that."

Brenda had waited for so long to hear those words that they now sounded hollow, especially when her thoughts were focused on Gabe Devane.

* * *

"How does someone go from helping old ladies in distress to being a serial murder suspect?" Ortega asked, gazing through the one-way window.

Leila shrugged. "Maybe he can answer that."

"What about the gun and shells?"

"They're being tested now."

"Why don't we see what he has to say?"

Leila looked at her boss, bypassing Seymour. "I think I'd like to talk to him alone."

"Sure you can handle it?" Seymour asked.

She took this as lighthearted. "I'm sure. We established somewhat of a rapport when doing the sketch of the mugger. Gabe may open up more with just me."

"Go for it." Ortega touched the window. "When his lawyer gets here, we'll send her in."

Leila wasn't sure what she could expect from the suspect, but if she could coerce a confession out of him, all the better. Assuming he was guilty of taking out three of his former colleagues.

She went into the interrogation room, armed with a tape recorder.

"Can I get you something to drink?" she asked in a pleasant enough tone.

"Do you have any vodka out there?" Gabe took a breath. "I think I could use something along those lines right about now."

Leila couldn't help but smile. "Sorry, afraid I can't help you there. Water, soft drinks, and coffee are all we have."

"Then I'll pass."

"If you change your mind, let me know." She sat the recorder on the table. "I understand you've already called your attorney. Do you mind if we talk a bit till she comes?"

Gabe scowled. "Why not? I already told you that you're way off base here. I had nothing to do with killing Douglas, Liz, or Larry. Asking me again isn't going to change that."

Leila could see he would be a tough nut to crack. And she didn't have much time to do it.

"I'd like to record this, if it's okay with you?"

He proffered an arm. "Whatever."

She turned the tape on. "Just for the record, did you shoot to death Douglas Brennan?"

"No!"

"Did you kill Elizabeth Racine?"

"No, I didn't!"

"How about Larry Nagasaka? Did you shoot him?"

"The same answer—no!"

Leila glanced at the mirror. "Tell me about the gun we confiscated from your condo. How long have you owned it?"

Gabe ran a hand across his chin. "About three months."

"And you got it from where?"

"A gun shop in Wailuku."

That would be easy enough to verify. "Why did you get a gun?"

Gabe pursed his lips. "To protect myself."

Leila looked at him. "Did you have anyone to fear?"

"Not anyone in specific. But as an ER surgeon, I see and hear things that have made me a little jittery insofar as becoming a crime victim. I figured having a gun at home would at least even the playing field should someone violate my space."

Leila wondered why so many people felt owning a gun would make them safer when, in fact, it was often the opposite.

"When was the last time you used the gun?"

"A few days ago at a firing range in Paia."

"How about before that?"

"The same place, but I can't tell you the exact day."

Leila peered at him. "Did you use it to gun down your enemies, Gabe?"

"Hell no!" His voice cracked. "You really think I'm some cold blooded murderer who took time out of his day to report a mugging?"

Leila had to admit that one stumped her. Maybe that had been his plan all along, in case they reached this point.

"I'm reserving judgment on that till we complete our investigation."

He sat back, face flushed. "I've made a few mistakes in my life, probably more than a few, but committing murder as payback wasn't one of them."

"We'll see about that."

Before Leila could delve into his whereabouts for the days and times in question, the door burst open and in came a dark haired, well-dressed Hawaiian woman.

"Don't say another word!" She eyed Gabe; then shot Leila a wicked look. "I'm Kim Yi, Mr. Devane's attorney. If he's said anything incriminating to you without benefit of counsel, you can be certain that—"

"He didn't confess," Leila cut in. "Your client has been cooperating, but was never asked to say anything he didn't want to."

Kim glanced at the tape. "I'd like to hear that for myself."

Leila turned it off. "We may be able to arrange that later."

"Then later is when you can talk to my client again. So unless you're prepared to charge him with something, we're ready to walk out of here."

Leila's nostrils flared, but she refused to spar with the woman.

They were interrupted when Seymour poked his head in the door.

"Can I have a moment?"

Leila favored Gabe and his attorney. "I'll be right back."

* * *

"What's up?" Leila asked Seymour as Ortega, Rachel, and Gil Delfino converged on them.

Seymour frowned. "Devane did purchase the gun legally and was licensed to carry it."

This didn't surprise her, given Gabe's ease in this regard. "He indicated as much. Anything else?"

Rachel stepped forward. "I checked with the range in Paia, and they do have a record of him being there three days ago and a couple of weeks before that."

"So that gives Devane an out as to why the gun had recently been fired," Leila said. But it still didn't necessarily exonerate him. She faced Delfino, who had tested the gun and bullets against those used to kill Brennan, Nagasaka, and Racine. "What did you come up with?"

"Probably not what you want to hear." He scratched his chin. "The gun belonging to the suspect has a barrel with a left hand twist with five lands and grooves. By comparison, the bullets from the murder weapon came from a barrel with a right hand twist and six lands and grooves. The ejection and firing pin marks on shell casings were also different compared to those recovered from the crime scenes. Bottom line is, we're talking about two different weapons."

"So Gabe's innocent." Leila felt a sense of relief, though no regrets in playing this by the book.

"Looks that way, unless he used a different gun."

They had found no other firearms in his condo or vehicle. As far as Leila was concerned, that was enough to turn the spotlight elsewhere, as she believed the real shooter still had possession of the murder weapon.

"I think we have to let him go," Seymour told her.

Ortega put a hand on her shoulder. "As much as we all wanted it to be over, something tells me you're glad it wasn't your Good Samaritan."

Leila offered a hint of a smile. "Guess I'd better get back in there with the news before Gabe's attorney has a conniption."

The fact that they were back to the drawing board made Leila more determined than ever to solve this case and put the true culprit behind bars.

CHAPTER TWENTY-NINE

At seven that evening, Leila sat in the club on Ka'anapali Beach with Jan drinking Mai Tais.

"So this Gabe wasn't the guilty party after all?" Jan lifted her glass.

"Technically he's still a suspect, given there was no love lost between him and the victims and with Gabe's whereabouts during the crimes still unconfirmed. But I'd have to say he's not at the top of our list right now."

"Who is?" Jan gazed across the table. "Or can't you say?"

Leila was used to her friend prying into police business. She was almost accustomed to dodging the questions as much as possible.

"We're keeping an open mind right now."

"It's scary to think someone is out there with a loaded gun just waiting to attack somebody else."

"I know. Hopefully we can stop things from getting to that point."

Jan touched her hand. "Just don't let it overwhelm you."

"It won't." Leila had no intention of becoming so stressed out that it affected her ability to do the job. Killers came with the territory, like it or not. The satisfaction came in making the system work, even if it didn't happen overnight. She tasted her drink and changed the subject. "I'm still waiting to meet your mystery man."

Jan smiled. "I'll invite you both over to dinner next week. How does that sound?"

"I can hardly wait." Leila nibbled a pretzel. "So what's he do for a living anyway?" She did say he was loaded. Was he a doctor?

"Erik's a high end real estate agent."

"Sounds impressive. Has he been on the island long?"

"About four months now."

Leila was happy to know he wasn't in the medical profession. Not to say their killer was a doctor.

"Are you serious about him?"

Jan laughed. "Probably as serious as you are about Blake."

Leila wasn't sure how serious things were between them. Maybe she was a little more into what they had than Seymour. Unless she was misreading him. Either way, it seemed to be working right now to the degree that both kept coming back to each other.

"So in other words, you're not looking to get hitched anytime soon?"

"Not if I can help it." Jan rolled her eyes. "What's with the twenty questions anyway?"

"Only ten questions," Leila quipped. "Just being nosey. Sound familiar?"

Jan chuckled. "Maybe a little."

"Thought so."

"Is this a private party? Or can anyone join in?"

Leila looked up and saw the reporter, Renee Bradley, standing there.

* * *

"Are you stalking me now?"

Renee Bradley might have thought Detective Kahana was only joking, had it not been for the serious look on her face. Well join the club. She was serious, too. Especially when there was a killer in their midst and the police were less than forthcoming in keeping the public up to speed.

"I wouldn't exactly call it stalking," she responded, essentially ignoring the other woman at the table. "As a reporter, I go where the story is."

"There's no story here." Leila wrinkled her nose.

Renee didn't expect her to simply roll over and make this easy. Any good reporter understood that getting information required skill and savvy. Along with plenty of persistence.

"I'd call arresting and releasing a triple murder suspect all in the same day a story, Detective. Why don't you give me just a few minutes of your time and I promise I'll get out of your hair."

Leila sighed and favored her friend. "Do you mind?"

"No, not at all. I'm seeing Erik tonight, so I'd better get going anyway." Jan got to her feet. "I'll call you about the dinner next week."

"I'm looking forward to it. Bye, Jan."

Renee waited for Jan to depart before taking her chair. She suddenly felt nervous one on one with the detective, but quickly regained her poise.

"Thanks for talking to me."

"Seems like you left me with little choice."

Renee saw this as a good sign. "Can I buy you another drink?"

Leila declined. "I hope you understand that all official statements go through our public relations officer."

"So this is unofficial?"

"Let's just say you'll get nothing out of me that could compromise the investigation or get me into trouble."

"Understood." Renee took out her recorder.

Leila lifted a hand. "Off the record, remember?"

Renee nodded reluctantly, putting the recorder back into her handbag and resisting the temptation to turn it on.

"What can you tell me about Gabe Devane that we don't already know?"

"He was a person of interest. Now we're looking elsewhere."

"So Dr. Devane is no longer considered a suspect?"

"All I can tell you is we're no longer actively investigating him. If any reason comes up to change that, we will."

Renee took that to mean Gabe Devane was not their man. "What about some of the other suspects you've interviewed?"

"What about them?"

"Is there anyone who you're more focused on?"

Leila dribbled her fingers on the table. "We're focused equally on all possible suspects in this case. When we have enough solid evidence to make an arrest, the press will know about it."

"Do you think the killer will strike again?"

Leila paused. "We can't rule anything out, but we're doing our best to prevent that from happening. You can be sure we're exhausting all efforts to find the killer and are confident it's just a matter of time until we make an arrest."

Renee made a mental note of that last statement. She had a feeling that was precisely what the detective wanted her to convey to the public.

* * *

Seymour debated whether or not it was a good idea to talk to Mele about their pending divorce without his attorney. It was still hard for him to believe they had even reached this stage. But that didn't change the facts as they were. Mele had chosen to live her life apart from him. He, in turn, had been forced to do the same.

After sucking in a deep breath, Seymour rang the doorbell. A moment later the door swung open and Akela greeted him with enthusiasm.

"Makuakane!"

"How's my little girl?" He knelt and took her into his arms.

"Great."

"Then that makes two of us."

Seymour looked up at Mele. She was clearly less than pleased to see him.

He got to his feet. "Hi."

Mele pursed her lips. "Akela, your father and I need to talk, alone."

Akela sulked.

"It's all right," Seymour told her, hating that she had to be caught in the middle of this. "I'll see you a little later, I promise."

He watched her disappear up the stairs; then turned to Mele to face the music.

"You really have to stop doing this," she said.

"Doing what?" As if he didn't know.

"It's not fair to her—or me."

His nostrils grew. "And you call what you're doing fair?"

"Maybe you should have thought of that when you decided to be unfaithful."

"You're right, but I can't undo what's already done."

She batted her lashes. "And neither can I."

Seymour refused to let this get out of hand. "I just came by to say I don't want this to turn into a battle of lawyers, taking away money that at the very least could go to our daughter's college fund."

He could tell this was an area where they shared the same sentiments.

"I'm listening."

"I won't contest the divorce. And you can have the house and whatever you want inside it. All I want is to be able to spend as much time as my schedule will allow with Akela. It doesn't have to be official or anything, just your willingness to work with me."

Mele gave a slow nod and Seymour felt a breakthrough in the iceberg that had existed between them. It gave him a glimmer of hope that maybe there were other inroads to follow.

* * *

Gabe had just fed Sal while wondering about his run of misfortune, when the bell rang. Had the police decided he was guilty after all and come back to re-arrest him? Or maybe it was another reporter looking for a story?

He opened the door and saw Brenda. She was smiling.

"I didn't expect to see you again," he said, assuming that the entire scenario as played out by the media had scared her off.

"Then you don't know me very well."

Gabe grinned. "I guess not."

"I'd like that to change."

Since no one else was standing in line to be with him, he could hardly turn down the offer and invited her in.

Sal came to check out the visitor.

"Hey, boy." She petted him generously and he ate it up, more at home with her than most.

"Would you like a drink?"

Brenda looked up. "Yes. I'll have what you're having."

He came back with two cocktails, passing one to her. "Do you want to ask me anything about what happened?"

Her lashes fluttered. "No. I never believed you had it in you to kill people."

"Do you always trust your instincts?"

"Not always."

Gabe wondered why she had chosen to this time. Would he have if the situation had been reversed?

"I'm glad you came."

She licked her lips. "So am I."

They ended up in bed for the next hour or so and Gabe was able to push aside the circumstances that led up to him becoming a murder suspect. He had no idea how this might affect his career, but would not shy away from doing what he did best, even though a cloud continued to hover over him regarding the murder of Douglas Brennan and two other former colleagues.

CHAPTER THIRTY

On Thursday morning, Leila and Rachel went to Napili to interview Diane Treadwell. She was amongst the mourners at Douglas Brennan's funeral and a single mother whose son died shortly after childbirth nine months ago due to alleged negligence on the part of internist, Elizabeth Racine, and Brennan as her medical advisor. Diane sued both parties and the Medical Association of Maui for the incident, with an undisclosed settlement reached out of court last month.

Leila couldn't even begin to imagine what the woman must have gone through after this tragedy. Had her grief turned homicidal?

"Wonder what I'd do if some medical mishap turned what should have been one of the happiest times of my life into a nightmare?" Rachel echoed her thoughts.

Leila cringed. "Let's hope neither of us ever has to find out."

They walked up to the second story unit of the beachfront Pacific Heights apartment complex.

Leila rang the bell and recalled her impromptu chat with the reporter last night. One could only hope the press was more of a help than hindrance in solving this case at the end of the day.

The door was opened by a tall, thirty-something woman with curly brunette hair.

"Diane Treadwell?" Leila met her eyes.

"Yes, that's me."

"Detectives Kahana and Lancaster with the Maui Police Department. We're investigating the recent deaths of Douglas Brennan and Elizabeth Racine."

"Oh." Diane twisted her mouth.

Rachel stepped forward. "Do you mind if we ask you a few questions?"

She hesitated. "I guess not. Come in."

Leila saw a TV on and a living area that was in general disarray, as though the resident were preparing to move.

"Thanks for your time," she said.

Diane blinked. "I don't know how I can help you."

Leila gave her a straight look. "We understand you recently sued Dr. Brennan and Dr. Racine for your child's death."

She reacted. "Yes, and it was settled."

"We learned about that. Unfortunately no amount of money in the world could bring back what you lost."

"You're right, it can't."

"Which is why we find it strange you attended Douglas Brennan's funeral," Rachel told her.

Diane looked away and back with hard eyes. "Maybe I just wanted to stomp on the grave of the man who was half responsible for killing my son."

"Or maybe you went further than that."

"Are you suggesting I killed him?"

"Did you?" Rachel's mouth tightened. "And while we're at it, did you also kill Elizabeth Racine as payback for her role in your son's death?"

"No, I didn't kill either one of them!" Diane snapped. "But don't think I never thought about it. I trusted Dr. Racine to do the right thing. And she put her trust in Dr. Brennan to give her the correct advice. The end result is that my baby died needlessly from hypoxic ischemic brain injury.

For a time, I was consumed with giving them a dose of their own medicine. Can you really blame me?"

"Killing the two of them wouldn't bring your son back," Leila said. "It would also be murder and you'd spend the rest of your life grieving in prison."

"I know." Diane's eyes watered. "I guess I went to Dr. Brennan's funeral as my way of saying I forgave him. I realized I was filled with so much hatred and bitterness it was bringing me down and I couldn't heal. This was a chance for me to try to put closure to a terrible time in my life." She wiped away tears and looked out the window. "I'm still trying to come to terms with my anger, but I'm getting better every day."

Leila glanced at Rachel, sensing she was thinking about her own tragedy of losing someone dear to her unexpectedly.

"Can someone vouch for your whereabouts when both victims were killed?" Leila gave her the dates and approximate times of the murders.

"I've recently become engaged to a wonderful pediatrician. His name's August Oroku. We've pretty much been inseparable lately, including the time you say Dr. Brennan and Dr. Racine lost their lives."

Leila made a mental note to check it out, but she had a feeling Diane Treadwell was not their killer.

* * *

At three p.m., Officer Natalie Yuen was doing her normal patrol while counting down the hours till her shift ended. The driver ahead increased his speed when she approached, but was still within the speed limit. He was driving a late model Malibu. There was a dent on the back bumper.

While this normally wouldn't have aroused her curiosity in and of itself, instincts told Natalie something wasn't right. Perhaps it was the way the driver kept checking his rearview mirror, as if having something to hide.

Or that she was on the lookout for more than one lowlife wanted by the police.

She ran a check on the license plate number and discovered it was a stolen vehicle.

Natalie turned on her blue lights. The driver immediately picked up speed, putting distance between them. He clearly had no desire to pull over. She turned on her siren and radioed it in before engaging in a full pursuit.

* * *

Rachel sat at the bar working on her third or fourth martini. She'd lost count. Rachel was drunk or getting there, but didn't give a damn. She felt like drowning her sorrows in alcohol. It was one way of coping with being alone and unhappy that actually worked for her, if only a temporary thing.

Tomorrow she could go back to being a widow cop. For now, she'd just like to forget about chasing bad guys and remember how much had been lost in her life when Greg died.

Rachel put the glass to her lips and squeezed her eyes shut while the alcohol burned its way down her throat.

"I think you like getting wasted almost as much as I do," someone said.

Rachel opened her eyes and saw a young man dressed in Western attire standing over her. He was gazing at her lasciviously.

"Beat it," she told him in a voice unmistakable in its disinterest.

"Not unless you let me buy you another one of those."

"I'd prefer to drink alone."

He grinned. "We could drink alone together at my place. What d'ya say?"

Her eyes narrowed. "I say leave me alone."

He laughed. "Now don't be like that. You and I can have some real fun. I promise I'll keep my pants on till you're ready."

He put his hand on her knee and Rachel reacted as she had been taught at the Academy. Using quick reflexes, she grabbed the man's hand and had it behind his back and him up against the bar in no time flat.

"I'm a cop, asshole, and could arrest you right now for harassment and stupidity." Rachel's heartbeat intensified. "Now be a good little cowboy and go find someone else to work you charms on. Do we understand each other?" She twisted his arm more and heard him whimper. "Yeah, I thought so."

She shoved him away and he mumbled something under his breath and stumbled off.

Finishing the rest of her drink, Rachel decided to quit while she was ahead. But she was in no condition to drive. The last thing she needed was to be pulled over by another cop for DUI.

* * *

Detective Fujimoto entered the interrogation room where the suspect sat. At twenty-one, Corey Quintana was already a career criminal, with motor vehicle theft the latest crime added to his rap sheet. Unfortunately for him, his troubles were only beginning.

But first, Fujimoto hoped to squeeze as much information out of him as he could.

"You're in a boat load of trouble, Corey." He sat down in front of him.

Corey sneered. "I'm supposed to be scared?"

"No, definitely not. You're too damned stupid for that, which is your problem. I can tell you, though, where you're headed, you ought to be scared. They're gonna be fighting over each other to see who has you for lunch. Auto theft is a serious offense. So is resisting arrest and possession of stolen property. Oh, and did I forget to mention we also found drugs in the vehicle you stole? In the absence of anyone else in the car, this is all on you, Corey. When you add it all up, you're looking at some serious time. In fact, you'll be lucky if you ever see daylight again."

This had clearly gotten his attention.

"What do you want?"

Fujimoto smiled. "That's more like it. We know you participated in some home burglaries, since we have your mug on a security camera. I want the names of everyone else involved and where they plan to strike next."

Corey rubbed his nose. "So what's in it for me?"

"Maybe we can drop some of the charges against you as a cooperating witness."

"I ain't testifying against anybody."

"You won't have to. Once we get them, we'll have more than enough to put them away for a long time. Whereas you'll get the chance to still be able to have a life before you're too old to know what to do with it." Fujimoto let him sit on that for a moment. "So do we have a deal?"

Corey shifted his eyes. "Yeah, man. But I want somethin' in writing."

"No problem." Fujimoto slid a notepad at him. "Give me what I want and you'll get your deal in writing. You have my word."

He watched as the suspect in his home burglary case was about to rat out his partners in crime, helping Fujimoto to break this case wide open. And Quintana was going down with the ship, whether he realized it or not.

* * *

Leila was slightly surprised to receive a call from Rachel, asking if she could pick her up at the bar. It was obvious to Leila her colleague had too much to drink, a problem that had apparently been escalating since the death of her husband.

Leila credited Rachel for being smart enough not to get behind the wheel of her car while inebriated. Both had seen the devastating results of drinking and driving firsthand.

Walking into the Puunene tavern, Leila spotted Rachel at the bar. A full glass of alcohol sat in front of her, but she made no effort to drink.

"Hey," Leila said.

Rachel colored. "Thanks for coming. I didn't have anyone else to call."

"Don't worry about it." Leila smiled sympathetically. "Let's get you home."

"What about my car?"

"I'll get someone to bring it." She volunteered Seymour for the job, confident he wouldn't ask questions for which he didn't necessarily want the answers.

Rachel stood on gimpy legs and Leila helped her out to the car.

During the drive, Leila decided to pry. "So what's going on with you?"

Rachel ran a hand over her mouth. "I guess I let the talk we had with Diane Treadwell get to me a bit. Losing someone you love can be a real downer, especially when it didn't have to happen."

"I know." Leila thought about losing her father and grandfather, the two most important men in her life to date. But neither were the same as losing a husband or child. "Have you seen anyone?"

"Yeah, but it doesn't always help."

"Maybe you should give someone else a try."

"Yeah, maybe I will."

Leila left it at that, but hoped Rachel was serious. She dreaded the thought of this impacting her career. They were already in the minority in the ranks and Leila didn't want to see those numbers dwindle.

Rachel lived in nearby Waikapu. Inside the Tuscan style home, Leila put Rachel straight to bed and she fell asleep quickly. She would likely have a hangover in the morning, but Leila had a feeling she'd gotten used to it.

CHAPTER THIRTY-ONE

The moment Leila stepped onto the lanai, she knew something was wrong. First there were shards of glass from a broken window. While the door was closed, there was evidence it had been damaged, as though forced open.

Her house had been broken into. Perhaps the burglars were still inside?

She heard a banging sound from within, indicating that was a likely possibility.

Backing away slowly till behind some flowering bushes, Leila got out her cell phone and reported what she believed was a burglary in progress.

"So it was your house they targeted," Fujimoto said after muttering an expletive.

Leila sensed he was not speaking in general terms. "Who are you talking about?"

"We've arrested Corey Quintana, part of a trio of home burglary punks. The other two decided to go for it without him. We only knew the area they were planning to hit and are just minutes away."

Leila heard more noise, causing her to flinch. "Well, you're not here right now and I'm afraid my house is being trashed. I'm not going to stand around and just let it happen."

"Now's not the time to go it alone, Kahana," he voiced succinctly. "Get out of there and let us do our job."

"Doesn't seem like you've done it very well to this point!"

"We know who they are and where they are now. We'll get 'em."

"Well, I suggest you hurry it up." Leila disconnected and pushed speed dial for Seymour's number. Earlier she had gone with him to drive Rachel's car home before they said their goodbyes for the night.

Or so she'd thought.

"Missed me too, huh?"

"Not in that way," she told him honestly. "I've got a little problem I thought you might like to hear about—"

* * *

Leila removed the department-issued Glock 23 pistol from her side strap. She was prepared to use it if necessary, to at the very least keep the burglars from getting away.

Fortunately, the Property Crimes and Robbery Unit had arrived to take the lead.

"They still in there?" Fujimoto asked.

Leila nodded. "Someone is."

"What type of treasures do you have?"

"Everything I own."

"Good answer. We'll try to save it all for you."

Leila sneered. "Yes, we will. I wouldn't dream of leaving this task entirely up to you."

Fujimoto grinned. "Didn't expect you would."

They stormed the house and arrested the suspects, neither of whom Leila believed were older than twenty-one, without incident. But not before they'd left the place looking like a war zone.

Leila could not believe her house had been hit by thieves. And for what? Things that would only be considered valuable to her. She could just imagine what her mother would say. Probably blame her, while hoping this would be the trigger to get her to move back home.

* * *

"Are you going to be all right?" Seymour gazed down at her as CSI collected evidence.

"Not sure," she admitted, hating that her space had been violated. It was bad enough that they were in the middle of a difficult homicide investigation. Now this. What could go wrong next?

"Don't sweat it. Could've been much worse. The important thing is they're in custody now and no one, especially you, got hurt."

He put his arm around her shoulder and Leila instantly felt better. She spied Fujimoto looking their way without comment.

"You're right," she told Seymour. "Unfortunately I still have to clean up this mess."

"But not alone."

She wasn't too proud to have his help. "Thanks."

Fujimoto walked up to them. "Looks like they cut the wires to your phone line, disabling the security system. You should think about investing in a wireless system."

Leila bit her lip. "Yeah, I'll do that."

He glanced at Seymour and returned his gaze to Leila. "We should be out of your hair in no time."

Leila wondered if Fujimoto was actually jealous when she'd never given him any reason to believe she was interested in him.

"Do what you need to. I don't want any wiggle room for them to get off lightly."

"You and me both."

After Fujimoto left, Seymour asked, "What's his problem?"

Leila batted her eyes innocently. "Don't know, don't care."

"Then why should I?"

"I don't really feel like cleaning this right now." She looked at him. "Do you mind if I stay at your place tonight?"

She didn't mean to put Seymour on the spot. Or maybe she did.

"Not at all," he said. "I'd love the company. And you can stay as long as you like."

Leila felt relieved. "Only till my place becomes livable again."

"Which could be a matter of interpretation."

Leila smiled. It was probably the closest he had come to indicating they were in a real relationship where each could actually depend on the other for something beyond a sexual connection.

Not that she had anything against sex with him. Far from it. But right now, she was content to have his companionship.

CHAPTER THIRTY-TWO

Adrianne Pompeo readied herself for a new job as a physician assistant at the South Shore ER. The pay was less than her last job, but the responsibilities were just as great and they seemed to respect her abilities more.

Adrianne mused about the deaths of Elizabeth Racine and Larry Nagasaka, followed by Douglas Brennan's demise. There would be no tears shed by her. As far as she was concerned, they all got what they deserved. That's what happened to people who thought they were better than everyone else. Or looked down on people like her and took them for granted, dismissing them without even giving it a second thought.

She hated being hauled down to the police station like a common criminal with those detectives thinking they had everything figured out. The truth was they didn't know the half of it. If so, their case would already have been solved and everyone could pat themselves on the back for a job well done.

Instead they were searching for something right in front of their faces and couldn't see it.

Adrianne flashed a devious smile while applying cherry lip gloss to her mouth. Her thoughts shifted to the new man in her life. His sexual desires were a bit kinky, even by her standards. But she could live with that, given his other qualities.

Ironically he was a doctor, but one she seemed in sync with for the ways that counted most.

A knock on the door gave Adrianne a start. She hadn't been expecting any visitors at this time.

It occurred to her that the detectives could be back, ready to harass her again in hoping to extract a confession.

When hell froze over.

Adrianne opened the door. She arched a brow. "Hi. I thought you didn't want to meet until after my shift." She was pushed backwards into the apartment. "Hey, what was that about?"

Adrianne recoiled when she saw the gun whip out and point at her.

"Whoa! Is this a joke or something?" Her voice trembled. "If so, it's not very funny."

Adrianne realized in that moment she had misplayed her hand and it would cost her dearly. Before any other thoughts could flood her head, she heard the pop. Then another in rapid succession.

She felt the piercing pain in her chest and crumbled to the floor. It was obvious to Adrianne she was about to be murdered.

And there wasn't a thing she could do to prevent it.

* * *

The doer watched as Adrianne Pompeo fell flat onto her face. Though seriously wounded with a pool of blood spilling from her back, she was still breathing and that could not be allowed.

Moving right over her, the doer took aim at the back of Adrianne's head and pulled the trigger again. Part of her head separated from the rest and the tremulous reflex movements of her body came to a halt.

Satisfied Adrianne had breathed her last breath, the doer grinned and then prepared to make a quick exit. It was important to stay ahead of the authorities at all costs. Failure was not an option.

With the mission completed, the doer sidestepped the corpse. The lights were turned off and door closed, before the intended escape route went as planned with no resistance.

* * *

Leila arched her back and relished the hot feel of Seymour's calloused hands caressing her nipples and breasts as she lowered herself onto his covered erection. She involuntarily contracted when he was deep inside her and watched the satisfaction light her lover's face. She began to move up and down him slowly, body trembling ever so slightly while her knees pressed against Seymour's hard nakedness. He began to stroke her pubis, driving Leila mad with delight.

"Kiss me," Seymour demanded, urging her down.

"I'll kiss you."

Leila fell onto his face with her mouth, kissing his eyelids, nose, and then finally his waiting lips. He seemed to take over from there, sucking her upper lip, then lower, before putting his tongue in her mouth.

She'd gotten used to his taste, turning her on even more as their open mouths pressed tightly.

Seymour easily flipped them over into the missionary position and propelled himself into Leila time and again as she met him halfway, running her fingernails across his back, fighting to hold off her orgasm for as long as possible.

When it came, her legs were splayed wide and body elevated from the bed, as Leila clung to Seymour's erection and absorbed his own powerful climax.

He fell on top of her and their sweaty bodies quivered together as the sounds of sex quieted.

"I think we managed to take my mind off the burglary," Leila murmured.

Seymour took a breath. "Maybe we ought to thank the burglars."

"I wouldn't go quite that far."

"Neither would I. Still, I'm glad you're here."

"Me, too."

Leila had never spent the night at his house. She wondered if it was a sign of things to come. Was Seymour really prepared to share his personal space with someone other than his wife?

Leila also considered the implications of breaking new ground for her in this relationship. She didn't want to get hurt, even if she was realistic about their future.

The phone rang.

Seymour cursed. "Better get that." He rolled off her and grabbed his cell phone from the nightstand.

Leila propped on an elbow while listening to him. It was obvious the news was not good for someone.

"What is it?" she asked when he hung up.

"Adrianne Pompeo was found shot to death tonight."

CHAPTER THIRTY-THREE

Seymour felt it was a definite downer to be called back to duty after making love. But this was precisely the situation he and Leila found themselves in with the news that Adrianne Pompeo had been found murdered. The fact that the M.O. had all the markings of the serial killer they were tracking made things that much worse.

Careful not to contaminate the crime scene, Seymour moved to other side of the corpse. She was lying flat on her stomach, fully clothed. He guessed she had been shot three times—once in the back of the head, execution-style. Like the others, the unsub obviously wanted to be sure Adrianne never saw another day.

"She probably knew her attacker," he told Leila. "With no indication of forced entry, we have to assume Pompeo let the killer in. Maybe she was expecting whoever it was."

"Either that or she was expecting someone else and got the surprise of her life."

"More like the surprise of her death." Seymour gazed again at the decedent. "Someone chose to silence her permanently."

Leila frowned. "But she wasn't a doctor. Why break the pattern now?"

"Maybe she knew something the killer didn't want to get out."

"Like the killer's identity?"

"That would be my first guess." He turned to the CSI at work. "I want this place combed from ceiling to floor for any clues the killer may have left behind."

"And anything else about the victim that can tell us what she couldn't that may have led to her death," added Leila.

They bypassed the police photographer documenting the death scene and made their way to the bedroom.

Seymour noted the bed was made, giving no indication it had been the scene of sexual activity prior to the murder.

He watched Leila pick up something with her gloves. "Looks like an appointment book," she said.

"Anything in it for today?"

"Says she had plans to meet a Victor after work—at eight a.m. for breakfast."

"So she must have been on her way out the door rather than coming home when the attack occurred," Seymour said. "Wonder if this Victor decided to make their date earlier?"

"Maybe we should ask him."

Seymour spotted the blinking message light on the phone. After donning latex gloves, he pushed the play button.

"Hi, it's Victor. Can't wait to see you again. Maybe we can pick up where we left off. See you soon."

It made Seymour think about where he and Leila had left off before they were interrupted. He glanced at her. "Sounds like he was really into Adrianne."

"Or wanted her to think that."

Seymour lifted the phone and saw the last message came from Victor Crowe at nine-fifty p.m. Or less than an hour before a neighbor heard gunshots and found Pompeo dead.

"Let's track down Victor. Now that the killer has upped the ante, it puts us and more possible victims in an even more unenviable position."

* * *

Turned out that Victor Crowe was a urologist who worked at Maui General. Leila and Seymour pulled him aside to talk.

"You said this concerned Adrianne?" he asked.

Leila studied the thirty-something, stocky man with a receding hairline and goatee. "I'm afraid we have some disturbing news. Ms. Pompeo was killed tonight."

"What?" His head snapped back.

"She was found shot to death in her apartment," said Seymour.

Victor wiped his mouth. "I can't believe this. Was it a break-in or what?"

"We don't think it was a burglary."

"Then why?"

Leila lifted her chin. "We were hoping you might be able to help us with that. Your message was the last one left on her voicemail. Also, we understand you had a date with her in the morning?"

"Yeah. We both work the night shift so I was going to take her out for breakfast."

"How long have you been seeing Adrianne?"

"Not long."

"And when did you last see her?"

Victor mused. "Two days ago."

Seymour stepped forward. "How long have you been at the hospital tonight?"

"Since eight o'clock."

"We'll need to verify that."

Victor's brows bridged. "You think I killed Adrianne?"

"It's just routine," Leila answered. "That said, everyone who knew her is a suspect until proven otherwise. I'm sure you understand."

He nodded. "Do whatever you need to."

"Did Adrianne ever tell you she was feeling threatened by anyone?"

"Not that I recall."

"Did you meet any of the people she knew?"

"Only a girlfriend. I think her name was Melissa."

Leila cocked a brow. "Would that be Melissa Eng?"

"Couldn't tell you her last name, sorry."

Leila described her.

"Yeah, that sounds like the woman I met," Victor said.

Leila exchanged looks with Seymour and wondered if it meant anything that Adrianne and Melissa happened to be friends—before one of them was eliminated from the picture.

Leila gave him her card. "If you happen to think of anything else that might be helpful, give me a call."

*   *   *

After they checked out Victor's alibi, Leila and Seymour left the hospital.

"What do you make of Pompeo being in bed with Eng, so to speak?" Seymour asked Leila.

"Not sure," she admitted. "Could be nothing more than two frustrated women who bonded over their shared misery. Or maybe they were both in on killing Nagasaka, Racine and Brennan, with one deciding she was better off going it alone since a dead partner in crime couldn't talk."

"If Eng was involved in this, you can bet her nephew Travis Takamori probably also played a role. Possibly as the triggerman."

Leila twisted her lips thoughtfully. "Meaning he or Melissa could decide to take the other out if fearful enough their blood bond wouldn't hold up under pressure."

"Let's bring them in and see if we're onto something before it reaches that point. Or maybe we'll discover we're looking in the wrong direction."

"Hey, Adrianne's definitely dead. All we can do is keep digging and hope we're not the ones who end up buried."

"Yeah, remind me to get out my shovel when we get back to my place."

Seymour wondered how long they would share the residence, as Leila's house was still uninhabitable, thanks to the thieves and vandals. He felt comfortable enough having her in his bed, even though Seymour would have preferred Mele next to him when he woke up in the morning. But miracles rarely occurred. Settling for the next best thing was not exactly a sin, even if it felt like one.

CHAPTER THIRTY-FOUR

Vice Detective Jonny Chung and his team surrounded the house on Hauoli Street in Ma'alaea. It had been under surveillance for two months as part of a drug sting operation. The goal was to put local drug dealers out of business, thereby scaring off dealers from the Mainland who might be thinking about setting up shop on the island.

Chung wanted this to go down as planned. Not only would a few arrests and confiscation of cocaine, crack, and methamphetamines make him look good with the department, it would be the perfect cover for taking a cut of the drug profits from bigger fish. He had set this up carefully, making sure the big drug dealers the department wanted most were nowhere to be found. Instead, he would give them some low level dealers and everyone could go home happy. Especially him.

With everyone in place, Chung considered what would happen were this to blow up in his face. It was worth the risk, considering what he gained in helping to finance his retirement someday.

He sucked in a deep breath and then gave the go ahead for the operation to move full steam ahead.

With guns drawn, the team barreled its way through the front and back doors, prepared to do whatever was necessary to anyone who resisted.

"Keep your hands up where we can see them!" Chung shouted, spotting Travis Takamori getting high.

Travis put his thin arms straight up and offered no resistance as other males and females were rounded up.

Chung was glad to see everyone was very cooperative, like they were sleepwalking. Or maybe they were scared to death of the police. Either way, the result was the same.

Chung approached a room at the back of the house. The door was partially shut. "If anyone's in there, better get your ass out here right now or face the consequences!" He positioned his weapon, nodded to fellow detective Hollis Schmidt, and kicked the door open.

"Don't shoot!" the woman said, her arms up.

He recognized her as the lady of the house, Melissa Eng, who with her nephew, Takamori, had a nice little drug operation going. Chung almost hated to have to put them out of business, as he would've welcomed getting a piece of the pie. But there were bigger fish in the sea.

"Get her out of here!" he ordered. "I'll make sure there are no stragglers hiding."

Schmidt nodded. "You heard the man, move!"

Chung waited till they were gone and quickly moved toward the closet where he'd been told some money would be left for him in a box.

He found it, riffling through the new hundred dollar bills, before stuffing them in his pocket. Resisting the urge to get greedy by taking some of the drug money left behind by users, he moved to the center of the room just as Schmidt returned.

"Everything all right?" he asked.

Chung gave a half grin. "Yeah. I checked the closet and didn't find any junkies hiding out. Let's get outta here!"

No sooner had they entered the front room when Chung saw Detectives Seymour and Kahana from homicide IDing themselves and entering.

What the hell were they doing here?

Chung smiled. "Hey, you two."

"What's going on here?" Seymour gazed at him.

"We just took down a drug house. Why are you here?"

Leila widened her eyes. "We came to talk to Melissa Eng in connection with a homicide tonight. Thought we might find Travis Takamori here, too."

Chung tilted his head. "What homicide?"

"Adrianne Pompeo."

Chung was aware of the case they were working on. "Afraid you're a little too late. They're both on their way to the station, charged with possession, dealing, and half a dozen other charges."

"How long have you been here?" Leila asked.

"If you're wondering about Eng and Takamori's whereabouts tonight, we've been staking out the house for hours. They've both been holed up inside all night." He knew this probably wasn't what she wanted to hear. "Eng and Takamori are definitely guilty of committing some serious crimes, but neither one took out Pompeo."

* * *

Hours later Leila was trying to get her house back in order following the burglary, with Seymour still on the job. She'd always considered the place a sanctuary ever since visiting her grandfather here as a child. Now that the reality of today's times had hit home, Leila could only hope an updated security system would make potential burglars think twice before invading her space again.

Convincing her mother of that was another problem altogether. As though equipped with telepathic skills or radar that something was wrong, she had called and compelled Leila to explain what happened.

"This is why I worry so much about you," Rena complained. "Things have gone from bad to worse in Maui.

If you can't even feel protected in your home, how can you ever feel safe there?"

Leila sighed, realizing she could only hope to mitigate the damage. "This could have happened anywhere."

"But it happened there—to you. What if you'd been home at the time? They could've killed you."

"Not if I killed them first. I'm a cop, Makuahine. I can protect myself."

"But not the house your Kapuna and Tutu loved dearly. Maybe next time they'll burn it down and take away the memories forever."

"There won't be a next time," Leila insisted. "We caught the burglars. They will be put away for years and the department will put more patrols in the area."

This seemed to satisfy her mother for the moment.

"Do you want me to come and help out a little?"

Leila was quick to respond. "I appreciate the offer, but I have things in hand."

"Well, I'll let you get back to it."

Leila promised to call her in a few days once some order was restored in her life. She hoped that included the case she was working on. With Melissa Eng and Travis Takamori no longer suspects in Adrianne Pompeo's murder, that meant they had to follow other leads in nailing down the killer.

* * *

At seven a.m., Rachel awakened with a throbbing headache. She vaguely remembered being put to bed by Leila, whom she'd called after deciding not to drive home from the bar.

Dragging herself out of bed, Rachel listened to her voicemail. She got the news Adrianne Pompeo had been killed last night.

Rachel had slept through the call. She could only hope there was no fallout from it. Work was pretty much all she had to look forward to these days. Losing a job she loved was something Rachel didn't even want to think about.

Not as long as she didn't have to.

She hopped in the shower and wondered who might have killed Adrianne and presumably the three doctors before her.

CHAPTER THIRTY-FIVE

Leila brought a cup of coffee for herself and water for Melissa Eng into the interview room. She'd never suspected the woman was dealing drugs along with her nephew, Travis Takamori. While this turned out to be good news in letting them off the hook as murder suspects, selling drugs on the islands was taken seriously by authorities.

"Here you are," Leila said, handing her the drink.

Melissa drank some water and frowned. "I was framed."

"I saw the evidence. It seemed pretty convincing to me."

"That's the whole point, isn't it? Police frame people all the time to get what they want."

Leila was amazed at how those caught with their hand in the cookie jar could still claim they were set up. Not that she could always discount the possibility, just not this time when twelve people were arrested in the sting with some already confessing to drug crimes.

"If you believe that's the case, I suggest you take it up with your lawyer. I'd actually like to talk to you about Adrianne Pompeo."

Melissa reacted.

"Do you know her?"

She hesitated. "Yes. Why?"

"Adrianne was found murdered last night."

Melissa shook her head. "No way!"

"Someone shot her to death in her apartment. We think it might have been the same person who murdered Larry Nagasaka, Elizabeth Racine, and Douglas Brennan."

Melissa's eyes narrowed. "If you're suggesting I killed Adrianne, then—"

"We know you didn't do it. Your house was under surveillance with you inside at the time of the murder."

"Then I don't understand what you want from me."

Leila sipped her coffee. "How did you and Adrianne meet?"

"She was staying at the Crest Creek Condominiums when I worked for the cleaning service," Melissa said. "We hit it off."

Leila wasn't too surprised about that, all things considered. "Did you ever talk about the doctors who were killed?"

"Yeah, of course. We felt we were singled out unfairly by the police."

"Seems like you just can't get a break." Leila nearly chuckled at the cynical comment. "Have you ever considered that everything you've experienced has been because of your own actions?"

Melissa pouted. "If you're through with me..."

"Did Adrianne ever say anything to you about having knowledge of the killings or killer?"

Melissa tasted the water; then met her eyes. "Can you help me out of this mess I'm in? And Travis, too?"

Leila peered back. "I can't make you any promises and won't. However, I can put in a good word with the prosecuting attorney that you were helpful in our investigation, if that's the case. Since Adrianne was your friend, I'm sure you'd like to do whatever you can to help, right?"

Melissa licked her lips. "Adrianne knew something, but didn't say what. She just told me it was all about revenge and making people accountable. I never asked her who she was talking about because I didn't want to know."

"Probably a good thing for you," Leila told her. "Otherwise you might not be around to deal with your current difficulties."

* * *

That afternoon Seymour entered the crime lab in search of Gil Delfino, who was examining the bullets removed from Adrianne Pompeo. Preliminary results from the autopsy found that the manner of death was consistent with the deaths of Nagasaka, Racine, and Brennan. Seymour had little doubt they were dealing with the same killer, but had to make it official.

He found Delfino headed in his direction. "Just the man I'm looking for."

Delfino half smiled. "If only you were female, a foot shorter, and a lot better looking, I might be all over that."

Seymour wasn't amused. "I'll settle for knowing what you've got on the bullets dug out of Adrianne Pompeo."

"Same old, same old. They came from a .25 caliber gun and had six lands and grooves with a right hand twist. Same ejection and firing pin marks, too."

"So you're telling me—"

"That the bullets definitely came from the gun used to shoot Racine, Nagasaka, and Brennan."

Seymour rubbed his forehead. "Why am I not surprised?"

"Hey, I'm just relaying the information and giving you a heads up that your killer is calculating and a dead-eye shot, if nothing else."

"I'll keep that in mind," Seymour said sarcastically. "I'll let you get back to it."

Seymour left with what he came for, but didn't feel any better about it. Someone was killing doctors, and now assistants, right under their noses and it was frustrating as hell. If he hoped to make lieutenant someday, this case couldn't drag on much longer.

* * *

"Did you get stuck or something?" Gina asked, looking up.

Ferguson had stopped moving while lodged inside her. He resumed his thrusts.

"No, my mind was just somewhere else."

"I wasn't really talking about your mind."

He grinned. "You just do your part and I'll do mine."

"You're the boss. I'm just a whore and happy to play whenever you pay."

She had become loose with her comments and he had no problem with that. He liked the easy communication between them. If only it were the same with Brenda, instead of turning into a battle of wills all the time.

But Ferguson had sensed some changes in his wife recently. She seemed less combative and more resigned to the status quo. He saw that as a good thing.

Or was there something more to it that he just hadn't figured out?

CHAPTER THIRTY-SIX

On Saturday, Leila was returning to the scene of the crime with Rachel. They were hoping to find any clues into Adrianne Pompeo's death the CSI might have overlooked.

"By the way, thanks for having my back yesterday," Rachel said from the passenger seat.

"You would've done the same for me."

Leila recalled telling Lt. Ortega that Rachel had been a bit under the weather. He bought it, which was fine by her. It was better for Rachel to get some professional help on her own than to make it mandatory.

But would she?

"You're right, I would have." Rachel paused. "I'm not a drunk."

"I didn't think you were." Leila felt she was definitely a problem drinker.

"Every once in a while, I need something to take the edge off."

"It's only a temporary fix."

"I know. Just give me some time to get things together."

Leila eyed her. "Take whatever time you need. But remember, it's your career on the line if you screw it up."

She had heard it all before. Her father had some issues with alcohol, blaming it on job stress. He eventually cleaned up his act. But not before the damage had already been done to his family.

Leila didn't want to see Rachel go down that path, though as a widow, her only family was a sister she apparently didn't keep in close touch with.

They arrived at the apartment, sidestepping crime scene tape.

"So what are we looking for?" Rachel asked.

Leila donned her gloves. "Anything that might give us a clue as to why someone decided Adrianne was better off dead. My guess is she got in over her head and it cost Adrianne her life."

"You mean like blackmail?"

"Why not? If Adrianne knew who the killer was, maybe she made the mistake of trying to profit from it."

Rachel put gloves on. "That could explain why the killer decided to go after a non doctor this time."

"Maybe. Unfortunately that still doesn't tell us why the unsub targeted the three doctors," Leila said, and began going through some of Adrianne's things. "Or if there are others still on the hit list."

* * *

Seymour got a message from his informant, Marty Mendoza, that he might have something for him in relation to a hot gun sold recently.

Entering the tavern, Seymour found Marty at his usual table.

"What's up, man?"

"You tell me," Seymour said.

"Have a seat and let's talk over a drink. What's your pleasure?"

Seymour sat, ordering a beer. "This better be good."

"Good enough, I think. Been asking around and came up with someone who's set up shop here from the Mainland. Seems like he specializes in untraceable handguns and ammo. Word is he sold a .25 caliber pistol and bullets to a very eager buyer about a week before the doctors met their Maker."

"I need a name."

Marty sucked on his scotch. "Kurt Landon."

"Where can I find him?"

"All over the island."

Seymour's brow furrowed. "You need to be more specific."

Marty showed his teeth. "I hear he's got an Upcountry place in Haiku. Can't tell you anything more than that."

"It'll have to do."

The drink came and Seymour paid. He slid the balance owed to Marty across the table. "It's all there and a little something extra."

He scooped it up. "As always, nice doing business with you, Seymour, even if I can't see your face."

Seymour gulped down a generous amount of beer before getting to his feet.

"You're probably better off not seeing the ugliness out there these days."

Seymour left with a strong desire to have a talk with Kurt Landon.

* * *

Ferguson went around the side of the house on Kuaha Road, gun drawn. If the suspect made a run for it out the back door, he'd be waiting for him.

He heard a dog barking inside. Guard dog, no doubt, for someone dealing in arms. Probably drugs, too. Ferguson hoped he didn't have to shoot the dog, but wouldn't hesitate if it came to protecting his own life.

He thought about his anniversary in two days. They usually celebrated by going out to dinner. Should they continue the tradition this time around? He had a feeling Brenda, like him, could think of better ways to spend their money. But that wasn't the point, was it? This was a chance to try and make the marriage work again.

Or had they already reached the point of no return?

Ferguson heard talking inside, before Seymour yelled, "He's heading your way!"

Quickly moving to a spot beside the back door, Ferguson sucked in a deep breath and waited till a large, thirty-something man lumbered out the screen door, half dressed.

With a head of steam, Ferguson dove into the man, the surge toppling both of them to the ground. Ferguson held the gun to the man's temple.

"Don't even think about making a move, unless you want to find out what it's like to have your brain matter splattered across the concrete."

He grabbed the man's right arm and handcuffed it behind his back, then the other.

Seymour ran outside. "You all right?"

Ferguson huffed. "Yeah, the suspect is secure." He heard more barking. "How'd you handle the dog?"

"I kept it at bay with a chair and got the hell out of there as fast as I could." Seymour eyed the suspect. "Kurt Landon, you're under arrest for dealing in illegal firearms..."

CHAPTER THIRTY-SEVEN

Leila faced Kurt Landon in the interrogation room. She wondered if he really was the key to solving their case. Seymour seemed to think so. She glanced at him as he leered at the suspect.

"You're in a lot of trouble, Kurt," she said to get his attention. "Aside from facing charges for the possession and sale of illegal weapons, one of the guns you sold may've been used to commit four murders. That would make you an accessory before the fact at the very least and could even lead to you facing trial as an accomplice."

"Hey, I had nothing to do with any murders," Kurt said nervously. "I only provide a product for self-defense. If people choose to use the guns unlawfully, I can't be held responsible for that."

"If you really believe that, you're in for a rude awakening."

While Leila didn't really expect the prosecuting attorney to throw the book at him as a direct participant in the homicides, should that prove not to be the case, she wasn't above tightening the screws to get his cooperation.

She eyed Seymour to take it from there.

"Personally, I couldn't care less if you spent the rest of your life behind bars," he said gruffly. "But there's a chance it might not come to that, assuming we get something useful from you."

Kurt wrung his hands. "What do you want?"

"We know you recently sold a .25 caliber gun to someone who wouldn't take no for an answer."

He cocked a thick brow. "Yeah, I remember. It was a dude in an expensive suit. When I asked what he needed it for, he said it was none of my business. I never argue with paying customers."

"Maybe you should have in this case. What can you tell us about this man?"

Kurt shrugged. "Just a man."

"You'll have to do a lot better than that," Seymour said.

Kurt licked his lips. "Tall, white, mid forties, gray hair..."

"Would you recognize him if you saw him again?"

"Probably."

Leila leaned forward. "I'm a sketch artist. Why don't you describe the man to the best of your ability and let's see if I can draw a reasonable representation."

Kurt rubbed his nose. "I can try."

Over the next fifteen minutes Leila drew a composite sketch, adjusted accordingly, till it was apparently right on the money.

"Is this the man you sold the gun to?" she asked.

Kurt studied the drawing. "Yeah, that looks pretty much like him."

Leila took a good look at the face that bore a strong resemblance to Kenneth Racine.

* * *

"I knew there was something about the man that rubbed me the wrong way," Seymour said as he mulled over the identification that had suddenly thrust Racine to the forefront of suspects.

Leila looked at him from the passenger seat. "There's no guarantee he's the man in the sketch or that Landon sold the gun to our killer."

"True, but I wouldn't bet against it. Racine certainly had motive for the first two murders and opportunity. I'm still trying to figure out why he would kill Brennan and Pompeo."

"Once we get Racine in custody, maybe he'll help us fill in the blanks." Leila paused. "Of course, what we really need is the murder weapon to sign, seal, and deliver this to the prosecuting attorney."

"I agree."

With a warrant already issued to search Racine's house and vehicle, Seymour was confident they would find the gun he used.

He was less certain as to whether or not Racine would own up to the crimes. Or, as medical director of the Behavioral Health Unit, would he seek to use psycho babble to justify his actions; hoping to somehow lessen the severity of the punishment he faced by a jury of his peers?

* * *

On the third floor at Maui General, Leila and Seymour were accompanied by uniformed officers as they found Kenneth Racine making his normal rounds.

He stopped dead in his tracks when he saw them approaching, brow furrowed. "What is it this time?"

Leila had a feeling he already knew the answer. "Kenneth Racine, you're under arrest for suspicion of committing multiple murders."

His rights were read and the suspect was handcuffed.

"You're making a big mistake," he insisted.

"You'll have every opportunity to prove that."

Kenneth growled. "This is absurd!"

Seymour got so close that their noses nearly touched. "I don't think so. I see guilt written all over your face." He motioned to the officers to take him away.

"The press will likely be all over this one," feared Leila.

"When are they not covering a case made for the headlines?" Seymour's eyes rolled. "Best we can hope for is to hold them at bay as long as possible while we continue to gather the evidence we need."

She saw that as a tall task, given that the media seemed to have eyes and ears everywhere these days. Still, Leila was more focused on catching a killer and making the medical practitioners, citizens, and tourists alike feel safe again in Maui.

* * *

Rachel held the search warrant in hand as they approached Kenneth Racine's house in Kapalua. Not too surprisingly, it was impressive with a palm tree lined driveway. All that glittered was not gold, since the doctor had some serious skeletons about to come out of the closet.

There was no indication anyone was home. Indeed, they had already been told Racine had been arrested at work. Still she went through the routine, shouting, "This is the police. We have a warrant to search the premise. Open up—"

When there was no answer, Rachel made eye contact with Ferguson and the accompanying officers. She gave the go ahead to force their way in.

They fanned out in every direction, looking for a .25 caliber firearm and shells in specific, but open to anything else that might be incriminating.

"Lots of places to hide something you don't want found," commented Ferguson.

Rachel nodded. "And sometimes it's right under your nose."

He dug inside a bookshelf. "Not sure Racine's that clever."

"That's obvious, considering why we're here in the first place."

After going over the place with a fine toothed comb, the news was not good. The murder weapon was nowhere to be found.

* * *

"No .25 caliber gun was located in the suspect's house or car," Ortega relayed bleakly.

"Uh oh." Leila made a face as they stood outside the interrogation room where Racine sat. "Maybe he's not our man after all?"

Seymour gazed at her. "I'm telling you that's not an innocent man sitting there. What he doesn't know about the murder weapon, he doesn't need to till the time is right."

Ortega nodded. "See what you can get out of him before the lawyer arrives. Just make sure it doesn't end up being thrown out of court."

"You ready for this?" Seymour asked Leila just before they went in.

She met his eyes, reading his hunger for her. Or was she projecting her own feelings onto him?

"Let's go for it."

Inside the room, Leila remained standing while Seymour took a seat across from the suspect. He put a recorder on the table and turned it on.

"So are we going to make this short and not so sweet, Kenneth?" Leila asked. "Or are you going to play hardball?"

His nostrils flared. "If you expect me to confess to something I didn't do, you're both crazy."

"Actually, we're perfectly sane. And I believe you are, too."

"Then you should know this isn't going to work."

Leila sighed, but stayed in control. "We didn't arrest you on a whim or prayer. We know you bought the gun used to kill the victims from an illegal gun dealer named Kurt Landon. And he's willing to testify to that." She'd gotten no such assurance, but hoped it would have the desired effect.

"I don't know what you're talking about." His voice shook.

"Oh come now, Doctor!" Seymour said. "We've got you dead to rights and no amount of denying it will change things."

The door opened and a tall, thin man in his sixties entered.

"I'm Leonard Fenkell, Dr. Racine's attorney." Behind glasses, his brows touched as he looked at the recorder. "You can start by shutting that damned thing off."

Seymour pushed the stop button. "We're not violating your client's rights. This is standard procedure."

"Not with my client."

"Whatever. We were just telling your client that he's bitten off more than he could chew."

"Is that so?" Fenkell uttered curtly.

Leila regarded him. "I'm afraid so. He purchased a gun and shot to death four innocent people. That's four first degree homicides. There's no turning back from the consequences."

"I didn't do it." Kenneth glared.

"The evidence doesn't lie."

"What evidence?" Fenkell flashed a look of skepticism.

"How about the murder weapon?" Leila threw out, hoping they would soon be able to back it up. "We've got fingerprints I'm betting will match your client's."

"All I did was buy the gun."

"Don't say another word," his attorney demanded.

Kenneth shot him a wicked look. "Shut up! I'm not taking the rap for something I didn't do."

Leila eyed Seymour quietly turning the tape back on. "Are you saying you purchased the gun for someone else?"

He looked up at her. "Yes."

"Who...?"

"Connie Nagasaka."

Leila exchanged glances with Seymour and back. "You're telling us Connie is the killer?"

"Yes!"

Seymour cocked a brow. "Do you really expect us to believe that?"

"It's true, I swear. The whole thing was Connie's idea. She was pissed Larry was sleeping with Liz. So was I. Connie begged me to get a gun and said she would make things right. I guess I was so consumed with rage, I went along with it, not thinking clearly."

Leila leaned forward. "Had your thinking improved any when Connie allegedly killed Douglas Brennan and Adrianne Pompeo, too?"

Kenneth ran a hand across his mouth. "Yes, but it was too late by then. I was already an accomplice."

Leila's irritation was growing. "So you figured it didn't matter how many others died after the first two because your hands were too tied to stop it?"

"I tried to talk some sense into her," he claimed. "But Connie had her mind made up, once they pushed her too hard."

Leila nodded at Seymour; then turned to Kenneth and his attorney. "You might as well make yourselves comfortable. It's going to be a long day."

CHAPTER THIRTY-EIGHT

"Are you buying his story?" Ortega asked outside the interrogation room.

Seymour looked through the window. "Could be the effort of a desperate man to try and save his own neck as much as possible."

Ortega looked at Leila. "What do you think?"

"Well, we haven't found the murder weapon yet. Could be he doesn't have it. Maybe she does. Wouldn't be the first time a woman and man partnered up to commit murder, no matter who pulled the trigger."

"You'd better get a search warrant to see if she has the gun, before she's tipped off that Racine's in custody and fingering her as the killer. She might decide to toss it in the ocean or use it on someone else."

Leila sighed. "If Connie is the killer, she probably wouldn't hesitate to go after anyone who got in her way."

Ortega's brow wrinkled. "That's what concerns me. Between the two of them, this has to stop now!"

"I'm hoping it will."

Leila favored Seymour and could see the strain on his face. Could he see the same on hers?

Connie Nagasaka was the next one to feel the heat and perhaps put the investigation to rest.

* * *

The doer was flipping through an investment magazine and thinking about nothing in particular, when something on the news registered.

"Dr. Kenneth Racine, medical director of the Behavioral Health Unit at Maui General Hospital, was arrested for the murder of his wife, Dr. Elizabeth Racine, and three others in the medical field. The police aren't commenting on what led up to the arrest. Or if other arrests will be forthcoming."

This unexpected turn of events threw the doer for a loop. What could the authorities possibly have on Kenneth to charge him with anything? Maybe this was merely a bluff to get him talking. Would he swallow the bait?

Or would the whole thing blow over in a day or two?

The doer decided it was best to err on the side of caution before the police figured things out and came knocking.

It was obvious there was only one thing that could make the case for them. The doer couldn't let that happen. Getting rid of the smoking gun would derail their investigation, regardless of what spewed out of Kenneth Racine's mouth.

The doer set about to locate the murder weapon.

* * *

Leila rang the doorbell of Connie Nagasaka's house. With lights on inside and her car in the driveway, it was clear the suspect was home.

"It's the police," she shouted, suspecting Connie had already heard about Kenneth Racine's arrest. If guilty as indicated, she would likely want to dispose of any evidence that could tie her to the crime.

Especially the gun.

Just when they were ready to enter the house forcibly, the door opened. Connie stood there in a long, silk robe.

"What is it?" she asked coldly.

"We have a warrant to search your house." Leila handed it to her.

224

Connie bristled. "Whatever for?"

"Evidence in relation to a murder investigation."

"I thought we had already been through this?"

"So did I, but things change." Leila regarded her sharply. "I advise you to stay out of the way and let us do our job."

Connie stepped aside and Leila went in, followed by Seymour and several officers.

"Check everywhere," Seymour ordered. "Particularly places you might not ordinarily think to look."

Leila watched the team fan out while keeping an eye on Connie. Could the woman actually be a multiple murderer working in tandem with the likes of Kenneth Racine?

"This is a total waste of time," Connie argued. "Hoping I killed my husband and his mistress won't make it so."

Leila met her gaze. "Who said anything about your husband and Elizabeth Racine?"

"Then who are we talking about?"

"Are you aware Kenneth Racine has been arrested in connection with the death of his wife and three others?"

Connie paused. "I heard about it. So?"

"So he had a very interesting story to tell."

Connie remained poised. "I thought you dealt in facts, not stories?"

"We do. And that includes checking out every new development, no matter how small."

Connie sneered. "Sounds like a perfectly good waste of manpower and taxpayer money."

Leila kept a straight face. "Probably, but that's not our call."

Connie folded her arms and Leila tried to read her mind. She suspected Connie was strategizing should this not go her way. Or maybe even if it did.

A female officer approached them, holding an item with a gloved hand. "Found something..."

Leila looked with interest at what appeared to be a .25 caliber gun, as Seymour joined them. "Where?"

"It was stuffed inside some tissue in a heating vent."

Leila glanced at Seymour and turned to Connie.

"I have no idea how that got there," she claimed.

Seymour narrowed his eyes. "I have a pretty good idea. Connie Nagasaka, you're under arrest on suspicion of murdering four people, including your husband, Larry Nagasaka."

Leila read Connie her rights while handcuffing her. "Looks like taxpayer money being well spent now."

Connie's face contorted irritably, but she stayed mute.

CHAPTER THIRTY-NINE

"I've never seen the gun before," asserted Connie. "I'm obviously being framed."

Leila stared at her in the interrogation room, unconvinced she was the innocent woman portrayed. But with the evidence against her purely circumstantial at the moment and a desperate Kenneth Racine fingering her as the killer, now was not the time to pass judgment.

"The gun's being dusted for prints. If yours show up, any credibility you have goes up in smoke."

Connie's mouth tightened. "You won't find my prints on the gun because I never touched it."

Leila peeked at the mirror with Seymour, Rachel, Ferguson, and Ortega on the other side before returning her gaze to the murder suspect. "According to Kenneth Racine, you two were in this together. He told us he bought the gun and you were the one who killed your husband, his wife, Douglas Brennan and Adrianne Pompeo."

Connie's mouth hung open. "And you believe him?"

"He seemed pretty damned convincing," Leila responded for effect. "Why would he lie?"

"Why wouldn't he? Isn't it obvious? Kenneth's simply trying to save his own neck by trying to set me up."

"So you're accusing him of planting the gun in your heating vent?" Leila asked.

"It's the only explanation I can think of."

Leila could think of another, but kept it to herself for now.

"Were you lovers?"

Connie batted her eyes. "Excuse me?"

Leila colored. "It doesn't seem that farfetched, since you were spending time together. Maybe that would explain how he could have snuck the gun in and hidden it."

Connie took a breath. "Okay, we had sex one time—when we were both feeling down about our spouses found dead together. It was a stupid thing to do and I regret it. Especially now that I know he's responsible for Larry's death and trying to make me the scapegoat."

"Are you sure you played no part in these murders, acting out of rage, jealousy, and desperation?" Leila asked.

Connie held her ground. "Positive. I'm not a killer, no matter what Kenneth might have you believe."

* * *

"We've brought Connie Nagasaka in," Seymour informed Kenneth and his lawyer, hoping to shake things up between the competing stories. "Looks like there are some holes in your prior statements."

Kenneth scowled. "What holes?"

"Well, for starters, Connie has denied shooting anyone. She says you planted the gun to cover your own tracks."

"She's lying."

"Funny, but she accused you of the exact same thing."

"I think we've had enough of this," his attorney insisted.

Seymour dismissed him. "That's up to your client." He angled his eyes at Kenneth. "If you'd rather have Connie Nagasaka spill her guts and say you were the one to murder four people, that's fine by me. And when you consider that you purchased the gun we believe was used to commit the crimes, you're in a very weak position here."

"I'm not going to allow her to pin this on me," Kenneth said. "Connie was the shooter in all four cases. She knows it and I know it. I'm willing to testify to that effect, or do anything I can to keep this from getting any worse for me."

Seymour stretched his jaw. It was obvious the two murder suspects were determined to blame each other. He wouldn't be surprised if both were actively involved in the murders.

"You're already way past that point," he told him. "You'd better hope the gun has her prints on it and not just yours."

Seymour wasn't hedging his bet in either direction.

* * *

At the crime lab, the results had come in on the gun.

Leila stood beside Seymour. She wondered if it was possible this gun wasn't the murder weapon. If so, it would make the case against both suspects pretty weak.

"I have some good news and bad news," Delfino said, scratching his pate.

Seymour cleared his throat. "Let's have the bad first."

"All right. There were no prints on the gun. So we can't say who used it and when."

"And the good news?" Leila dared ask.

"The gun is a .25 caliber. I test fired bullets and compared them to those taken from the victims. They had the same six lands and grooves with a right hand twist. They also had identical ejection and firing pin marks."

"So you're saying—" began Seymour.

Delfino cut him off. "Yes, this is definitely the murder weapon in all four homicides."

Leila gave a tiny smile. They had the weapon and the two killers. But which one pulled the trigger?

As though reading her mind, the forensic examiner said, "I may be able to help you out on one other little matter... I told you it was possible through measuring electrochemical reactions from touching the metal that we might be able to isolate fingerprint patterns on a bullet, if lucky. Today was our lucky day. I was able to get a pretty good partial off a bullet fragment taken from Adrianne Pompeo. I put it in the computer to check for a match."

"What did you come up with?" Leila was eager to get the answer. "Or should I say who?"

"The print belonged to Connie Nagasaka."

Seymour grinned. "Guess this definitely isn't her lucky day!"

"She's certainly boxed herself in a corner with no escape," Leila said. "We've just made the case for murder against Connie and Kenneth Racine; though it turns out he wasn't the triggerman after all."

* * *

Leila sat across from Connie Nagasaka, wondering if she actually believed she would be able to get away with murder. Incredibly this seemed to be the case for most killers. Overconfidence and mistakes ultimately caught up with most of them.

"You were right, your fingerprints weren't found on the gun," Leila said. "Unfortunately you weren't as careful with the bullets. One of the bullets you used to shoot Adrianne Pompeo had a partial print. Turns out it was a perfect match to your fingerprint."

Connie favored her with a wicked gaze while seemingly trying to come up with something other than empty words.

Leila had no such difficulty. "It's over, Connie. We know that you and not Kenneth killed them, though I promise he won't get off the hook anytime soon. If you want to tell me why those four people had to die, I'm willing to listen."

Connie sucked in a deep breath and her eyes became slits. "Yes, I killed them because Kenneth was too weak to do what we both wanted. Neither Larry nor Elizabeth deserved to live after carrying on like they did right under our noses. It was a fitting way to end their lives."

Leila could only roll her eyes. "But why kill Douglas Brennan?"

"Because he wouldn't leave me alone. Somehow Douglas felt with Larry out of the picture he could continue to make sexual advances toward me. When I refused, he threatened to tell the police that Larry was convinced I would kill him one day and get away with it." She chuckled. "I couldn't allow him to ruin things for me by giving him another reason to dig deeper."

Leila looked at the mirror and could imagine what they were thinking on the other side as she got into the head of a serial killer.

"And Adrianne Pompeo?"

"That bitch made the mistake of trying to blackmail me." Connie's nostrils flared. "She was another one of my husband's conquests and claimed he told her during pillow talk that I was an expert markswoman. She put two and two together and demanded $100,000 to keep her mouth shut. Instead, I ended her miserable life!"

Leila knitted her brows. "And in the process you ended your own life as you know it."

She stood and signaled to a waiting guard to take the prisoner away.

Even in victory, Leila was left with a sour taste in her mouth. As always, she knew it would pass in time.

CHAPTER FORTY

That night Leila joined her colleagues at a Kahului club where a live band played traditional Hawaiian music. She was glad to enjoy some down time after solving the case that saw four people gunned down in cold blood. It was also nice to be able to spend time with Seymour in a social setting where they could openly be more than just partners.

She wondered how long it would last. Having survived the challenges of a difficult investigation was a good sign.

Leila stuck a pretzel at him and he bit off a generous piece. She finished the rest.

"Who can ever predict how things will turn out?" She grabbed another pretzel. "I certainly wouldn't have guessed Connie Nagasaka and Kenneth Racine would join forces to retaliate against their spouses lethally; and, apparently for Connie, anyone else who got in her way. But hey, what do I know?"

"No more than the rest of us, I'm afraid," Seymour said over a mug of beer. "I'd say we definitely dodged a bullet or two bringing them to justice."

Ferguson raised his mug. "I'll drink to that. Talk about femme fatale. I sure as hell wouldn't want to be on that woman's bad side."

Rachel laughed. "Thought you liked to live on the wild side, Ferguson? Or am I getting you and Seymour mixed up?"

Ferguson chuckled. "No wild side here. Brenda keeps me on the straight and narrow."

"Good for you."

"Yeah, I guess so." He quickly changed the subject. "I hear Nagasaka has hired a high powered attorney to defend her."

"She'll need it and then some," Leila said. "With Kenneth Racine prepared to testify against her and some solid evidence, this will be hard for Connie to walk away from."

"Doesn't mean she won't give it her best shot." Seymour put his hand on the table. "I'm sure the lawyer will try to get her confession thrown out; claim it was coerced, manipulated or whatever."

"No amount of legal maneuvering is going to change the outcome. The facts speak for themselves," Leila said.

Rachel nodded in agreement over a Virgin Mary. "I'm just wondering how Connie plans to pay for the pricey help. She can forget about an insurance payout now that she's being charged with her husband's murder. And I'm betting Larry Nagasaka's sister will do all she can to challenge Connie for control of his assets."

"Something tells me that Connie already planned for every contingency in her life," Leila said. "Even murder. Unfortunately pathological jealousy proved to be her undoing."

"None of us are gonna lose any sleep over that." Ferguson took a swig of his beer.

Seymour followed suit and cast his eyes on Leila.

She gave him a tiny smile before turning to the band. They were playing, *Mele O Ku`u Pu`uwai*.

Leila sang along in her head, feeling content to be where she was at this stage in her life.

* * *

A week later, Officer Kelly Long responded to a domestic disturbance call at a condo on Ka'anapali Beach. He drove there barely awake after putting in overtime lately to make extra money in anticipation of the kid he had helped conceive. But he wouldn't complain. It was worth the sacrifice.

Carol seemed to be making a concerted effort to keep things good between them. The least he could do was prepare himself for being a good father and hope he didn't let their child down.

Long walked up to the condo just as a half naked woman ran out. Her face was bruised and blonde hair knotted.

"Are you Courtney Brennan?" he asked, as she had made the 911 call.

"Yes." Her voice was a whimper.

Long recalled reading about the ex-wife of CEO Douglas Brennan, who had been gunned down in front of his home last month.

"Can you tell me what happened?"

"My boyfriend, Henri, beat the hell out of me—for no reason."

Long frowned. As though there could be any reason for a man hitting a woman. Or vice versa.

"Is he inside?"

"Yes. Afterward he passed out on the bed."

"Had he been drinking? Or using drugs?"

"Both."

Long eyed her. "How about you, Ma'am?"

"I had a couple of glasses of wine." She began to cry. "He never hit me before or..."

Long pursed his lips. "We'll try to make sure he never hits you again. Why don't we go inside and you can show me where he is."

She hesitated. "I don't want to see him."

Long understood as best he could. "I'll protect you from your boyfriend," he promised.

"I just want him out of my house—forever!" Courtney sniffled while leading the way.

"What's Henri's last name?"

"Alfonso."

She took him to an upstairs bedroom and Long found the man sprawled face down on the bed and naked.

"Was there a sexual assault?" Long thought to ask.

Courtney colored. "Yes."

"Are you willing to press charges?" Though that should have been a given, it never was when it concerned intimate violence.

She dabbed at her eyes before responding firmly, "Yes."

Long gave her a sympathetic nod. "We'll get you checked out at a hospital. First things first. Wait here."

He drew his gun, approaching Henri. When he gave no indication of being awake, Long pounced on top, keeping him down with his weight.

He quickly grabbed Henri's arms and handcuffed him as he began to stir and realized what was happening.

"Why don't you assholes ever pick on someone your own size and gender?" Long said with asperity. He couldn't imagine laying a finger on his girlfriend.

Henri muttered something incoherent. Long dragged him to his feet.

"You're under arrest for domestic battery and sexual assault."

Long would probably add resisting arrest to the charges just to make sure he'd get as much time for this as possible.

In the meantime, he hoped Courtney would choose her mate more carefully in the future.

* * *

It was ten p.m. when Seymour found himself at Mele's door. He suspected her reaction would be less than cordial, as had been the case of late. But it was where he needed to be at this moment.

She opened the door and was obviously surprised. "Blake—"

"I know it's late."

"Akela's in bed."

"I figured that." He paused. "I came to see you."

Seymour expected her to rant and rave before sending him on his way. Instead she let him in.

"You see me," Mele said. "Do you have something to say?"

"Yeah, I still love you."

"Don't do this—"

"I doubt I'll ever stop loving you, no matter what happens." His gaze lowered to her face. "Tell me you don't love me anymore and I'll leave."

Mele averted her eyes for a moment, before looking at him. In saying nothing, she told Seymour everything he wanted to hear.

He cupped her cheeks and brought their lips together. She made no attempt to push him away. They just stood there kissing for a while before Seymour felt it was safe to take this to the next level. He scooped Mele into his arms and carried her to the bedroom, their mouths still locked.

It was what Seymour had hoped would happen this night. He didn't dare look beyond to the implications concerning his relationship with Mele or Leila.

He could only think about the moment at hand.

* * *

Leila watered her bamboo and orchid plants before curling up on the sofa to catch the news and enjoy a glass of wine. She thought about Seymour. Things were going pretty good for them and she was happy to have him in her life as a partner and lover. She hoped, if he let her, to spend more time with Akela. For all Leila knew, the girl might be the closest thing to a daughter she would ever have.

At least while she was involved with Seymour. Leila didn't discount the possibility of having children of her own someday, should the right man come along. She was still young and fertile. Something told her Seymour was not interested in going there with her. Or had she misread the way he felt about their relationship?

And Leila still had to win her mother's approval of her choice of man. Seymour would be a hard sell, but maybe once she got to know him....

Leila focused on the TV screen when the newscaster began to speak.

"A twenty-one-year-old tourist, Amy Lynn Laseter, has been reported missing by her best friend. Ms. Laseter's rented car was found abandoned near a North Shore wooded area about a mile from the Spreckelsville motel where the women were staying. You may recall that earlier this year another woman was found strangled to death in the same area in a case that is still unsolved. So far there is no indication of foul play..."

Leila felt a lump in her throat. She had worked that case. It was one of the few to have stumped her. The killer was still out there, perhaps gloating.

Had Amy Lynn Laseter met the same fate as Marcia Miyashiro?

# # #

Bonus Excerpt of R. Barri Flowers' bestselling mystery novel

MURDER IN HONOLULU
A Skye Delaney Mystery
(available in print, eBook and audio book in Audible,
Amazon, and iBookstore)

CHAPTER ONE

The name's Skye McKenzie Delaney. I'm part of the twenty-first century breed of licensed private investigators who live by their wits, survive on instincts, and take each case as though it may be their last. The fact that I double as a security consultant for companies in and around the city of Honolulu, where I reside, gives me financial backup not afforded to all private eyes. This notwithstanding, I take my work as an investigator of everything from cats stuck in trees to missing persons to crimes the police can't or won't touch very seriously. If not, I wouldn't be putting my heart, soul, and body into this often thankless job.

I also happen to be happily divorced—or at least no longer pining for my ex—and not afraid to get my hands dirty if necessary in my business. I get along with most people, but won't take any crap from anyone should it come my way.

Before I became a security consultant/private eye, I used to be a homicide cop for the Honolulu Police Department. Stress, fatigue, burnout, and a real desire to get into something that could provide more financial security and flexible hours, without the downside and depression of police work and know-it-all authority figures, convinced me to change careers.

During my six years on the force, I spent my nights earning a Master's Degree in Criminal Justice Administration. I'm hoping to get my Ph.D. someday when I no longer need to work for a living and can devote my time to further educating myself. In the meantime, I'm getting an honorary doctorate in private detectiveology, where every case can be a real learning experience.

On and off the job, I carry a .40 caliber or 9-millimeter pistol Smith and Wesson—depending on my mood. And I'm not afraid to use either one if I have to, as it sure beats the alternative of ending up as just another private dick on a cold slab in the morgue.

If I were to describe myself character-wise, the words that come to mind are feminine, adventurous yet conservative, streetwise though I often rely on intellect to get me over the hump, and kick-ass tough when duty calls.

I've been told on more than one occasion that I'm attractive—even beautiful—and sexy as hell. I leave that for others to decide, but I'm definitely in great shape at five-eight, thanks to a near obsession with running and swimming, along with not overdoing it with calories. I usually wear my long blonde hair in a ponytail. My contacts make my eyes seem greener than they really are.

I recently celebrated my thirty-fifth birthday. All right, in truth, it wasn't much of a celebration. I spent the entire day holed up in my house with my dog, Ollie, contemplating the future and happy to put much of my past behind me. That included my ex-husband, Carter Delaney, whose greatest contribution to my life and times was making me realize that no man was worth sacrificing one's own identity and integrity, even if it meant losing him in the process.

I did lose Carter five years ago, after deciding I had no desire to share him with his mistress (and probably others I didn't know about). It was a decision I firmly stand by today and am definitely the better for.

At least I convinced myself that was the case even as I came face to face with the subject in question on a muggy afternoon at the end of July. I had just filed away some papers when he walked into my office literally out of the blue. It was his first visit to my office since I joined the ranks of private eyes. I had once worked for the man as a security consultant. That turned into lust, sex, love, marriage, and divorce, and now we were little more than distant acquaintances.

The tremulous half-smile that played on Carter's lips told me that he was not entirely comfortable being there. I felt just as awkward for probably the same reason: the *ex-spouse syndrome*, which would forever keep a wall of regrets and painful memories between us, thick as molasses.

Never mind the fact that Carter Delaney was still every bit the physical specimen I had fallen in love with another lifetime ago. Tall, fit, handsome, and perennially tanned with dark hair and gray eyes, he almost looked as if he had just stepped out of the pages of Good Looking Digest. Though it was hotter than hell outside, he was decked out in an Italian navy designer suit and wing-tipped burgundy leather shoes. He glanced at the expensive watch on his wrist as if he needed to be somewhere else.

At thirty-eight, Carter Delaney was a successful businessman. A former Honolulu prosecutor in the career criminal division, Carter had walked away from the job after excelling at it for the lure of cold hard cash in the world of commerce. He had turned his smarts and acumen into a successful Internet-based international trade company.

It was during the early stages of this success that I entered the picture. Carter had hired me, wanting to have the best security devices for both his home and business. The rest, as they say, is history.

At least it was.

We had managed to avoid running into each other for nearly a year now, which suited me just fine. I wasn't looking for history to ever repeat itself, so quite naturally my curiosity was piqued as to why he was here now. Rather than appear too overeager, I decided to wait and let him take the lead.

"Hi," I said tonelessly as I eased back into my chair and scooted it up to my gray workstation desk. I shuffled some papers to at least give the guise of being busy. In fact, I was going through somewhat of a dry spell right now with the sluggish economy and all. This was particularly true on the private eye side of things, where potential clients seemed more willing to go it alone or rely on an overworked criminal justice system to solve their problems.

I wondered if Carter was here for a social call or if he was looking to hire me as a security consultant again.

"Nice office," he said, though the words seemed to squeeze through his tight-lipped smile.

I agreed with his assessment, as I'd paid enough for the roomy one-woman, air-conditioned unit in a high rent downtown office building that had all the tools of the private eye trade.

Carter hadn't taken his eyes off me since entering the office. It made me just a little uncomfortable. I wondered if he was trying to undress me with his penetrating gaze, as if he hadn't seen the merchandise before.

Either way, it was not winning him any brownie points, if there were any left to win.

I glared at him and said dryly: "Glad you like what you see."

He immediately turned his eyes downward, as though searching for something. When he looked at me again, Carter's smile had faded as he said, clearly for my benefit:

"I've been meaning to stop by, see how things were going, but between work and—"

I was only too happy to bail him out in this instance, though I had the feeling he was stalling. For what, I had no earthly idea.

"Don't torture yourself, Carter," I told him. "It's a little late for a guilt trip. Or have you forgotten that we're not married anymore?"

At least not to each other. Six months to the day after our divorce was finalized, he and the mistress tied the knot. Rumor had it she was pregnant at the time. Rarely did I take rumors seriously but, sure enough, the newlyweds did produce a baby girl shortly thereafter. I didn't want kids—at least not until I had done the career thing first. Carter didn't want to wait for me or my career.

To this day, we've never discussed whether that was the beginning of the end or just the beginning of his wandering eyes. Either way, it did little to erase my self-doubts, what might have been, or what had transpired since.

"Like it or not, a part of us will always be married, Skye," he declared, "at least in spirit."

"I don't think so," I said, sneering. "In spirit or otherwise. What's done is done."

"Maybe you're right." He rubbed his chin thoughtfully.

"Do you plan to tell me why the hell you're here?" I decided to be blunt, since he seemed willing to take his own sweet time. And in my business, time was money. He didn't have to know that it was only trickling in at the moment. "Or am I supposed to guess what reason my ex-husband might have for paying me an office visit?" I asked.

I honestly couldn't think of any reason for him to be there. Other than maybe to check out my office digs out of curiosity or get a glimpse of what he'd given up back in the day.

He chuckled. "Still as impatient as ever, I see."

I frowned. "Guess some things never change..."

We eyeballed each other for a moment or two of stubborn reflection. Finally, he asked coolly: "Mind if I sit?"

I indicated either of two brandy-colored cluster armchairs. He sat down and for some reason I was glad that my desk separated us.

Carter sat there staring blankly at me, as though in a trance. I stared back and waited with uneasiness at this unlikely get together.

I suddenly felt compelled to ask: "So how's your wife and...?"

At about the same time he was saying: "I'd like to hire you..."

My question could wait. If I hadn't known better, I thought I just heard Carter Delaney actually say he wanted to hire me! If the notion wasn't so absurd, I might have burst into laughter at that moment. Instead, I forced myself to say: "I'm listening—"

He shifted in the chair unsteadily. "I think Darlene is cheating on me..."

He was referring to wife number two. I'd always detested the idea that someone named Darlene took my place in his life. It was as if her name was *darling*—somehow making her more endearing than I ever was to him.

Apparently, a certain someone must have concurred.

I resisted the urge to say what goes around comes around. *Oh, what the hell,* I thought. *Let's hear what else he has to say.*

"Really?" I said. "Now isn't that a terrible thing to suspect—" I couldn't resist smiling when I said it, in spite of myself.

Carter peered at me beneath thick, dark brows, clearly annoyed and perhaps embarrassed. "I'm not looking for sympathy or amusement," he said.

I got serious again. "Could've fooled me." A well-timed sigh. "Exactly what is it you want from me?" I dared ask, almost afraid of his answer.

He recomposed himself, and after a moment or two said: "I'd like you to follow her around, see where she goes, who she talks to..."

I suddenly found myself laughing, almost hysterically, probably to keep from crying. When I finally stopped, I said: "You can't be serious!" But something told me he was. "You don't really expect me, of all people, to spy on the very bitch-slash-bimbo you left me for, do you?"

His brow furrowed. "Can you lay off the name calling? I was hoping this would be a bit more civilized—"

I was almost enjoying this. *Almost.* "Get real, Carter. You didn't come here for civility. That ended between us the day you decided I wasn't enough for you."

He gave me a quizzical look. "Remember who kicked out who? It's not like I'm asking you to do something illegal. Isn't this the sort of work a private investigator does? Or is my money not green enough for you?"

I leaned toward him; anger building up that I thought had been buried for good. "Don't patronize me! It's not about money. It's about respect! You've got a hell of a lot of nerve showing up in my office and asking me to snoop on your wife. I'm afraid I don't come *that* cheap—" I took satisfaction in making that abundantly clear to him.

He actually seemed shocked by my reaction, and maybe even hurt. "Dammit, Skye, I didn't come here to insult you. I came because I need your help." He batted those charming eyes at me emotionally. "You think it was easy for me to come to you with my, uh, problem? Hell no, it wasn't, but I did because I thought you'd understand."

"Sure, I understand all right," I told him. "You're feeling betrayed, humiliated, and agony over your suspicions. Am I right?" I was sounding like a still bitter ex-wife and found it to be oddly refreshing.

Carter sighed, sounding exhausted. "You're never going to give up the spiteful ex-wife routine, are you? What happened between us is history. Right or wrong, I can't do a damned thing about it now." He hoisted to his feet so fast he nearly toppled over. "I guess it was a mistake coming here. I thought you were professional enough to take on *any* case without letting your personal feelings get in the way. Obviously I was wrong." He turned his back to me and headed for the door.

Carter always had an incredible way of being able to manipulate people—especially me—into seeing things his way. Not this time! I was not about to be conned into feeling guilty or unprofessional because I refused to take a case that was far too personal and could only stir up feelings that I would just as soon forget, if that was possible.

I stood and asked what seemed like a legitimate question under the circumstances. "Why me? Surely you could have found some other private eye in Honolulu to follow your wife around—one who didn't happen to be your ex-wife."

He turned around and gave me a look that implied the answer should have been as obvious to me as it was to him.

"Do you even have to ask why?" He clenched his jaw. "The last thing I want or need is to make public to already jittery investors *my* private business...or the fact that I think my wife—the mother of my three-year-old little girl—is cheating on me. You're the only private detective I felt I could count on for a *discreet* investigation that wouldn't come back to haunt me." He lowered his head. "I guess in some ways it already has—"

I suppose I took it to heart that he trusted me enough to feel that I would handle such an investigation with the utmost discretion. But, all things considered, I wasn't sure that I could trust myself as much.

"I can recommend someone—" I offered as a goodwill gesture.

"Don't do me any favors," Carter muttered irritably as he turned toward the door, gave me a final heated glare, and vanished much the way he had appeared.

I slumped back down into my chair, angry that he had put us both in an unenviable position. In truth, things had not been all that great for us even before the other woman entered the picture. Carter's obsession with getting ahead at all costs and his insistence on meticulousness in every aspect of our lives clashed heavily with my somewhat lower aspirations and lack of perfect order in my life. And our differences over when children should become part of the picture hadn't helped matters either.

The final straw came when I learned of Carter's affair and the reality that he didn't really seem to give a damn that the cat was out of the bag. It was more like a big relief to him. And when confronted with the option of me or the other woman, he was unable or unwilling to make what I believed to be the intelligent choice.

I sought to hold my ground where it concerned my ex. It had been over between us for a long time. I owed him nothing but the painful memories of days gone by. Neither of us had even pretended to be friends once our relationship had officially ceased. (I even turned down a generous divorce settlement, preferring to leave the marriage with only what I brought to it. At the time, it seemed like only a clean break could allow me to regain my dignity.) What was the point when we had gone too far beyond friendship to go back?

As far as I was concerned, that overused cliché applied perfectly when I thought of Carter Delaney. He had made his own damned bed and now had to lay in it—but not with me!

* * *

The privilege of sharing bed space with me in the post Carter Delaney era currently belonged to Ridge Larsen. A homicide detective for the Honolulu Police Department, Ridge had transferred from the Portland Police Bureau in Oregon just after I had gone into early retirement. He was forty, divorced, and handsome in his own rough-hewn, square-jawed way with crafty blue eyes, a shaven bald head, a thick dark moustache, and six foot three inches of solid muscle.

Ridge and I had been dating for the past six months. I wouldn't exactly call what we had serious, insofar as my wanting him to put a ring on my finger. Being on my own for some time, I had become extremely possessive of my independence and privacy and was in no hurry to share my space with anyone on a permanent basis. Ridge seemed to understand and fully accept this, being of the same mind after a disastrous marriage, which probably accounted for half of why we seemed to work so well together.

The other half was that he tolerated my infrequent but not very pretty mood swings, knew when to leave me alone, was a great cook, and an even better lover.

An added fringe benefit of having Ridge around was that he came in handy during those not so rare occasions when I needed official snooping or able-bodied assistance in the every day and sometimes dangerous world of private investigations.

"I've never had the pleasure of meeting the current Mrs. Carter Delaney," hummed Ridge in bed, his strong arm holding me close to his taut body, "but from what I've heard, the former prosecutor's wife is hot stuff."

I jammed my elbow into his ribs and watched him wince. "I wouldn't know about that," I said tartly. "And now is *definitely* not the time for you to fantasize about my ex-husband's wife."

The afterglow of making love for the past hour was dimming quickly.

Ridge groaned. "I wouldn't dream of fantasizing about anyone but you these days." He planted a nice kiss on my lips. I enjoyed the taste of him. "I only go for pouty ones with long blonde hair and a smokin' hot body."

I soaked in the compliment and felt my annoyance beginning to wane.

Ridge sat up and asked nonchalantly: "So are you going to take the case?"

I looked at him dumbfounded while partially covering myself with a satin sheet, as if he hadn't already gotten a bird's eye view of every inch of me. "What case?"

"Delaney versus Delaney," he said cutely. "Sounds like pretty routine stuff to me." He grinned. "Let's face it, it took guts for him to come to you of all people for help."

I couldn't believe my ears. "Give me a break! Guts or not, why the hell would I want to find out for poor Carter if his wife is fooling around on him?"

"What are you afraid of?" Ridge asked.

"I'm not afraid of anything," I insisted. Except for maybe not being in full control of my own life at all times, I thought. But I knew it didn't work that way in the real world. We were all victims of circumstances for which we often had little to no control.

Ridge eyed me suspiciously. "You don't still have the hots for your ex, do you?"

I stared at his chest, then into his eyes, rolling mine. "What do you think?" He gave me that look all men have—the one that says they need to hear the words of reassurance. "No, I'm *not* still hung up on Carter Delaney," I said with an edge to my voice. "You of all people should know that, Ridge. I don't make a habit of sleeping with one person while fantasizing about another—" I hoped that would erase all doubts.

It didn't.

"Prove it," Ridge challenged me, "if only to yourself and maybe to Delaney. Take his case just as you would any other client. After all, it's just business, right?" He twisted his lips and added: "Who knows, you might even find it therapeutic."

I sneered at him. "Thanks for the advice, Dr. Phil."

He grinned crookedly. "Just wait till you get my bill. I don't come cheap."

I could vouch for that, as his expensive tastes included having a sometimes difficult girlfriend.

Reluctantly, I climbed out of his king-sized bed and gathered up my clothes that were scattered about the floor as if a tornado had passed through.

"What are you doing?" Ridge asked with a frown.

"I'm going home," I told him.

"Why? I hope it wasn't anything I said or didn't say."

I slid into my jeans and zipped them. "It wasn't. I have to feed my dog—"

He got out of bed. "Can't it wait—maybe for a couple of hours?"

"No," I said. "Ollie starts to get antsy when he goes practically all day without eating." I looked around, but couldn't find my cami, which seemed to work to Ridge's advantage.

He came up behind me and wrapped massive arms around my waist. "Are you sure you aren't just a little pissed at me?"

I wriggled out of his arms and gave him a sincere look. "There's nothing to be pissed about."

At least not with you, I told myself, reserving that for my ex at the moment.

Ridge looked relieved. "Good. I just don't want you to throw away Delaney's money for all the wrong reasons."

He was starting to press his luck and my patience.

I sighed and told him: "This may come as a surprise to you, but what's wrong for one person may be totally right for another—"

So maybe I was a little pissed at Ridge for seeming to represent the typical male in sizing up the situation. It was as if there was no room in the scheme of things for emotional baggage or ethical principles where it concerned making money. I wasn't sure I bought into that or if he really did.

I found my top, which had somehow ended up beneath Ridge's black denims. He gathered up his clothing.

"Any chance we can start the night over?" he asked lamely.

I couldn't help but smile at the thought. "Don't ask more of yourself than you're capable of delivering."

"Try me," he dared.

Though a repeat performance was pretty damn tempting, I grinned and said, "Isn't that what I just did?" while glancing at the wrinkled bed coverings that betrayed the hot and heavy activity that had taken place there tonight.

"At least let me drive you home," Ridge offered.

"My car will get me there just as quickly," I said, and kissed him lightly on the mouth. "You can walk me to the door, though."

He grumbled and hugged me as we walked in step through his ranch style home on Keeaumoku Street in the Makiki section of Honolulu that wasn't far from my office.

I could never be upset with Ridge Larsen for very long. His intentions were usually anything but self-serving. Yet I couldn't help but wonder if by pushing me into this case, he was more motivated by his own insecurities than any self-doubts I may have had.

My instincts told me that both were likely to be tested before this thing was over.

CHAPTER TWO

I left Ridge's house at eight o'clock, feeling a bit worn down for a day that had begun with Carter and ended with Ridge. At the moment, I was happy to be going to my own little piece of paradise, where I did my best thinking alone.

I had a one-year-old Subaru Forester that fit quite nicely into my current monthly payment budget. I drove to Waikiki, where I owned a nice house on a palm tree lined, dead-end street not far from the beach. I purchased the two-story plantation style home shortly after my divorce was finalized from an elderly couple who decided to move back to the mainland. It was my good fortune to be in the right place at the right time to get the property, which had been well maintained and reminded me of the home where I grew up on the island. My parents had been beach bums who island hopped before settling into Oahu and having me.

I could hear my dog barking when I pulled into the driveway. Ollie was a five-year-old German Shepherd, named after my late uncle who was as mean as a junkyard dog and ornery as ever. In fact, more often than not, Ollie was just the opposite—sweet and gentle as a lamb, as long as he was not provoked.

Opening the front door was all he needed to make me eat my thoughts, as Ollie literally attacked me. Okay, so it was just his way of playing and asking me "Where the hell have you been all day?" Or maybe "I'm hungry as a dog. What's for supper?"

We ended up wrestling for a few minutes before I turned on the ceiling fan in the living room, then fed Ollie his favorite dog food. He wanted more, but I wasn't about to let him get fat on me. That wouldn't help either of us.

After freshening up and changing into a sleeveless shirt and denim shorts, I allowed my sore feet some freedom from footwear, padding barefoot across the hardwood floor and into the kitchen. I made myself a salad and ate it with two slices of wheat bread and a glass of red wine. Ollie loved to hang out on the kitchen's cool ceramic tiles more than anywhere else in the house.

However, the kitchen floor still took second place to the backyard. When he began to grow restless, I got the picture, letting him out of the house to run around in our nice sized, fenced in yard. I joined Ollie a few minutes later and tossed a Frisbee around for him to chase, making sure he stayed clear of my vegetable garden.

Back inside, I watered the flamingo flowers, vanda orchids, and heart leaf philodendron I kept throughout the house, which helped give the place a Hawaiian botanical garden look.

By the time I was ready to call it a night, I had tucked Ollie in his basement hideaway, read a couple of chapters of a John Lescroart novel, and watched the news.

Before drifting off to dreamland, I had more or less decided that, for better or worse, I would take on the task of spying on the current wife of Carter Delaney. Business was business, I convinced myself, even if it happened to involve my ex-husband and his ex-mistress. I still hadn't decided if I wanted his suspicions to prove false or right on the money.

Only time would tell...

# # #

Bonus Excerpt of R. Barri Flowers' bestselling psychological
thriller

KILLER IN THE WOODS

(available in eBook and audio book in Audible, Amazon, and
iBookstore)

CHAPTER ONE

He hadn't planned to kill this one. But then she caught his
eye. Or more like his ear. A man would have to be deaf not
to have overheard the pretty, young Latina yapping away on
her cell phone in the booth across from his like she owned
the place.

"Can you believe I have to work tonight?" She batted
obvious fake eyelashes, as if dumbstruck at the notion. "I'm
gonna be there all by my lonesome just staring at the four
walls, girl. What a drag! Oh well, if I get too bored, I'll just
call Andres and he can keep me company...or at least his
sexy voice will."

He pretended to be oblivious to her conversation while
eating. Out of his periphery, he watched as she headed for
the cashier.

He waited a bit before following.

After paying for his meal in cash, he stepped outside and
breathed in the distinct smell of late summer in the Pacific

Northwest. It was just past seven-thirty and the sun was beginning to set for the day, but it wouldn't get dark for a while.

He spotted the object of his attention just as she was about to get into her car. Without drawing attention to himself, he moseyed over to his vehicle and followed her from a safe distance.

The press had dubbed him "The Woods Strangler." He would've preferred "The Man With A Serious Axe To Grind," or better yet, "A Cold, Calculating Killer!"

Grinning, he looked in the rearview mirror at his dark eyes staring back, before seeing the woman pull into an office building's parking lot. For a moment, he considered it might be too dangerous to go after this one. He hated the thought of allowing his inner demons to rise above common sense and survival instincts. But the adrenalin rush, dark impulses, temptation, and opportunistic nature of the prey attracting the predator got the better of him.

He caught the door to the building just before it closed, but too late to catch the elevator—and her. He glanced about inconspicuously, seeing no one and trying not to be seen. Looking up at the numbers, he saw that the elevator had stopped on the third floor. Scanning the small entryway, he spotted the stairwell and headed toward it.

* * *

Sophia Pesquera opened up the Blossom Dating Service and prepared for her routine of answering the phone, working the computer, and greeting those who showed up at their door for assistance in the competitive dating arena. She and a girlfriend had started the business a year ago, eager to cater to the upscale lonely, desperate, and just plain unlucky men and women in Bluffs Bay where it concerned matters of the heart. It had turned out to be a smart move as single, attractive, and highly motivated people were only too happy to use their agency to try to find love.

This included Andres Hernandez, an advertising executive, who was incredibly good looking though lacking somewhat in his social skills. Sophia had tried to set him up with someone else, but his attention was solely on her. So what could a woman do who had struck out herself in the love department on more than one occasion?

She went with the flow. Now Andres was her man and she couldn't be happier about it.

Sophia sat at her desk and turned on the computer. She decided she couldn't wait a moment longer to talk to Andres.

"Hey, baby, it's me," she said, immediately perking up at the sound of his voice.

* * *

He passed by several businesses, instinctively dismissing them. Then he came to something called the Blossom Dating Service. Though slightly turned blinds obscured his vision, he saw enough to know he had come to the right place.

He looked around for any unwanted company. Seeing no one, he took a deep breath and, clutching the doorknob with a handkerchief, twisted till it opened. He entered a small office with two desks. Only one was occupied.

She was on the phone, probably talking to Andres. The nameplate on her desk read: Sophia Pesquera. When she looked up at him, she seemed more irritated that he had apparently interrupted her conversation than afraid. There was no indication that she recognized him from the diner.

Good. He wanted to keep things simple.

"Call me back in ten...no, make it fifteen," she said before hanging up.

Giving him her full attention, Sophia forced a smile and asked, "How can I help you?"

He thought about it for a moment or two, before removing the silk scarf from his pocket. Flexing it, he responded, "The better question is: how can I help you? I don't think you want to know—"

When Sophia realized that he wasn't there to find a date, she impulsively sprang out of her chair.

He quickly came up behind her before she could react, and draped the scarf around her neck, tightening it in a viselike grip. He enjoyed the feel of her struggling to break free.

But it was not to be.

A vein bulged in Sophia's temple as she gasped desperately for air, her arms flailing. All she could think of was that Andres would never get to know what might have been between them. If only some crazy man had not chosen her to die...

He literally lifted Sophia up off her feet, which swung helplessly in the air. Her body grew tense and shook wildly, before turning pliable. Her erratic breathing stopped, and he knew it was over.

For this one anyway...

CHAPTER TWO

"There's no evidence the victims knew each other or the killer," said Homicide Detective Dennis Cramer of the Bluffs Bay Police Department. "All the killings appear to have taken place in The Woods and each time the victim was alone when attacked. The latest victim was attacked in her office. The victims were not sexually assaulted. Given the seemingly random nature of the killings, with the perpetrator picking targets as they become available, the news is not good for law enforcement or the residents of The Woods—"

Selene Herrera was unnerved by the recent murders. When she and her husband Quinn moved there two months ago, they thought it was a safe, comfortable environment—each having previously experienced violence in their lives.

But that all changed when the first killing occurred not long after they had purchased their home in The Woods, an affluent community within Bluffs Bay. The relaxed, peaceful atmosphere had been shattered over the summer with the strangulation murders of several local women.

Selene first heard about the latest victim on the news last night. She had been found lying face down in her office. Like the four previous victims, she had been strangled while apparently putting up little resistance.

Fearing she might become a potential target of this serial killer, Selene had taken it upon herself to bring the community together to try to fight the monster who had left them all on edge.

A sense of outrage and panic threatened to boil over inside The Woods Community Center on this warm Saturday afternoon. While there was heated debate over whether the killer lived amongst them or was a stranger who took advantage of easy entry into the gateless subdivision, most residents agreed that the problem was too serious to ignore or leave to the authorities to resolve alone.

Detective Cramer looked pained as he said, "We've gotten dozens of calls with descriptions and other information on possible suspects. We're evaluating all leads and take each one seriously. I ask for your patience while we conduct our investigation. In the meantime, the best thing any of you can do right now is use common sense to protect yourself. Stay off the streets at night, keep doors and windows locked, and your eyes and ears open for anything or anyone suspicious; and women should not be alone, if at all possible..."

He was interrupted by a boisterous voice. "How can you expect us to be patient?"

Selene watched as Marvin Bonet stood up two chairs over from her.

"Someone is killing our women and you don't seem to be doing a damn thing about it!" Marvin pointed an accusing finger at the detective.

Dennis's head snapped back as if he had run into a wall. "Look, I understand your irritation," he said. "But we're not the enemy here. The department is working round the clock to stop this killer before he strikes again."

"Well that's not good enough," Marvin persisted. "I think every man and woman here should arm themselves to protect their families."

"I knew he was going to embarrass me," Elisa Bonet whispered in Selene's ear, referring to her husband. "Marvin just had to make a complete fool of himself—and me by association."

"He's only expressing what a lot of people feel. We're all frustrated," Selene whispered back. She put a reassuring arm around her friend's shoulders before refocusing on the detective.

"That's probably the worst thing to do, under these circumstances," Dennis cautioned. "An inexperienced person with a loaded gun is only asking for trouble."

Selene watched and listened as the two men went back and forth; each holding his own, before Marvin wisely relented and sat down.

Dennis said a few parting words and then nodded at Selene. That was her cue to take the podium. She rose, standing directly in front of Quinn, who flashed an encouraging smile. They had been married for a little more than two months now and it was the second marriage for both.

Selene's first marriage had lasted five years. She had been a victim of domestic violence and suffered through the classic battered women's syndrome. Her ex-husband's abusive behavior had been blamed on a lifelong drinking problem; then the stress of making bad business decisions. Selene had attributed the battering to her being too stubborn for her own good and not jumping whenever he told her to, causing him to lash out in anger.

Soon it became apparent to Selene that she wasn't the cause of the abuse—he was. He had long harbored resentment towards headstrong women who reminded him of his domineering mother, who had been abusive towards him. When that was compounded with his drinking and an inferiority complex, it gave her ex more than enough excuses to hit Selene as often as he pleased.

After one serious beating that landed her in the hospital with a concussion and broken ribs, Selene had had enough. She finally got the courage to leave the man she'd once loved while she was still able to stand on her own two feet.

Selene's prayers for being able to pick up the pieces of her shattered life were answered twofold. One was using her experience to help other abused women when she became the director of a local battered women's shelter.

The other was when she met Quinn Herrera eight months ago. He'd immediately impressed her as a man of principle and conviction, along with being handsome and charming.

They hit it off right away. Quinn was a bestselling author of mystery novels and nonfiction books on the Pacific Northwest. A year earlier, he had lost his wife tragically in a drive-by shooting that was a case of mistaken identity.

Selene believed adversity had made her and Quinn that much stronger and was the propelling force behind their meeting, falling in love, and getting married. They had both been given a second chance at love and had taken it for all it was worth.

She smiled at Quinn, trying not to show how nervous she was.

He winked and patted her hand lightly. "You'll do just fine."

Taking him at his word, Selene strode to the podium.

Selene stood before her friends and neighbors. She had never been particularly comfortable as a public speaker. But with the practice of speaking to women's groups in the fight against domestic violence, and Quinn's encouragement, she had become more at ease in the role of speaker. And, in light of the recent wave of murders to hit The Woods, she was determined to do her part to fight a common enemy.

Selene sucked in a deep breath. "Thank you all for coming, especially on such short notice. It's a tough way to get to know each other better, but circumstances haven't left us much choice. Everyone here has a responsibility to band together when someone—especially a killer—threatens the safety of our families..."

# # #

Bonus Excerpt of R. Barri Flowers' bestselling legal thriller

STATE'S EVIDENCE
A BEVERLY MENDOZA LEGAL THRILLER
(available in eBook and audio book in Audible, Amazon, and
iBookstore)

PROLOGUE

She was a real piece of ass...

He could feel his arousal through tight jeans. He had
been watching her, following her, getting to know her every
move till it was time to do what had to be done.

He could have taken her any time he wanted, crushing
her pretty skull between his strong, calloused hands, as easily
as one might flatten a piece of dough. But it was more fun
and stimulating to bide his time like a shark might before
going after a helpless fish. Or even a human. He knew
exactly where she was every minute of the day.

And night.

Why rush a good thing?

He considered killing a person a work of art. Like the
Mona Lisa. It required skill, finesse, courage, determination,
and a vision.

He had been born with these talents thirty-two years ago in East L.A.'s Latino community. Surviving the mean streets there had required every bit of his artistic skills, and then some. With his mama a whore and his daddy a wife-abusing heroin addict, he had literally been left to fend for himself as early as he could remember.

Joining a gang had allowed him to sharpen his skills. He imagined he had taken out or seriously injured maybe a dozen or more rival gang members by the time he was fifteen. He considered it all in a day's work. It was either them or him. Which was a real no-brainer.

But he knew he was going nowhere fast in L.A.'s war zone. Between the rival Latino gangs and the black gang bangers fighting for territory, respect, or just for the hell of it, he saw no future there. Sooner or later he figured a bullet or blade would have his name written on it in blood—unless he quit while he was ahead.

Which was precisely why he had given up the hood and gang life and fled the city before he turned eighteen. He ended up in Northern California in a town called Eagles Landing. By comparison to the urban jungle he'd left behind, it was fairly laid back and boring as hell.

Still, he didn't miss his homeboys one bit. No damned way!

He'd hooked up with distant relatives and was cool with a few dudes in Eagles Landing.

But even that was fleeting. It didn't take long for him to realize he operated much better on his own, apart from keeping a roof over his head in living with a broad. This way he got to keep all the profits and pleasures from doing what he did best—killing people.

It was a rush like no other. Even better than getting off inside a bitch. Or the almost orgasmic feel of cocaine going into his veins. He killed for hire or just plain old desire. It made no difference to him. What counted most was that once he had targeted someone for death, it was just a matter of when, where, how, and sometimes how much.

He contemplated those very things as he studied the nice looking broad through the window of her fancy home. She was maybe thirty, slim, with a big ass and even bigger breasts. Her yellow hair was permed with fluffy curls and she had full red lips. He imagined kissing that mouth, then sticking his tongue inside. Or better yet, having that mouth go down on him and do its thing.

Before he gave her a taste of death.

She was sitting at the dining room table with her husband. He was a few years older than her, dark haired, and seemingly uncomfortable in her presence, as though he didn't belong.

He looked away from the man back to his wife, watching a while longer, as he devised his strategy for her demise. A rush of adrenalin poured through him at the prospect, knowing the time was getting near to put the plan into action.

But first he wanted to allow her a bit more false sense of security. It was always that much more exhilarating when his victim realized that the perfect little world she or he had created was about to come crashing down around them and there wasn't a damned thing that could be done to prevent it.

Except maybe hope you got run over by a bus first. Or dropped dead of a heart attack, sparing yourself from meeting up with him.

Short of that, the person was his for the taking. And he fully intended to do just that.

Only a matter of time.

Yes, let her feel secure in her comfortable house. With that husband of hers there to protect her. Wouldn't do her one bit of good.

She would never live to see the light of day.

CHAPTER ONE

The jury foreman looked tense as she responded to the judge's terse question, "Have you reached a verdict?"

The juror, an attractive Jordanian professor and mother of five, risked a furtive peek at the other jurors, as if for final confirmation. Then she raised her big brown eyes to the bench. "Yes, we have, Your Honor—"

Judge Sheldon Crawford was in his mid-fifties, but looked younger with a cappuccino-toned face that was without wrinkles save for a barely perceptible crease stretching across his forehead. He had short salt and pepper hair, and deep gray eyes that rarely seemed to blink. Focusing them on the juror, he instructed her to hand the verdict to the bailiff.

Judge Crawford had a reputation as a tough judge, routinely doling out the stiffest penalties the law would allow. Needless to say, prosecutors and their constituents loved him and the justice rendered. Whereas, defense attorneys and their clients feared coming before the judge, often doing all they could to avoid his court, including plea bargaining at virtually every opportunity.

Beverly Mendoza, co-counsel for the State, fidgeted in her seat. It was so quiet you could hear a pin drop. Her intense green eyes studied the faces of the jurors, trying to get a hint as to what direction they had taken. Admittedly she hadn't a clue and was too smart to make any presumptions.

The case involved a woman accused of murdering her lover by pushing him off a 320-foot cliff. Her defense was that they were just fooling around—*love play*, she had called it—when he accidentally fell to his death. The fact that she didn't report him missing for two weeks seemed incidental. As did his million dollar life insurance policy, which had only recently named her as the beneficiary.

Beverly gazed at the thirty-year-old defendant who sat there cool, calm, collected, and incredibly confident.

Does she know something I don't?

Could this jury have possibly let her off the hook?

Meaning the prosecution would have failed to prove its case. *And I'd have a loss on my record that would be hard to swallow and harder to justify.*

She snapped her head back, causing her long, straight brunette hair to bounce against the gray jacket of her Anne Klein linen suit. Her eyes landed on her co-counsel, Deputy District Attorney Grant Nunez. His Afro-Latino profile was classic with chiseled, caramel colored features and a round head that was shaven bald. He wore a tailored dark brown suit that fit well on his muscular, tall frame. Grant was forty—eight years older than her—and in line for a judgeship by all indications. Losing this case would not help his chances.

Nor would it bode well for Beverly's career. Sensationalized cases would always be remembered for the winners and losers, no matter how many other battles were fought and won, especially when lawyers were always looking ahead in their careers. She had aspirations of being a district attorney someday. Or maybe even a judge.

Right now, assistant district attorney for Wilameta County would have to suffice.

Sensing her stare, Grant swiveled his head, slanting his cool sable eyes at her. If he was worried, he didn't show it. Instead, he gave Beverly a devilish smile that she knew was less about the proceedings than it was about them. They had been dating for four months now, though it had only become sexual in the last four weeks. Both had survived bad previous relationships and, once they had overcome their fears of failure and the unknown, had succumbed to mutual desires that left Beverly shamelessly wanting him every chance she got.

But getting her twelve-year-old son to approve of Grant had proven to be a far more formidable task. Jaime was very protective of her and did not want to see his mother get hurt—again. To him, Grant was someone who threatened the life Jaime had known for most of his young life, where it had pretty much been just the two of them.

Perhaps even more difficult for Beverly to deal with was losing her mother five years ago to breast cancer and now watching her father wasting away with Alzheimer's disease. It left him but a shell of his former and proud self as a Latino who was used to being a macho man in command of his life and times. Sometimes she wished it would be over with for him so her father wouldn't suffer anymore; other times Beverly wanted him to hang on for as long as he possibly could. After all, having part of a father and grandfather to her son was preferable to none at all.

Wasn't it?

Beverly's mind shifted back to the attention Grant was giving her, as if they were the only ones in the courtroom. She willed herself to avert his lascivious gaze that had managed to cause her temperature to rise, and focus on the important matter at hand. Judge Crawford read the verdict to himself. He passed the slip back to the bailiff, giving no indication by his dignified facial expression as to what it said.

Beverly felt butterflies in her stomach as she usually did whenever a case was about to be decided. It represented weeks or months of hard work and in an instant would culminate for all parties concerned. Later there would be the penalty phase. And then, in all likelihood, appeals, and more decisions to come.

But for the moment it didn't get any more exciting and tension filled than this.

Once the bailiff had returned the verdict to the jury foreman, the judge faced the defense table and stated levelly, "Will the defendant please rise—"

She obeyed him, springing to her feet and running thin fingers through short crimson hair before taking a breath and awaiting the judge's words that would change her life for the better or worse. Standing alongside her was her attorney, Cassandra Fielding, a forty-something, ex-prosecutor, who had put up a strong, sympathetic defense. No doubt she had an eye on a hefty percentage of the insurance payments, mused Beverly. Provided they ever came.

Judge Crawford nodded at the jury foreman. "You may read the verdict."

The woman put on her glasses, almost for effect, took a deep sigh, and looked down at her trembling hands. "We, the jury, find the defendant, Suzanne Landon, to be guilty of murder in the first degree—"

The courtroom erupted in cheers from the family of the victim. Beverly let out a sigh of relief and saw victory spread across Grant's face in a big grin. The two hugged as co-counsel might be expected, formally and professionally. There would be time later for a much more private celebration.

The newly convicted murderess was led away in handcuffs, tears of disbelief or disappointment flowing down her reddened cheeks. Before leaving the courtroom, she shot Beverly a contemptuous gaze, which the prosecutor dismissed for all it was worth.

Sticks and stones may break my bones, but hateful glares won't hurt me.

Justice was not always blind. Not today anyway.

* * *

"We did it!" Grant Nunez declared magnanimously. He had Beverly cornered in his office, right between two file cabinets. The door was locked and might just as well have had a DO NOT DISTURB sign on it. He certainly had no intentions of being interrupted till they were done.

At six-three, he hovered over Beverly by almost seven inches. But that didn't detract from the presence she had as a woman. With her Selma Hayek looks and a hot, taut body all her own, it was all Grant could do not to want to be with Beverly 24/7.

He'd settle for twenty-four minutes and seven ways to make love to this woman who turned him on like no other with both her mind and sexuality, inside and out of the courtroom.

"Never thought for a minute we wouldn't," Beverly declared between kisses.

"You're not a very good liar." Grant put his hands on her firm breasts through her silk blouse, causing Beverly's nipples to tingle.

"So sue me," she murmured, "but only after you make me come."

"Whatever you say, Counselor." He put his tongue in her mouth. "Never let it be said that I don't believe in the spirit of cooperation."

"Maybe that's why we make such a great team."

"Maybe."

Beverly tasted spearmint from his tongue, and gave him hers to play with. She put a hand to his pants, feeling the hardness of Grant's erection begging to be released. She was only too happy to oblige, unzipping him, even as his hand went under her skirt and began to caress between her legs. She pulled him out and held firmly as if her own, stimulating the shaft.

"Umm..." She heard the sound utter between their mouths, unsure who it had come from.

Her back stiffened when Grant slipped fingers inside her panties and then into her. She spread her legs while leaning against a file cabinet, urging him on and giving back as much in touching his penis. Beverly bit her lip as he began to stimulate her, causing her to nearly scream with pleasure.

Instead, mindful they were somewhere where noise could be easily heard, she managed barely more than a whimper. While still holding his throbbing erection, Beverly looked Grant ravenously in the eye. "Condom?"

He removed one from his pocket and placed it in her palm, content to see her take the lead. She quickly removed the foil and slid the latex over him and climbed atop Grant's sturdy hips, wrapping her arms around his neck.

Beverly inserted him inside her. "Make love to me," she demanded in a desperate voice, the sense of urgency spreading across her body like a bolt of lightning.

"It would be my pleasure, baby," he husked, and held onto her slender waist while plunging himself deep into her as she absorbed the thrusts while slamming herself back against him with equal zest.

Her orgasm came quickly and a second one shortly thereafter at about the same time that Grant climaxed with a rush of breath and a violent shudder. Both were breathing heavily, and Beverly could feel Grant's heartbeat pounding as they clung to one another till the experience had come to a mouths smacking, bodies perspiring, satisfying conclusion.

"We need to win as a team more often," Grant said contentedly, giving Beverly another long kiss.

She kissed him back and climbed off him. "That may not be possible," she teased, "if you're a judge."

"True," he said, removing the condom and zipping his pants. "But look at the bright side, baby. When and if that day ever comes, just imagine what fun you and I could have in the judge's chambers."

Beverly pushed him playfully. "You're insatiable!" She put her clothes back into place; then brushed her hair.

He laughed. "And you're not?"

She blushed. "Maybe it's the effect you have on me, darling, that makes me crave your body."

He chuckled again. "I have been known to have that effect on women."

"Oh, really?" Beverly met his eyes with a touch of jealousy. As far as she knew they were exclusive. If they weren't on the same page there, she wanted to find out before this went any further.

Grant sensed that he'd used the wrong choice of words and quickly sought to rectify that. The last thing he wanted was to ruin this relationship, something he'd managed to do too easily in the past. Only none of the previous women in his life could hold a candle to Beverly Mendoza and he wouldn't have it any other way.

"What's important is that this is the first time it's really meant something to me," he said in earnest. "I don't take that lightly, Bev, and I'm definitely not looking at anyone else."

She smiled, feeling a sense of relief and maybe a little left over insecurity. "But you will tell me if you change your mind."

"I won't change my mind," he promised. *Not as long as there's the possibility that we can really go somewhere with this.*

"Neither will I," she added. She was enjoying his company more than she had any man's company in some time. She was in no hurry to ruin a good thing.

Grant straightened his tie. "So how about if I take you out to dinner for a victory celebration? Sex always leaves me famished."

"Can't," Beverly said apologetically, putting fresh lipstick on after he had taken it all off. "I promised Jaime pizza tonight." She couldn't help but think that though only twelve, her son sometimes seemed like he was twenty-five with his maturity and rapidly growing body.

Grant grinned wistfully. "Did I tell you that I love pizza?" *And would love to get to know your son better, if you'll let me.*

Beverly squirmed guiltily, knowing he wanted more than what they had. And so did she. But right now her son was still her top priority. As were his feelings on the subject.

"Jaime just needs a little time adjusting to someone else in my life," she offered contritely.

Grant looked like a wounded puppy. "How much time does he need—the rest of *your* life?"

Beverly touched her nose thoughtfully. "Not much longer, Grant," she hoped. "It's been just the two of us for so long, he's trying to come to terms with the fact that someone else is now in my life who's very important to me."

Beverly realized that along with wanting to protect Jaime, she was also trying to protect herself, from being hurt and abandoned, as they had been by his father.

Grant furrowed his brow while trying to be understanding. "Seems to me it's time you let someone else take down that wall you've built around the boy."

"Please be patient, Grant," Beverly implored softly, not wanting to spoil what just happened by applying too much pressure either way. "I just want what's best for everyone—you included." She kissed him on the mouth. "Call me."

Even as she said that, Beverly knew that it sounded like she was afraid of commitment. Was she? Not that Grant had ever suggested he wanted a commitment in so many words. Or maybe she was confused over the terms *commitment* and *exclusivity*. Didn't they mean the same thing in a relationship? Like her, Grant had been married once before. He had no children and didn't seem entirely comfortable at the prospect of ever marrying again. But she was pretty sure he cared for her, beyond their sexual compatibility.

Beverly wondered if that was that enough to constitute a real and trusting relationship at the end of the day—a relationship that included her son as an intricate part of the team.

Would it ever be enough?

* * *

Grant showed Beverly out the door, waved good-bye, and settled back into his office musingly. She was the first woman he'd been with who gave as much as she took—both sexually and as a prosecutor. He was damned glad to have her on his side in both departments.

Should he be offered a judgeship, as expected, it would be all the more reason for them to mesh, without the competitive thing as trial lawyers that brought them together and could potentially tear them apart.

Grant's focus shifted to other issues on his mind. He picked up the phone and buzzed his secretary.

"Get the D.A. on the line," he ordered.

A moment later, the heavy voice said, "Yeah, Grant, what's up?"

He sighed and glanced out the window musingly. "We need to talk—"

# # #

Bonus Excerpt of R. Barri Flowers' bestselling hard-boiled thriller

DEAD IN THE ROSE CITY
A DEAN DRAKE MYSTERY
(available in print, eBook and audio book in Audible, Amazon, and iBookstore)

CHAPTER ONE

I'd just stepped out of the restaurant, the greasy food still settling in my stomach, wondering if I was ever going to get out of the Rose City, when I saw her approaching with a tall man. I did a double take, barely believing my eyes, but trusting the sudden racing of my heart.

It was *her*—Vanessa King. Still as gorgeous as ever. How many years had it been? Ten? Eleven? Too many to even want to think about. Yet that was all I could do at the moment, especially when she was the best thing that ever happened to me. And I'd thrown it all away for reasons I couldn't explain.

If only I could turn back the hands of time, things might have turned out differently. Me, Vanessa, and all the joy we could bring to each other.

The day we met years ago was forever ingrained in my mind for more reasons than one...

* * *

The dictionary defines fate as "unfortunate destiny." Once upon a time, I didn't buy into forecasts of doom and gloom, much less associate it with my life as a private eye and even more private individual. But then I took on two seemingly unrelated cases and one bizarre thing seemed to lead to the next and even I began to wonder if I was somehow tempting fate.

Before I begin my fateful tale, let me introduce myself. The name is Dean Jeremy Drake, or D.J. for those close enough to be called friends or kin. Otherwise it's simply Drake. Some call me a pain in the ass. Others see me as a half-breed with an attitude. I prefer to think of myself as a forty-one-year-old, six-five, ex-cop turned private investigator who happens to be the product of an interracial affair.

My parents, who have both since gone to heaven, couldn't have been more different. My father was Jamaican black, mother Italian white. But for one steamy night they found some common interests and ended up with me for their trouble.

I admit I can be a pain in the ass with an attitude, or a gentle giant with a perpetual smile on my square-jawed face, depending on which side of the bed I wake up on. But that's another story. Let's concentrate on this one for now.

It was raining like the second coming of Noah's Ark on that day at the tail end of July. I was sitting in my Portland, Oregon office, my feet on the desk as if they belonged there. The Seattle Mariners were on the tube playing the Oakland A's in sunny California. With three innings to go, the Mariners were getting a major league ass whipping, 11-0. To add insult to injury, there was a rumor that the players were planning to go on strike next month.

Who the hell needed them anyway? I'd had just about all I could take from greedy players, and owners who never seemed to tire of bleeding the fans dry. For me, this was merely a tune-up for the mother of all sports—football. The exhibition season was due to start next month in what might finally be a winning season for the Seahawks, my adopted team and a three hour drive away on a good day with light traffic.

The Mariners had finally gotten on the scoreboard with a solo shot when I heard one knock on my door and watched it open before I could even say come in.

A tall, chunky, white man entered wearing a wrinkled and dripping wet gray suit. He had a half open umbrella in one hand that looked as if he had forgotten to use it, a leather briefcase in the other. "Nasty out there," he muttered, and let out a repulsive sneeze.

"Tell me about it," I groaned. You didn't live in a city like Portland if you expected sunny, dry weather year round, though a soaker like this was pretty rare in late July. I was still partly distracted by the game, when I asked routinely: "How can I help you?"

That's when he walked up to me, stuck an I.D. in my face, and said: "Frank Sherman, Deputy District Attorney for Multnomah County—"

Only then did it dawn on me that I knew the man. Or at least I used to. Like me, Sherman was an ex-cop in his early forties. He had made that relatively rare jump from law enforcement to criminal law, while I had chosen private investigation work as my answer to justice for all. The closest I'd come to law school was the B.A. I'd earned in Criminal Justice from Portland State University. This hardly made me in awe of the man before me. He had gone his way and I had gone mine. Right now, it looked as if our ways had converged.

"Narcotics, right?" I asked, taking my feet off the desk.

He nodded proudly, and ran a hand through wet, greasy dark blonde hair. "And you were homicide?"

"Seems like two lifetimes ago," I exaggerated. In fact, it had been six years since I turned in my badge and the stress and strain that went with it for a lesser, more independent kind of misery. That Sherman could identify my department meant he had done his homework or my reputation preceded itself. I chose to believe the latter.

"At least we made it out on our own two feet." Sherman looked down on me with big blue eyes and a twisted smile. He was heavier than I remembered him, by maybe fifteen pounds. No, make that twenty. I turned off the TV to give him my undivided and curious attention. I did maybe a quarter of my work for the D.A.'s office, but I almost always went to them rather than the other way around.

"So is this a social call?" I asked, but seriously doubted. "Or have those unpaid traffic tickets finally caught up with me?"

He lost the twisted smile, and said directly: "I'd like to hire you, Drake—on behalf of the State. Mind if I sit?"

I indicated the folding chair nearest to him—a flea market pickup that was a bargain. "I'm listening..."

Sherman laid the briefcase on the desk, opened it, and removed a folder. "It's the dossier on Jessie *The Worm* Wylson," he explained, handing it to me. "He's wanted in connection with the sale and distribution of narcotics and methamphetamines. This bastard is personally responsible for most of the drugs poisoning our city and turning our kids into junkies!"

I looked at the face of a bald, dark-skinned black man on the dossier. It said he was thirty-five, six feet tall, and one hundred and seventy-five pounds. Wylson was a resident of Portland and had been in and out of jail most of his life for an assortment of drug and theft charges.

Even if I believed he was the scum of the earth, I had trouble buying that this one dude was behind most of the drugs floating about the city. In my book, that distinction belonged to the Columbia drug cartels and the rich Americans who made getting drugs into this country as easy as addicts getting crack on the inner city streets.

"Why do they call him The Worm?" I had to ask.

Sherman shrugged. "Heard someone gave him that name while he was in the joint, probably because he always seems able to worm his way out of trouble." He scowled. "Not this time."

There was something sinister about Sherman's, "Not this time." I took another look at Jessie The Worm Wylson, before shifting my gray-brown eyes to the man on the other side of the desk. "If I find him—which I assume you'd like me to do—what makes you think he won't manage to slip away again?"

Sherman shifted somewhat uncomfortably. "It's a chance we're more than willing to take," he said evenly, "provided you can locate his ass. If I have my way, once he's in custody, Wylson will be in a cheap, wooden box the next time he gets out." He sneezed then wiped his nose with a dirty handkerchief. "So what do you say, Drake, will you take the case?"

I glanced once more at the dossier and the man called The Worm. It seemed like a simple enough investigation. But I knew that no investigation ever turned out to be that simple, especially when it involved the district attorney's office. In fact, finding anyone on the streets of Portland could sometimes be like searching for a hypodermic needle in an urban jungle.

For some reason, I found myself hesitating in jumping all over this case. Like most P.I.'s, I liked to go with my instincts. And, from the beginning, there was definitely something about the case that rubbed me the wrong way. Maybe it was the surreptitious meeting with a member of the D.A.'s office outside the D.A.'s office. Or perhaps it was uneasiness in taking on an investigation that I presumed was still active with the Portland Police Department. Experience told me that they didn't take too kindly to meddlesome private eyes muscling in on their territory.

Sherman seemed to be reading my mind. "If you're wondering why you instead of one of our regular investigators, the answer is simple. I want this asshole off the street! I was told that you do things your own way, and not always within the guidelines you learned as a cop. We both know that sometimes the guidelines can be a bitch when it comes to justice for all." He sucked in a deep breath. "I'm willing—unofficially—to do whatever it takes to find Jessie Wylson. Of course, the D.A.'s office will cover all of your regular fees and expenses."

The private investigation business had been fairly good to me by the standards of most trying to make a living as dicks for hire. I managed to stay one step ahead of my debts and have some money left over for recreation. But business had been lean of late and the bills never went on holiday. I could hardly afford to pass up a cash-paying reliable client, assuming that at least a minimal standard of acceptability was met. This one seemed to qualify, though barely.

"Can I keep this?" I held up the dossier, which was my way of saying I was on board.

Sherman smiled. "I was counting on it." He stood and pulled a card from his pocket, handing it to me. "Keep me informed, Drake. If and when you find him, I want to be there to personally slap the cuffs on."

I wanted to remind Sherman he wasn't a cop anymore. But I gave him the benefit of the doubt that old habits died hard, and said: "I'll be in touch."

Once the Deputy D.A. left me all by my lonesome, I turned the TV back on. Mercifully for the Mariners, the game was over. Final score: A's 14, Losers 3.

* * *

The sun had begun to peek through the clouds by the time I left my downtown office which was not far from the Riverplace Marina. It was on the third floor of a building that seemed to house everything from a psychic hotline office to a Jenny Craig weight loss center. I wasn't complaining though. The rent was affordable and most of the tenants tended to mind their own business.

I was wearing a jogging suit that fit well on my six-foot-five body and my Nike running shoes. People asked me all the time if I ever played basketball. I usually responded truthfully with, "I was lousy at basketball, but give me a baseball bat and I can hit the ball ten miles." That almost always left them speechless.

I liked to think that I was in pretty good physical condition for the forty and over crowd. Jogging was my forte, so to speak, these days. It was a carryover from my days on the force. Before they brought in all the high tech exercise equipment to keep everyone lean and mean.

I half-jogged, half-walked the two miles on the street parallel to the Willamette River, till I reached my apartment building. It was not far from the Hawthorne Bridge—one of several bridges that connected the city that was separated by the river. Since Portland was so beautiful and pedestrian friendly, I favored being on foot to driving or light rail.

Home for me was an old brownstone on Burnside Street. It was old, but comfortable. Most of the residents fit the same profile: single, divorced, or widowed *and* available, over thirty-five, and professional in some capacity.

Just as I was entering the building, exiting was another tenant who I seemed to pass by every other day lately. I didn't know her name or anything about her, but I liked what I saw. She bore a strong resemblance to Halle Berry, only she was better—and sexier!

She looked to be in her mid-thirties with jet-black curly hair that grazed her shoulders, cool brown eyes, and an oak complexion. She had a streamlined, petite figure that I could imagine cuddling up to on a lonely night. If there were such a thing as my ideal woman, she was probably it.

Though my mouth always seemed to go dry whenever I got near her, I managed to utter: "Hello."

She gave me a faint smile in return, perhaps flattered, but obviously unimpressed. I tried to convince myself that she was just having a bad day. Some other time, pal.

I climbed three flights of stairs before I reached my one-bedroom apartment. It was pretty much what you would expect of a single, male, private investigator: not particularly tidy, cluttered, bland, and sorely in need of a woman's touch. The "right" woman just never seemed to come along and volunteer her services.

I showered, shaved, and stepped into one of two cheap suits I wore on the job. This one was navy blue and the most broken in. I combed my short, black hair that was sprinkled with more gray than I cared to admit. Since high school, I'd had a thick coal black mustache. It was probably the best part of me and hung just over the corners of my mouth, tickling me whenever I yawned.

Dinner was some leftover KFC drumsticks, canned pinto beans, and milk. Afterwards I caught a bit of the news on TV, glanced at the front page of the *Oregonian*, and pondered my newest case.

* * *

Pioneer Courthouse Square was the place to be if you wanted to mingle with your neighbors and tourists alike, be right in the heart of downtown Portland, and catch some of the city's best free sidewalk talent.

Nate Griffin had made a name for himself as the Rose Clown, in reference to the annual Rose Festival held in the city. He did everything you expected of a clown and more, including cartwheels, telling bad jokes, and giving an often distorted, comical history of Portland. Nate also happened to be my best street informant ever since my days on the force. Sometimes he was helpful, other times helpless. At twenty-nine, he had succumbed to a life mostly on the streets after off and on bouts with alcohol and drug abuse, and failed opportunities to better his life.

The Rose Clown was in full costume and makeup when I saw him on the Square working his magic on anyone who cared to watch and listen. Nate was tall, lanky, dark, and bald. One wouldn't recognize him when looking at the clown in a baggy outfit, white curly wig, green painted face, and big red nose.

He acknowledged my presence with a half-hearted nod. I dropped a few dollar bills into his bucket that was sparsely filled with mostly dimes and quarters. He finished a terrible rendition of a rap song before giving me a moment of his time.

"They love you, Nate," I told him encouragingly, "even if your singing stinks."

"It's all in the ears of the beholder," he said, smiling and showing off a gold front crown. Then he looked into his nearly empty bucket and seemed to do an about face. "Guess I could use some work on my chords."

Guiltily I dug into my pocket and came out with a couple more dollars, dropping them into the bucket. "Maybe this will help—"

He wet his full lips. "Thanks, D.J. Times are tough these days."

"For *all* of us," I said with a sneer.

He peered at me suspiciously. "So what brings you my way?" He chose to answer his own question, fluttering his false lashes. "You probably missed seeing my pretty face!"

"Don't believe that for a minute," I said firmly. "I'm not into clowns, pretty or not." It had been about six weeks since I'd come his way. If there was anyone who could find out where Jessie Wylson was holed up, it was Nate and his seemingly endless network of street contacts.

I removed the photo of The Worm from my pocket and laid it on Nate's palm. "Know him?"

He studied the picture as if it held the secret of the universe. "Should I?"

"His name is Jessie Wylson. They call him The Worm."

"Ugly dude," commented Nate bluntly, his brow furrowed.

For once we agreed on something. Nate was still staring at the photo when he asked: "Why you looking for the man?"

I decided to be straight with him. "He's wanted by the D.A.'s office for drug trafficking, among other things."

Nate scratched his fake nose, then sniffed like it was clogged with a white powdered substance. "So why come to me?" he asked, as if he hadn't a clue.

"I need to find him." My mouth became a straight line. "And I need *your* help—"

Nate's eyes popped wide. "Don't know the man. Don't want to know him, 'specially if he's got the D.A. on his ass. Sorry." He handed me the photo as if glad to be rid of it.

I had a feeling he was holding back on me, but didn't press it—yet. "Ask around anyway," I insisted. "Maybe you'll get lucky."

"Can't make no promises," he hedged. "But I'll give it my best shot—for you."

"I'll check back with you in a couple of days."

"That soon?" He rolled his eyes. "What do I look like, a miracle worker?"

Gazing at the Rose Clown, that wasn't exactly the first thing to come to mind. I told him: "The sooner you give me what I want, the sooner I'll leave you alone—for a while."

Nate went back to what he arguably did best and I headed to my favorite nightclub, satisfied that I had at least put the wheels in motion to find the man known as The Worm.

CHAPTER TWO

Jasmine's was located right on the Willamette River. The jazz supper club was owned and operated by Gus Taylor, Vietnam vet, friend, and the ninth wonder of the world. He hovered somewhere in the neighborhood of three hundred pounds on six feet, three inches of flab. His salt and pepper beard was thick, as were his brows over large brown eyes. His head was shiny bald like Mr. Clean.

Jasmine's had the best jazz in town. Gus had named it after his late wife who was his pride and joy. I couldn't remember a time dating back to my days as a rookie officer when I didn't come to the club and leave feeling genuinely uplifted. Tonight was well on its way to following suit. The featured singer looked like a young Diana Ross, but had a voice that sounded much more like Billie Holiday than Ross ever did in "Lady Sings the Blues."

"What's shakin', D.J.?" The boisterous voice was none other than Gus himself, who often doubled as bartender, waiter, janitor, and security guard.

"She is!" I declared from my stool, while my eyes remained riveted on the singer who called herself Star Quality.

"Don't even think about it," Gus warned me. "She's too hot for even you to handle."

"I wouldn't doubt it," I said, finishing off my beer.

"How 'bout another?"

"Why not?"

Gus filled two mugs. "Why don't you come and work for me, D.J.?" he said as if he really meant it.

I raised a brow. "You mean you want me to *sing*?"

"Not if I wanna stay in business," he quipped. "I was thinking more along the lines of security."

I looked at him like he was half crazy, though I suspected he was dead serious. "Thanks, but no thanks, Gus. I'm afraid I'm not cut out to break up bar brawls."

"Don't knock it till you've tried it," he said. "You hang out here almost as much as I do. Why not put your talent to good use?"

"I thought I was," I responded with serious sarcasm, and tasted the beer.

Gus leaned at me from across the bar. He could tell that I was a little pissed. "Don't get me wrong," he said apologetically, putting froth to his mouth. "I'm not knocking what you do to earn a living. We need some of our own doing the private eye bit. 'The Man' sho ain't gonna bust his ass to find out whodunit, especially not in the part of town where most of us live. But you, my man, could do better than that. And I could use a man with your background and guts to help keep law and order around here. Think about it, D.J. That's all I'm askin'."

I already had thought about it, but saw no reason to tell him at that moment. Good intentions aside, I didn't quit the force to wind up checking I.D.'s for the proper drinking age. "I'll think about it," I lied.

He left it at that and went to jaw with another patron. I refocused my attention on Star Quality and became lost in her velvety, soulful voice.

* * *

The Worm's last known address was a house on Thirty-Third Street and Drummond, an area in Northeast Portland that was known more for its crack houses and gang bangers than its law-abiding citizens.

That next morning I paid the house a visit, figuring I might hit the jackpot the first time around and catch The Worm with his pants down. Not that I really believed I could be that lucky. If it had been that easy to locate Jessie Wylson, Sherman could have—and probably would have—done the job himself.

Wearing my alternate P.I. suit, this one dusty brown, with a tan shirt and thin brown tie, I rang the doorbell. It seemed that dressing the way people expected detectives to dress—somewhat rumpled and sleazy—made it easier to get a little cooperation from those least apt to give it.

There was a beat up Olds Cutlass in the driveway. From the looks of the house, with its peeling paint and overgrown lawn, it was as if no one had lived there in years.

I heard a rustling noise inside. It sounded more like a snake than a worm. But I was taking no chances. I placed my hand close to the .40 caliber Glock I kept between my waist and pants. I had never been accused of being trigger-happy as a cop or P.I., but that didn't mean I wasn't ready and willing to confront any dangerous situation that came my way.

The door slowly opened. A walnut-skinned woman in her early thirties stuck her face out. Her short, permed dark hair was highlighted with blonde streaks. The way her sable eyes squinted like taking a direct hit of bright sunlight suggested that I had disturbed her beauty sleep. A terrycloth white robe was loosely wrapped around her voluptuous body, revealing enough cleavage for my eyes to get sore.

"What?" she asked brusquely.

"My name's Drake," I said tersely. "I understand Jessie Wylson lives here."

Her brow creased. "He ain't here. Ain't seen him for weeks."

I glanced around skeptically and then back at her. "Who are you?"

She batted her lashes as if to say *Who's asking?* "Used to be his girlfriend."

"Anyone else home?" I asked guardedly, my hand still within reach of the Glock.

"I live by myself," she hissed.

"Do you have a name?"

She hesitated, regarding me suspiciously, before saying in a higher octave: "Nicole."

"Nicole, do you expect me to believe that even a low-life drug dealer like The Worm would dump a lady as fine as you?" I figured that would elicit a meaningful response.

She gave me a coquettish grin and seemed genuinely flattered. Then her face became an angry machine. "I dumped the bastard after he stole from me—every chance he got."

"Maybe the biggest mistake of his life," I offered, almost feeling sorry for her. "Do you know where can I find him?"

Her nostrils ballooned. "You askin' the wrong person. I'm not his damned keeper—not anymore." She sighed raggedly. "If there's nothin' else, I got things to do."

I was not altogether convinced that she had no knowledge of Wylson's whereabouts, but gave her the benefit of the doubt—for now. "Your ex-boyfriend's wanted on drug charges," I said coldly. "I'm not a cop, but I've been hired to bring Wylson in if I can find him." My eyes sharpened on her. "If you know where he is, you'd better think twice about keeping it to yourself. He's not worth going to prison for." I slipped my card in her cleavage for a perfect fit. "Give me a call if you hear from Jessie or happen to remember where he's hiding out."

* * *

By afternoon I had finished up some paperwork from a previous case. I rewarded myself by running. There was an unexpected joy in feeling the stress and strain course through my entire body as I pushed myself to go the extra mile, so to speak.

I took the long way home—about four miles along the river—leaving me exhausted and regenerated. I finished my run by cooling down and walking about the last quarter of a mile.

As I approached the front of my apartment building, I noticed a cab pull up to the curb. *My ideal woman*, the attractive lady whose name I still didn't know, got out of the back seat. She was wearing a gray business suit that flattered her nice figure. She reached in the back seat and came out with a painting that seemed nearly as tall as her. With obvious difficulty, she began to carry it toward the brownstone.

"Let me help you with that." I took full advantage of the moment, catching up to her in looping strides. *Maybe this was the break I'd been hoping for to get to know this angel.* I grabbed the painting before she could say no thanks.

"Thank you," she said in a shaky, but appreciatively soft voice. "I think this one was just a bit too much to handle."

I looked at the painting. It was a scenic landscape of Mount Hood and the surrounding area. I was not exactly a connoisseur of the arts. I wondered if she was the artist. The apartments in our building hardly seemed large enough to hold such a painting.

"Where to?" I asked. For one of the few times in my life, I was actually intimidated by someone. Her attractiveness, grace, and sensuality really did a number on me.

"I'm in 427," she said with a slight smile that revealed small, straight white teeth and thin sweet lips.

She even smelled good, as I got a whiff of her perfume. Definitely not the cheap stuff.

We took the elevator up and neither one of us seemed to have much to say. For my part, saying the wrong thing seemed worse than saying nothing at all.

"Do you live here?" she asked, seemingly out of courtesy, and apparently oblivious to the fact that we had been practically bumping into each other every other day for the last two months.

I nodded. "Third floor."

She smiled ingenuously. "Thought I'd seen you before. I suppose it's a good thing you came along when you did."

"If it hadn't been me, it would have been someone else," I muttered like an idiot.

She gave me a look to suggest that she agreed.

The elevator doors opened and I followed her to the apartment.

"Just set it there," she pointed to an empty wall in the living room.

I did and we stared at each other for seconds that seemed like hours. I started to ask her if she wanted to go for a drink, but something told me I wouldn't like her answer. So I kept my mouth shut. There was plenty of time to get to know this lady. *Why rush a potentially good thing?*

"Well, I'd better get going now." The words crept from my mouth as if they were stuck in cement.

She did not argue the point. "Thanks again. Maybe I'll see you around."

I nodded miserably, and left without even finding out her name or telling her mine.

At the mailboxes, I discovered that her name was Vanessa King. It seemed to fit her. This was another possible step in the right direction for me.

# # #

Look for these and other great mystery and thriller novels by R. Barri Flowers in print, eBook, and in audio.

ABOUT THE AUTHOR

R. Barri Flowers is a bestselling, award winning author of more than fifty books, including mysteries, thrillers, romance, young adult, true crime, and criminology. Recent mystery fiction titles include MURDER IN HONOLULU: A Skye Delaney Mystery, DARK STREETS OF WHITECHAPEL: A Jack the Ripper Mystery, DEAD IN THE ROSE CITY: A Dean Drake Mystery, KILLER IN THE WOODS, STATE'S EVIDENCE: A Beverly Mendoza Leal Thriller, JUSTICE SERVED: A Barkley and Parker Mystery, and teen mysteries, DANGER IN TIME and GHOST GIRL IN SHADOW BAY.

Recent true crime titles by the author include SERIAL KILLER COUPLES, THE SEX SLAVE MURDERS, and MASS MURDER IN THE SKY: The Bombing of Flight 629.

Mr. Flowers is the recipient of the Wall of Fame Award from Michigan State University's renowned School of Criminal Justice. He has appeared on the Biography Channel's *Crime Stories* and Investigation Discovery's *Wicked Attraction* series.

The author is busy at work on his next mystery novel, SEDUCED TO KILL IN KAUAI.

Connect with R. Barri Flowers online through Facebook, Twitter, YouTube, LinkedIn, MySpace, CrimeSpace, and at www.rbarriflowers.com.

CPSIA information can be obtained
at www.ICGtesting.com
Printed in the USA
LVHW010238151221
706269LV00024B/721

9 781475 202847